I0823290

THE FINAL SCORE

BOOKS BY DON WINSLOW

The Final Score

City in Ruins

City of Dreams

City on Fire

Broken

The Border

The Force

The Cartel

The Kings of Cool

The Gentlemen's Hour

Satori

Savages

The Dawn Patrol

The Winter of Frankie Machine

The Power of the Dog

Looking for a Hero (with Peter Maslowski)

California Fire and Life

The Death and Life of Bobby Z

Isle of Joy

While Drowning in the Desert

A Long Walk Up the Water Slide

Way Down on the High Lonely

The Trail to Buddha's Mirror

A Cool Breeze on the Underground

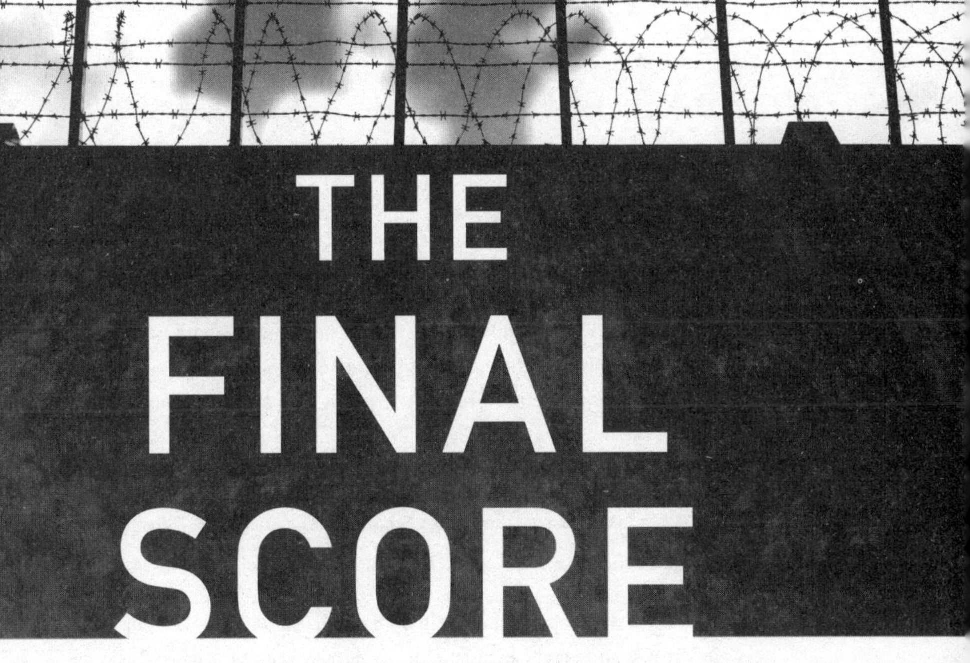

THE FINAL SCORE

· SIX SHORT NOVELS ·

Don Winslow

wm
WILLIAM MORROW
An Imprint of HarperCollins*Publishers*

 For information, address HarperCollins Publishers, 195 Broadway, New York, NY 10007. In Europe, HarperCollins Publishers, Macken House, 39/40 Mayor Street Upper, Dublin 1, D01 C9W8, Ireland.

HarperCollins books may be purchased for educational, business, or sales promotional use. For information, please email the Special Markets Department at SPsales@harpercollins.com.

hc.com

FIRST EDITION

Designed by Kyle O'Brien

Title page art © Marko Aliaksandr/Shutterstock

Library of Congress Cataloging-in-Publication Data has been applied for.

ISBN 978-0-06-345042-4

Printed in the United States of America

25 26 27 28 29 LBC 6 5 4 3 2

To Perry Carter Winslow, my grandson, with the wish that his life be full of wonderful stories

To this I witness call the fools of time,
Which die for goodness, who have lived for crime.

—William Shakespeare, Sonnet 124

CONTENTS

FOREWORD

TO SAY DON WINSLOW'S VOICE is unique doesn't do him justice. Don, unlike most of us who ply the trade, isn't bound by one voice, one style, one tone, one tense, one genre or subgenre. Don is a chameleon in the best possible sense, and regardless of the colors or camouflage with which he paints his characters, no matter if it's in the guise of a cartel moll, a corrupt NYPD detective, a local mob soldier, or a private investigator, Winslow's work glistens without ever calling attention to the man behind the curtain.

Perhaps only another writer can fully appreciate how difficult a magician's trick it is to write brilliant, powerful prose—sometimes brutal and graphic, at other times sly and comical—without the reader once losing track of the action or thinking about the person who put those words on the page. In Bruce Springsteen's anthemic "For You," he refers to the person about whom he's singing this way: "You could laugh and cry in a single sound." He might just as well have been singing about Don Winslow.

From the moment I picked up *California Fire and Life*, the first book of Don's I read, I have been hooked and in awe of my friend and colleague. Earlier, I referred to Don's refusal to be pigeonholed in any aspect of his work. He has set books like *The Dawn Patrol*—the ones I think of as philosophical surfing PI novels—among a group of surfers along the California coast. There's *A Cool Breeze on the Underground*, set in London. There are the intense drug trade novels, like *The Border* and *The Cartel,* set in various Mexican locales. He's walked his readers along the gritty, dirty-fingernail backstreets of New York City in *The Force.*

To say he sets his novels in these places is again to not do his work justice. His novels are not set in a time and place, they are *of* their time and place. He gets the details right so that the reader feels he or she is part of the action, not simply observing it. Whether it's the scents of gun smoke and atomized blood in the jungle air in the wake of a battle between rival cartels, or the feel of bobbing in the Pacific waiting for the next big wave with your buddies, or the post-theft buzz of pulling into a garage to switch cars with the blare of passing sirens echoing in your ears, Don doesn't simply engage his readers. He immerses them in the scene, embeds them in the moment.

And here's the thing: no matter where he sets his novels, no matter the characters, Don gets the language right. He knows the slang, the patter, the rhythm of the streets, wherever those streets might be. His characters talk the talk and walk the walk, because Winslow knows that a surfer would say "epic macking crunchy" and gets that the reader will comprehend through the context he's supplied.

What I love about Don is that he respects his readers, that while he takes his subject matter seriously and does everything to make sure his work is accurate, he never takes himself too seriously. The reader is always a line away from humor, but that humor, often dark, is never Don trying to be clever or to draw attention to himself. It's a reflection of life, appropriate to the moment and often meant to catch the reader unexpected for what is to come next. Although I read *The Force* years ago, one brief exchange between a corrupt NYPD detective and the head of a local drug gang has always stuck with me.

"You took Pena [a rival gang leader] off the count for me," the drug dealer, Carter, says to Detective Malone.

"And not so much as a muffin basket."

A reader might then anticipate an exchange of witty barbs between the two. Maybe in someone else's novel, but not Don's. What ensues instead is a discussion of community, our history of slavery, and the prison-industrial complex. That's Don Winslow, because at the core of his work is his humanity and his clarion call for us to care more for the least of us.

Don is an audacious writer, a man willing to work without a net. As a colleague, I can't help but admire a man who has the gall and guts to rework the story of Helen of Troy into a trilogy about warring gangs in Providence, Rhode Island. He's a man willing to write a one-word or a six-sentence chapter. A writer who will play with tenses so that the reader is simultaneously disoriented and sucked directly into the heart of the story. For these reasons and twenty more, I was excited to hear about his new collection of short stories, *The Final Score.* Excited because I knew exactly what to expect and know I'll still be surprised at every turn.

Called a hard-boiled poet by NPR's Maureen Corrigan and the noir poet laureate on HuffPost, ***Reed Farrel Coleman*** *is the* New York Times *bestselling author of thirty-plus novels, including six in the Jesse Stone series for the estate of the late Robert B. Parker. A former executive vice president of Mystery Writers of America, he is a four-time recipient of the Shamus Award for best PI novel and a four-time Edgar Award nominee in three different categories. He has also received the Authors on the Air Book of the Year, the Scribe, Audie, the Macavity, Barry, and Anthony Awards. Reed lives with his wife on Long Island.*

THE FINAL SCORE

THE FINAL SCORE

JOHN HIGHLAND IS GOING TO die in prison.

He's been found guilty of armed robbery, in this case of an armored car. That's twenty-five years, federal time, which means he'll serve at least 85 percent of the sentence. Twenty-one years. He's coming on sixty now, so he might get out when he's eighty.

Or not.

The judge will more likely hit him with the three-strikes provision and put him away for the rest of his life.

Out on bond until the sentencing in a month, Highland knows he's going to leave that hearing in bracelets and go straight inside.

And never come out.

"We know this for a fact," Highland tells Jamal. They're standing out on San Clemente Pier and the sun is sparkling on the Pacific Ocean. "So there are things I need to take care of."

Jamal misunderstands him. "Don't worry. When we find LeBlanc, we'll take care of him."

LeBlanc was the getaway driver on the job that went south. The problem was that he got away by himself, leaving Highland at the scene, and then turned government witness. He's off in Utah or Arizona or somewhere, selling time-shares or aluminum siding or what-the-fuck-ever.

"Revenge is for screenwriters," Highland says. "I have *real* concerns."

"You going to run?" Jamal asks.

Highland shakes his head. "I put the equity on the house up for the bond. What's Jewel going to do, live in the street? As it is, I don't know how she's going to pay the mortgage, the taxes . . ."

In addition to the prison sentence, there'll also be a fine. Could be as much as a quarter million.

"I feel bad for you, John."

"It's Jewel I'm worried about," Highland says. "The life I've given her, the least I can do is see she gets to grow old in her own home. Maybe she meets some citizen, they take walks on the beach, play pickleball, go bird-watching, I don't know."

Even though it's Southern California and they're by the beach, Highland is wearing a gray linen suit and a white dress shirt. His one concession is the open collar with no tie.

It's a rule of his.

Dress tight, work tight.

Jamal is more casual in a short-sleeved teal polo shirt and khaki trousers. The shirt doesn't hide the little potbelly he's been developing the past few years—unlike his old friend Highland, who hits the gym every morning like it's church.

"Jewel would never get with another guy," Jamal says.

"She should," Highland says. "That eight-year bit I did, she stayed faithful. I told her she shouldn't, she should find someone while I was in."

"That's not Jewel."

No, it isn't, Highland thinks.

She's the best.

They got married when they were kids, nineteen years old, and she's stuck with him through all of it.

He was hoping to take her to Paris for their fortieth anniversary.

Now that's not going to happen.

All he can do for her now is make her secure.

But most of his money is on vacation in Tahiti with his lawyers.

The legal fees, the trial, the appeals, the bond—Highland's string is played out. He's delayed incarceration for as long as he could, and it's left him nearly broke. Now he needs money for the prison commissary account, which makes all the difference in the quality of life inside. Far more important, he needs enough money for Jewel to live comfortably.

There's something else, too, if he's being honest with himself. And if there's any time for being honest with yourself, it's now, Highland thinks.

He doesn't want to go out a loser.

All his life it's been him against the world, and for the most part he's won, maybe the most successful high-level heist guy ever to play the game. Sure, he lost a couple, did his bits like a man, but for the most part he scored the big money and walked away with it.

At the end of the day, though, the world has beaten him.

And he can't tolerate that.

It's not enough to just pull off a score.

He needs to pull off *the* score.

So when he sits in the joint for the rest of his life, he does it as a legend. He knows that he's still himself.

That the world can't beat John Highland.

"Thirty-four–twenty-eight," he says.

"What?" Jamal asks.

"Thirty-four–twenty-eight," Highland repeats.

"I'm still not following."

Highland says, "Super Bowl Fifty-One. Seventeen minutes left in the game, the Patriots were down twenty-eight to three."

"Okay."

"Final score?" Highland says. "Thirty-four–twenty-eight. Patriots."

I have seventeen minutes left, Highland thinks.

And I'm down by a lot.

But all that matters is the final score.

HIGHLAND TELLS JAMAL the target he wants to hit.

Jamal just stares at him.

Then asks, "Are you out of your fucking mind?"

There's a reason the Castle has never been robbed.

"Because it can't be done," Jamal says.

The aptly named casino is a fortress, sitting atop a hill in the middle of freaking nowhere, on a reservation out in the backcountry east of San Diego. It's unexpected—an hour and change by car from downtown and you're driving past horse and cattle ranches, Native American reservations, with hills and mountains as high as six thousand feet. In the southernmost part of California, it can snow in the winter.

So why the hell would you have a casino out there?

Because every year, drug users in the United States send something like $60 billion to the Mexican cartels.

In cash.

More cash than the Mexican economy can absorb, so a lot of it comes right back to the States and it all needs to be laundered. It gets invested in real estate, banks, hotels, restaurants . . .

And casinos.

A casino is a freaking laundromat.

The process is simple.

Drug money comes into the casino through the back door.

The cartel sends people who bet at selected tables. These bettors win. They might lose a few hands or a few rolls for appearance's sake, but overall they win the rigged games and they win big.

They cash in the chips and get paid out in the drug money, which then goes back to its original owners clean.

The casino keeps 6 percent for its troubles.

The money from those six points doesn't show up anywhere—not on the books, not on annual reports, and sure as shit not on tax forms.

So whether it's the 94 percent or the remaining 6, if it gets stolen, no one is going to report it to the police.

It's the perfect score.

Except . . .

It can't be done.

The first obstacle is the location, off a two-lane blacktop that runs north–south, with an even narrower, winding two-lane road that switchbacks up to the casino parking lot.

So there's only one way in—and more importantly only one way *out*—which can be easily blocked with a single vehicle.

The security cameras in the parking lot are perched high on metal poles, so they can't be manually disabled. Likewise, cameras are everywhere inside, including the closed-circuit-television "eye-in-the-sky" surveillance that is a feature of every casino so that it can monitor dealers and players for cheating.

Or armed robbers bursting in.

And forget about doing a Danny Ocean and taking out the power—the casino has redundant generators that turn on automatically in case of a power failure. You'd have to disable three separate systems, with giant generators protected behind chain-link fences topped with barbed wire.

And, of course, the casino has security guards, some of them armed with handguns.

"What about the vault?" Jamal asks.

There are two of them, Highland explains—one for the casino's legitimate cash, the other in a back security room for the dirty money.

Both modular, specifically built for the casino, heavy steel inside reinforced concrete. Heavy-duty locks, motion sensors, biometric scanners on the combination dials that only open to authorized fingerprints, retinal scanners to even get into the vault room.

"Forget about the vault," Highland says. "Once the money gets into the vault room, it's too late."

So they have to hit it on the way in.

The cartel doesn't use armored cars to bring the cash in because it doesn't want the attention. Instead, it uses food delivery trucks and brings the cash in through the kitchen.

"The lettuce comes in with the lettuce," Jamal says.

Highland doesn't smile.

He's pulled off the two-lane blacktop a mile from the casino. They don't go to the casino itself because it has NORA (Non-Obvious Relationship Analysis) facial recognition technology that would pick them up and run a background check, alerting security to the presence of two high-level holdup men.

The cartel does dummy runs, Highland explains. Some of the trucks have cash, others don't. They vary times and routes. Sometimes they come up through the San Ysidro border crossing, other times through Tecate.

"It's random," Jamal says.

"Nothing is random," says Highland.

The cartel people track the vehicle from the moment it leaves Mexico. They mix the crews on the trucks so they don't know or trust one another enough to pull a rip, and they all have families in Mexico who are basically hostages. The man riding shotgun is authorized to blow the driver's head off if he looks like he's going rogue. The guards are locked in the cargo compartment from the outside, and only the contact in the casino has the combination to open the door.

The door is also locked from the inside. When the truck arrives, the head guard inside the cargo compartment gets a text with a code.

So does the guy at the casino. The casino guy has to give the correct code or the door doesn't open and the truck turns around and leaves.

"So you're waiting for them," Jamal says. "Move in fast and blow the door open."

Highland shakes his head. "The guards have automatic weapons, and they'll shoot it out to protect the money and their families. I don't want a bloodbath."

I have enough guilt to die with as it is, he thinks.

Moreover, the cartel uses a follow car—an SUV loaded with gunmen—that stays a few car lengths behind the truck and closes in as it drives up the switchback to the casino.

If you hit the delivery truck when it pulls up to the casino, you'd just be gunned down from behind.

"No weaknesses," Jamal says.

There are always weaknesses, Highland thinks.

The cartel creates the first one itself by tracking the truck.

First, it tracks only the trucks carrying the money, not the decoys. So if you can hack the tracking system, you know which truck has the cash. Second, if you do hack that system, you know exactly when the truck is coming.

"So what?" Jamal asks. "So you know which truck has money and when it's coming. You still can't take it down."

"We're not going to hit the truck," Highland says.

"We're not hitting the vault and we're not hitting the truck," Jamal says. "What the hell *are* we going to hit?"

Highland is a reader.

He picked up the habit on his second stretch, becoming a denizen of the prison library.

He mostly reads history.

Specifically, military history.

More specifically, the history of World War II.

Highland devoured every book on the subject in the library, and when he finished he started over and read them again. When he got out, he bought books and stocked his home bookshelves.

Ask Highland any question about WWII and he could answer you.

Except he won't.

Highland believes that knowledge should be closely held—that until necessary, you shouldn't let people know what you know.

But in this case, he thinks it's necessary.

"Do you know why," he asks Jamal, "German U-boats were so successful?"

"No," Jamal says, "for some imponderable reason I don't."

"Because they preyed on shipping lanes," Highland says.

He goes on to explain that convoys carrying vital military supplies from the US to England didn't just sail all over the Atlantic but used relatively narrow shipping lanes, determined by currents and weather. So the German submarines sat in the shipping lanes and picked them off.

"You're saying that the casino money goes through a shipping lane," Jamal says.

"The food deliveries go into the kitchen."

"Sure."

"From the kitchen they can't just walk cartons of cash disguised as food across the casino floor without raising ugly questions," Highland says. "There's a back corridor that runs from the kitchen to the secret vault room."

"And you're the U-boat waiting in the corridor." Which raises more questions than it answers, Jamal thinks. How do you get into the corridor? More importantly, how do you get out?

There's another vital question.

"Where did you get all this information?" Jamal asks. "Who do you have on the inside?"

"You don't need to know that," Highland says, "until you tell me that you're in."

"If I'm going to risk my ass on a final score," Jamal says, "I need to know now. Call it part of my decision-making process. Who is it?"

•

SUMMER REDBIRD FINALLY walks out of the casino to her car, a black Mercedes S-Class, in the employee parking lot.

It's been a long day, starting with a meeting at nine in the morning, and it's now eleven-thirty at night. But that's a typical day for Summer—as the executive casino manager, she's responsible for virtually everything that impacts guests on the casino floor, in the hotel and in the restaurants. It's also her job to keep the big rollers happy and coming back, and to seek out new big players and entice them to the casino.

Summer is well-suited to the work. Tall and leggy with long, shining black hair, dark eyes and an aquiline, slightly hooked nose, she resembles a sexier version of an Indian Disney princess, although the last employee who called her "Pocahontas" . . . well, actually he called her "Pocahon—" because he was fired before he got the last syllable out of his mouth.

Charming, smarter than hell, and with a head for numbers, she's worth every cent of her $75,000 annual salary, plus bonuses when she raises the ATP—the average amount players spend—which she does every year.

Summer likes her money. She knows what having money means because she knows what *not* having money means. Growing up poor right here on the reservation with two alcoholic parents, she decided at an early age that wasn't going to be her life. ("We grew up on Hamburger Helper," she has said, "often without the hamburger.") She studied her way to a scholarship at SDSU, double majored in business management and accounting, and because the casino had to hire a certain percentage of reservation people in executive positions, Summer was a natural choice. She started as a hostess and quickly moved up to her present job.

At which she is very good.

Her staff likes, admires, respects and fears her. This last because she has a quick trigger finger. “I’ve never regretted firing anyone,” she’s said. “I’ve only regretted not firing them sooner.”

You do your job for Summer or you don’t have your job.

But if you do that job, she has your back all the way. She’ll back you against customers, upper management, whomever, doesn’t matter.

Take the meeting this morning, when Summer went head-to-head with the chief of security.

“There’s a customer constantly harassing my female servers,” Summer said. “Where is security?”

“How is that a security threat?” the chief asked.

“How is it *not*?” Summer asked. “A server has a right to bring a drink without this guy grabbing her boob.”

“What do you want my guys to do?”

“Remove him,” Summer said.

“He’s a big player,” the floor manager said. “Have you looked at his ATP?”

“I have,” Summer said. “I can bring in someone else who will spend as much money without assaulting my servers.”

“ ‘Assaulting’?” the floor manager asked.

“That’s what it is.”

The security chief said, “In this business—”

“Do you want to remove him?” Summer asked. “Or do you want *me* to do it? Because if I do it, he’s going out horizontally, not vertically.”

They believed her.

That afternoon she came into the nineteenth hole after playing her once-a-week Wednesday round at a course out in the desert.

Highland caught her eye as she sat down at the next table with her Arnold Palmer.

“How was your round?” he asked.

"Subpar," Summer said, letting the ambiguity stand. "Yours?"

"I don't play," Highland said. "I just like looking at the course. And this is the best restaurant around."

He gestured to the empty chair at his table and she sat down. Summer was accustomed to men hitting on her and she used it to her advantage. The man was expensively dressed, he could be a player.

"The best restaurant around is at my casino," she said.

"You own a casino?"

"I'm the executive manager."

"I'll bet you're very good at it," Highland said.

"See, you've already won your first wager," Summer said. "You might like blackjack, but I see you more as a poker player."

She handed him her card.

Highland looked at it.

"Let me ask you something, Summer Redbird," he said. "Are you happy?"

At thirty-two, Summer's the youngest executive casino manager in the country.

But she's not going any higher.

Gordon Matthews, the casino controller, has told her as much.

"I know you want my job," he'd said one night over a few drinks at the bar.

"I do want your job," Summer said. "But not *your* job. I want to be a controller, but not here."

"Where, then?"

"Las Vegas."

One of the big casinos.

"Let me save you some heartache," Gordon said. "There are dozens of Indian casinos, and you could probably get that job in any one of them. But the Vegas casinos? They're all controlled by big corporate interests, who are going to see you as a token. You're a female and you're Native American. Be happy with what you have, Summer."

It pissed her off. So she said, "So what if I do want *your* job?"

He gave her one of his patented sleazy smiles. "Well, that's not going to happen."

Summer knew why.

Old Gordo felt so secure because he was the linchpin for bringing in dirty money.

The cartel's man in the casino.

Old Gordo had been trying to get into her pants for two years, and he'd get talkative when he'd had a few drinks and was trying to impress her. He dropped sly hints about his connection to dangerous, powerful people, about big money, dark secrets that he couldn't share with her but the mystery of which she should find irresistibly seductive.

Of course Summer had discerned most of this already, she's not an idiot. She knows every freaking fork and spoon in that kitchen, so she knows when "food" shipments come in that never make their way into the refrigerators or freezers.

And she observed what was happening on the casino floor, too. While not her direct responsibility—that was the floor manager—she could see that players were consistently winning who shouldn't be and that these winnings weren't showing up on the reports.

"Stay in your lane," Gordon had told her. "Food, beverage, hospitality, customer relations. Some of these big players, if they don't want to talk to you, you don't talk to them."

And at certain times, she should stay the fuck out of the kitchen.

"What you don't know," said Gordon, ever a font of clichés, "can't hurt you."

Which is, perhaps, the stupidest of clichés.

What you don't know can hurt the hell out of you.

For instance, what Gordon didn't know was how unhappy Summer was.

Now she looked at John Highland. "Am I happy?"

"Are you?"

"No," Summer said. "I'm not."

"You can walk away now," Highland said. "Nothing will happen. You don't know who I am so you're no threat. You're perfectly safe."

There was a long silence, then Summer said, "You targeted me."

"It's my business to know these things," Highland said. "You're a brilliant young woman working under a jerk like Gordon Matthews, and you've hit the glass ceiling. You make good but not great money, and you have to watch millions of dollars in cash come through the doors and none of it sticks to you."

"So you've heard the rumors," Summer said. "About the money laundering."

The rumors that the Castle is a cartel laundromat have circulated in the criminal underworld for years. No one has ever acted on them because the casino is thought to be impregnable.

"Are they true?" Highland asked.

"Are you a cop?" asked Summer.

"In the age-old game of cops and robbers," Highland said, "I'm one of the latter."

Her eyes widened.

But just a little bit.

"CAN WE TRUST her?" Jamal asks now.

"Can we trust anyone?" Highland says. "Besides each other? Anyway, what choice do we have?"

"Not to do this."

"Not a choice."

"A bank," Jamal says. "A different casino. Even another armored car. But not this."

"Why not?"

"Because it can't be done."

"Which is exactly why we should do it," Highland says. "They think they're invulnerable. They're arrogant. And arrogant people get careless."

"Even if we pull it off," Jamal says, "it won't be the cops after us, or even the feds. It'll be the cartel, and they'll never quit. I'm not taking that kind of risk for my share of, what could it be, three or four million?"

"Probably more like five," Highland says. "So you're out."

"No," Jamal says. "I'm in. I can't let you do this alone."

Highland's relieved. He needs Jamal. Needs a veteran, someone he can trust not to panic and bolt or start spraying bullets around. And someone he can trust to get Jewel her share.

That's Jamal, without doubt.

It's a solemn promise between them—if something happens to one, the other will take care of his family.

Six big scores together.

Seven years in Q together.

They're like brothers.

More than brothers.

They go over it and over it.

The key is the corridor that runs between the kitchen and the vault room.

Fine, great.

But how do you get into it?

"Only Matthews opens the door from the kitchen into the corridor," Highland says. "A retinal scanner unlocks the door."

"We have to be inside the corridor *before* he opens that door," Jamal says.

"Thoughts?"

"It reads the retina, right?" Jamal asks. "Not the whole face?"

"That's my understanding," Highland says. "But the guard

outside the vault room has a monitor. He can see Matthews open the door."

"First problems first," Jamal says. "I'll do some research."

Highland considers it done. If Jamal does the research, it will be spot-on. "We'll need a driver."

ISA ALMAZAN HITS the gas pedal.

Hard.

The Dodge Charger, that iconic ride of Hollywood bad guys, responds with a roar.

Isa, all five-two of her, braces her back against the seat and grips the steering wheel, aiming for the ramp that should give her the trajectory to make it over the culvert and onto the ramp across it.

If she's off, even by the slightest angle, the car could miss the opposite ramp and crash into the side of the culvert.

Which would not be good.

Isa hits the near ramp dead-on, then feels the car launch into the air. The natural tendency is to look down, but she resists, keeping her head pointed straight at her target.

Control the head, she knows, and the rest will follow.

Control the *mind* and the rest will follow.

Not that she can see the opposite ramp—she can't now because the car is tilting up—but it's critical to keep her focus on the landing site.

Stick the landing, she thinks, like one of those gymnasts.

Now it's just faith, confidence and faith, that she's done it all right—done her prep work, made sure that the mechanics did theirs, gone through each step a hundred times so that the actual execution is just a matter of muscle memory.

It feels as if she's in the air for a long time, then—

BAM!

The car hits the opposite ramp.

Perfect.

But the impact jars her back, compressing the lower vertebrae, which hurts and concerns her, because the last thing she wants is another surgery. She has blue-chip SAG-AFTRA health insurance, but surgery is always risky, the rehab long and painful, taking her out of work for an extended time. And her partner, Lisa, would be pissed.

Isa gently pushes on the brake, turns the wheel and puts the Charger into a sliding stop.

She hears applause through the tiny earpiece, then, *"Cut! Beautiful, Isa!"*

"Are you going to need another one?" she asks into the little microphone taped under her blouse.

"No, that was perfection. That's a wrap."

Good, Isa thinks. She pulls off the blond wig that made her resemble the white star whose publicist will doubtless claim she does her own stunts. Actually, the actress is a pretty decent chick, Isa thinks, not a diva at all.

She gets out of the car and climbs into the Jeep that pulls up beside her.

"Great as usual!" Blake, the stunt coordinator, says as she climbs into the passenger seat.

"What did you expect?" Isa asks. "Is lunch out? I'm fucking *starving*."

On her way to the lunch table, she sees a tall, portly Black man in a pink polo shirt, khaki slacks and Dodgers baseball cap.

"Jamal!" she says. "*Long* time."

"Too long."

"You want to have lunch with me?" Isa asks.

"Do *I* want to have lunch?"

"Silly question."

They hit the lunch table and make small talk through the chicken Caesar salad and the ice cream sundaes.

Isa eats like a wolf coming off Lent.

Jamal looks at her tiny frame. "Where does it go?"

"Adrenaline," she says. As they walk back to her trailer, Isa asks, "So what brings you here?"

Because it isn't nothing. Jamal Rahim Mobley never does anything for no reason.

"How," Jamal asks, lowering his voice, "would you like to make a shit ton of money?"

"WE'LL NEED ANOTHER gun," Jamal says.

"I don't like it," Highland says. Every added gun is just another chance that it will get used.

"Whether you like it or not," Jamal says, "we have to have it. Both of us will be in the corridor. We'll need someone to control the kitchen. And we'll need another pair of hands to get the money out."

Highland knows Jamal is right.

He usually is.

But it's a problem, because most of the good guns are retired, inside, or dead. Petrocelli is sitting on a beach in Nassau, Mays is doing fifteen to twenty in Victorville, Carlson has been in Green-Wood Cemetery for five years now.

"What about Mays's kid?" Jamal asks. "Colt."

"He's what, eighteen?"

"Try twenty-six."

"How did that happen?" Highland asks.

"All by itself," Jamal says.

"I remember the kid as a hothead."

"Kids grow up," Jamal says. "We did."

"Has he done any real work?"

"A bank out in Bisbee," Jamal says. "A truck hijack up near Redding. Word is they used motorcycles to get in and out. Both clean. No shots fired."

That means something to Highland. What you want in a gun is a guy for whom pulling a trigger is the last possible resort. "You know where to find him?"

COLT MAYS RIDES in on a sweet right-hand break off Brooks Street in Laguna Beach.

Not a big wave, to be sure, but with a nice shape to it.

He looks up and sees a man in a gray linen suit standing on the concrete landing.

Which is unusual.

Then, board under his arm, he walks up the steps and recognizes him. "Uncle John?!"

He looks like his old man, Highland thinks. Same thick coal-black hair, dark eyes, movie-star good looks, lean muscles visible even beneath the blue wetsuit. "Hello, Colt."

The kid suddenly looks concerned. "Is my dad—"

"He's fine," Highland says. "But you should know better than me."

Colt smiles. "Yeah, I should be better about—"

Highland says, "Let me buy you lunch."

"There's a girl waiting back at the crib."

"She can go another hour without her heart breaking," Highland says. "Let me buy you lunch."

"I have clothes in my ride."

Highland waits while Colt peels off the wettie, wraps his waist in a towel and does that surfer thing of getting dressed without exposing himself.

Highland takes him to Las Brisas, atop the bluff overlooking the bay, and gets a table outside away from other diners. After they order, Highland gets right to it. "Uncle Jamal tells me that you've taken up the family trade."

"If my dad sent you—"

"He didn't."

"So you're here to do what?" Colt asks him. "Warn me off it? Tell me I'm going to end up like he did?"

"No," Highland says. "I came to find out if you're a serious person or if you're just playing Johnny Jackoff."

"I'm serious."

"Then I may have something for you," Highland says.

"What?"

"Go up and visit your dad," Highland says. "If he signs off on it, then we'll talk."

"How do I find you?"

"I'll find you." Highland stands up.

"What about lunch?"

"You eat mine," Highland says. He walks away.

"I'M NOT GOING to play Brando here," Tom Mays says to his son on the phone through the thick glass, "tell you I'd hoped for something different for you, president or senator or some bullshit. You don't have the brains anyway."

"So Uncle John . . ."

"I'd trust him with my life," Tom says. "I *have.* So I'd trust him with yours. But listen, dummy. You do what Uncle John and Uncle Jamal tell you. Nothing less, and sure as shit nothing more. That way you don't get yourself or anyone else . . . you know what I mean."

"I know."

"You seen your mom lately?"

Colt shakes his head. "She's doing some real estate guy."

"Watch your mouth," Tom says. "She's your mother."

A week later, Colt is getting off his Kawasaki H2R—four-stroke supersport, at 300 horsepower the fastest street-legal bike—at the Taco Bell when a black Porsche 911 Carrera pulls up beside him.

The driver's-side window comes down.

"Next Tuesday, ten A.M.," Highland says. "I'll pick you up here. Be on time."

"I will."

"And lay off the bike," Highland says. "Last thing I need is a gun with a broken wrist."

Window goes back up, car drives off.

Okaaaay, Colt thinks.

IT'S A LONG drive out to Brawley.

If you fly over it, say on the short flight from San Diego to Phoenix, you look down on brown desert and then all of a sudden you'll see neat emerald-green rectangles around the town of Brawley.

Alfalfa fields.

Irrigated by canals dug from the Colorado River during the Depression.

The rectangles don't stay green by accident. The alfalfa can be overrun by noxious weeds unless you spray them.

Which is why Highland and Jamal are driving out to Brawley.

They find the little airstrip five miles outside of town off a dirt road. There's a hangar and a mobile home that serves as an office. Harley's Ford F-150 is parked outside.

An airplane and an old Bell 47 helicopter that Harley works on as a hobby sit in the hangar.

Harley steps out of the trailer to greet them.

Thin sandy hair down to his shoulders, straw cowboy hat, old boots, a joint dangling from his lips.

Jamal gets out of the car. "Willie Nelson over here!"

"Don't be making fun of Willie," Harley says. "Still the best."

It's a toss-up, Highland thinks, who smokes more weed, the Red Headed Stranger or Harley, but he doesn't question it anymore. Highland once asked Jamal, "Can Harley fly when he's high?"

"I know he can't fly when he's not," Jamal said.

Turned out to be the case.

Harley "Extraction" Jackson can put an aircraft down on the sixteenth green of a mini golf course and is utterly fearless.

Maybe it's the weed.

Whatever it is, there are a lot of guys walking around today because Harley could and would take an aircraft into heavy fire in Afghanistan, set it down on the edge of a cliff, wait while they loaded the wounded on board, then get it out and back to base, no matter how shot up it was.

Harley's own Purple Heart is buried in a drawer somewhere in the trailer.

Now he sprays alfalfa crops and occasionally flies a ton or two of marijuana in from Mexico, just a few miles down the road.

"Who's that behind the tinted glass?" he asks. "If Jamal is here it must be John Highland. Batman and Robin, although which is which I can't never tell."

"We take turns," Highland says, getting out. "How's the crop-dusting business?"

"For shit," Harley says. "Everyone's scared to death of Roundup these days. I guess they want to capture the weeds and rehabilitate them. You boys want to come in, smoke up?"

"Going to pass on the smoke," Jamal says.

"So you're in training," Harley says. "What's the job?"

"What else?" Highland says. "An extraction."

Another word for "extraction" is "getaway."

ASHVIK PATEL'S OFFICE is on the inland side of the Pacific Coast Highway in Laguna Beach, above a fairly decent coffee place and a more decent surf shop.

Both are important to him.

Necessities, really.

The office is unmarked, just a street number beside the door, and few people know what Ash really does there or what his business is, other than that it has something to do with computers. Those who do also know that if Ash ("I could have gone with Vic, but I went with Ash instead") isn't in his office, he's across the PCH on his shortboard.

Thick black hair combed up into an anachronistic but effective Pat Riley, eyebrows and lashes a catwalk model would kill for, and smoldering lamps beneath them that have lit the way to more than a few bedrooms, Ash holds the unofficial yet very real title of "Handsomest Straight Man in Laguna."

"I don't even try to compete with the gays," Ash has said. "It's futile. Those guys are beautiful."

Ash has done contract work for the federal government (the Department of Defense, the CIA), a few foreign regimes and the occasional high-level robber like Jamal Mobley.

What they all have in common is a need for Ash's services and the ability to pay for them.

Now he sips on a cappuccino (decent, not great) as he looks across his desk at Jamal.

"You want me to do *what*, now?" Ash asks.

Three days later, Jamal hands him a phone with a photo of the door into the corridor.

Ash takes a quick look and says, "You're in luck. I know this baby. They went on the higher end of the mid-scale techno—it only reads the retina, not the face. Now I'll need a high-res, close-up digital photo of Matthews's eyes."

"If I get you that," Jamal asks, "you can beat the scanner?"

"It won't be cheap," Ash says.

"*I'm* cheap," Jamal says. "That's why I have the money."

GORDO'S OUT COLD.

I literally fucked him unconscious, Summer thinks.

She gets his slacks off the chair and finds his cell phone in his pants pocket. Looks back to make sure he's still out and then calls the number Jamal gave her. When it goes through she clicks right off, puts the phone back into his pocket.

Then she gets her own phone out of her bag, gets back on the bed and straddles him. *"Gordon!"*

Gordon Matthews's eyes pop open. "What the—"

Summer takes the photo on her phone.

"I just wanted a souvenir," she says. Then she gets off him and starts to get dressed. It's an answer to that tired, age-old drunken party question about what you'd do—*who* you'd do—for a million dollars.

They're in an unsold hotel room at the Castle that she commandeered for the event.

"You didn't take a dick pic, did you?" Matthews asks.

"There's no magnification on this lens," Summer says. "So no."

"Nice," Matthews says. "So how many souvenir photos do you have?"

"I haven't counted."

"That many, huh?"

"And now comes the slut shaming," Summer says, buttoning her blouse.

Then he flat-out leers at her. "So, how was I?"

"Good."

"Good?"

"Good is good," Summer says. "Take the win."

"So after work tonight?" Matthews asks.

"This was a one-time deal," Summer says. "We wanted to get it out of our systems, and it's out of mine."

"But maybe it's not out of mine."

"Not my problem, Gordo."

"You're pretty cold for a woman named Summer."

"I didn't name myself." She sits down on the bed and puts on her shoes. "You got lucky, Gordo. Don't push it."

Like, if you're sitting on nineteen, don't ask for another card.

ASH EXAMINES THE photo.

"Will this work?" Jamal asks.

"Should do."

"'Should' isn't good enough," Jamal says.

"You'd prefer a different word?"

"'*Will*,'" Jamal says.

Ash smiles and looks at the photo again. "This will work."

So he has the eyes.

Now he needs the face.

The kid plays the keyboard like Parker played the sax.

Fast.

Fingers flying with intent.

Highland watches, switching his attention from the kid's hands to the computer monitor, where Summer's photo of Gordon Matthews's face becomes a whirling 3D scan. The screen splits, and on the right half Highland sees a photo of his own face, then it becomes a scan, then—

The two merge.

The kid plays the keyboard for another minute and then lifts his hands, sits back and looks at Highland.

"Now what?" Highland asks.

"Now I run this into the 3D printer and, voilà, you have your mask."

"Will it convince people?"

"Not his mother or his girlfriend," the kid says, "but someone looking briefly at a monitor? Shit, if the guy himself sees this in a monitor he'll think it's him."

"Let's do the others."

Photos of Jamal and then Colt whirl on the screen, are turned into scans, and the kid asks, "Who do you want? Denzel? Fishburne? For the other guy, Pitt, Gosling?"

"Whatever's easier."

"Denzel and Ryan it is."

He goes back to banging on the keyboard.

Highland pays him in cash.

THEY MEET OUT at Harley's airstrip, away from curious eyes.

Jamal pulls Google Maps up on his laptop. "Here's the Castle. Isa, notice the road up?"

She nods.

"Here's where the delivery truck will pull in."

He magnifies the picture to show the back entrance to the kitchen. "They bring the money in here. It's the same door we'll use to come out. Isa, your job is to get between the truck and the follow car, cause a diversion. We'll need ten minutes. Then you head for the extraction point."

She nods again. Isa is not one to waste words.

"John, Colt and I will go into the kitchen early," Jamal says. "Summer will get us uniforms."

Summer nods. No one will think anything of new kitchen help—the turnover since COVID has been constant.

"She'll create a quick distraction," Jamal says, "while John and I use the retina device to open the door to the corridor. John and I will go into the corridor. Colt waits in the kitchen until Matthews comes with the crew carrying the money and opens the door. As soon as the last of the guys with the money goes through, Colt will close and lock the door behind them. John and I will take the money, Colt opens the door and covers while we go out. Colt will follow and cover our six."

Colt asks, "What if the follow-car gunmen make it up there before we can clear?"

"That's on you," Jamal says. "Lay down enough cover fire to see us through—just give us two minutes—then take off and make it out to *here*."

He shifts the screen to show a hill to the east of the casino. "We hump it up here to the plateau. Then it's a one-point-four-mile run to the extraction point *here*."

Jamal moves the pointer around a flat clearing in the otherwise heavy brush.

"What are we looking at?" Colt asks.

"A fifty-acre grow field," Jamal says. "A primo cannabis farm, hidden in the brush. Harley, can you set the plane down on this?"

"I could land a B-52 there."

"Without running lights."

"I'm a bat."

"And take off again?" Jamal asks.

"If you make it there," Harley says, "I'll get you out."

"Where will the plane take us?" Colt asks.

"You'll find out when you're on board," Highland says. "Don't take it personally. The more information everyone has, the more danger everyone is in."

"Hell," Harley says, "he won't even tell *me* where we're flying to."

"You'll have enough money to go anywhere in the world you want," Highland says. "*Do* anything you want."

Jamal hands out new Apple watches. "Once we go, we won't be in touch. Everything goes by the clock. Use the stopwatch feature. The route on foot from the Castle to the extraction point is already programmed into navigation."

"What's the next step?" Colt asks.

"We wait," Jamal says, "until we get word of the next shipment. We'll be in touch. In the meantime, study the maps and the diagrams until they're burned into your brain. Then delete them."

"Lay low," Highland says. "Don't get into or even near any trouble. And work on your cardio. It's a steep climb up that hill, and when the plane is ready to go, it goes. It won't wait for you."

"Everyone good?" Jamal asks.

Everyone's good.

They start to head home.

Highland walks up to Colt as he's getting on his bike. "What did I tell you about that?"

"You said lay off the bike."

"Was I unclear?"

"I don't own a car," Colt says.

"Lay off the bike," Highland says.

Colt salutes him, steps on the starter and roars off.

"We should drop him," Highland says to Jamal.

"Too late," Jamal says. "Too late to find a replacement, and he already knows too much."

ON THIS JOB, Colt Mays will make more money than he's ever seen.

But you know what's better than more money?

More money.

Colt briefs his own crew.

The boys he did the Bisbee bank with, the Redding armored car job.

Travis Kellogg, Cooper D'Amico, Brad Rodriguez.

Good, tough kids, all of them. Surfers, bikers, Brazilian jujitsu guys, they can handle themselves. They're in killer shape and they're young.

Colt figures it this way:

It's a generational thing. Uncle John and Uncle Jamal have had their time. Their methods are outdated, soft. The way to take this delivery truck is to take it, grab this Matthews, make him open the truck door, and slug it out with the bitches inside.

Fast, hard, direct.

Get away on the bikes.

Colt's KTM 450 SF-X can do 123 mph, and he can ride it that fast, no problem.

No one is going to catch him at that speed.

But the "uncles" have set it up differently and Colt has to go along.

To a point.

The extraction point, to be precise.

"The plane will land in this field," Colt tells his guys, pointing at his tablet screen. "I'm the last one up, they'll wait for me."

"How can you be sure?" Travis asks.

"Because Highland's my 'uncle,'" Colt says. "He has this 'honor' thing. You guys get in place early, wait in the brush on the edge of the field. When I get there, we take them down, grab the cash and hike down to the fire road—*here*—where we left the bikes. Questions?"

"What are they carrying?"

"Dunno, but I know they ain't carrying what *we're* carrying." AR-15s, MAC-10s, grenades—enough firepower to take out all of them and the plane, if necessary. "They'll give it up."

"And if they don't?" Cooper asks.

Colt shrugs. The answer is obvious.

"You really okay with killing your *tío*?" Brad asks.

"He's about to go in for life," Colt says. "I'd be doing him a favor."

One way or another, it's John Highland's final score.

"I'LL BE GOING away for a couple of days," Highland says.

Jewel looks up from the book she's reading. "You report in a week."

"I know."

They're standing in the living room of their house in Cardiff-by-the-Sea. A big picture window onto the ocean, about a mile down the hill.

"Where are you going?" Jewel asks.

Highland doesn't answer.

She knows what his silence means. "I wish you wouldn't, John."

Highland never tires of looking at his wife. Now more than ever because he's trying to burn her image into his brain to sustain him through the years coming up. The strawberry-blond hair, the green eyes, the spray of freckles beneath, the slightly crooked nose. She's always been beautiful to him; there are still moments when he'll look at her across a room and his heart just stops.

Now he edges her feet to the side of the hassock and sits down in front of her.

"I have to," he says.

"No, you don't," Jewel says. She knows why he's going to do what he's going to do. "I'll be okay."

"You deserve more than 'okay,'" he says. "This life I've given you. It hasn't been fair to you."

"I knew who you were when I married you," she says.

There's a sadness in her eyes that's been there since the first miscarriage. Then the second and the third, and then they gave up.

"I'm sorry I could never give you children," she says.

"You gave me you," Highland says. "More than I ever dreamed."

"Then don't go."

"You know that—"

"I know," Jewel says. She knows he's not getting out. "But at least I'll be able to visit you. We can still see each other."

"We will."

"Not if something happens to you."

"Nothing is going to happen to me," Highland says.

"Because you're John Highland."

"And don't you forget it."

Highland gently pulls her up and they go into the bedroom to make love.

She's asleep when he slips out of the house.

ASH HEARS THE little alarm ding. Looks on the screen and reads the transcript of the call to Matthews's phone.

It's a Mexican number.

Then he texts Jamal.

"Your Dasher is on the way with your order."

Funny guy, Jamal thinks.

He texts Highland.

HIGHLAND SITS ON the bed in his motel room paying half attention to a hockey game on the television.

The text comes from Jamal. "Go."

ISA GETS HIGHLAND'S text. "Go."

HARLEY SETS THE spliff down long enough to look at the phone.

"Go."

Okaaaay, he thinks.

SUMMER HOLDS THE phone after the text comes in.

For the first time in her life, she feels something like cold feet.

COLT SETS HIS phone down and smiles.

Looks at his boys. "Mount up."

ASH WATCHES THE delivery truck's progress, a beeping light on his screen coming north on the 2. They're on the same phone they used to call Matthews, so Ash can track them.

Across the border at Tecate.

East on the 94 . . .

West for a few miles on the 8 . . .

North on the long, curvy road through the mountains on the 79, into the little town of Julian.

Ash texts: "Twenty-two minutes."

Highland parks the car—a freshly stolen nondescript Toyota—in the casino lot and pulls his Gordon Matthews mask over his head.

Checks his image in the mirror.

It will do.

He gets out of the car and glances at the Hummer parked in the corner of the lot.

Isa gives him the slightest nod.

As Highland walks to the casino's kitchen door, he feels more than sees Jamal and Mays—Washington and Gosling—fall in behind him.

They stride into the kitchen.

The Mexican kitchen crew doesn't check them out closely. Not ever wanting to be seen, they see nobody.

"*¿Dónde está la jefa?*" Jamal asks no one in particular.

One of the cooks points to the back of the kitchen at Summer.

Highland and Jamal walk over to her.

She leads them to the last big walk-in freezer. The door to the corridor to the vault room is in the back.

Highland takes out the iPhone that Ash gave them and holds it up to the retina scanner.

"*Inshallah,*" Jamal says.

God willing.

Highland's thinking the same thing. It feels like an eternity, but in reality it takes only a couple of seconds until he hears a click.

The door unlocks.

Then slides open.

He and Jamal walk in.

Summer walks out and goes back into the casino.

Her job is done.

Highland barely hears Ash through the little earpiece underneath the tight mask.

"*Truck on-site.*"

Gordo walks through the kitchen and out the door.

Takes his cell phone out and looks at the text he just got. Steps up to the back of the truck and says, "Five-seven-five-three-three-eight-zero."

Waits while the guy inside checks it against his code.

The truck door opens.

AR-15s point at him.

"Let's go," Gordon says.

Five men pile out of the truck, each carrying a large cardboard box labeled ACHILLES FOOD SERVICE.

"How much?" Gordon asks.

"Ten million," the lead guy says.

Gordon whistles. It's twice as much as usual.

The lead guy shrugs. "Super Bowl weekend."

They go into the kitchen.

Isa hits the gas pedal.

Steers the Hummer down the corkscrew road that leads up to the casino.

She sees the headlights of the cartel follow car coming up, jerks on the steering wheel, and the Hummer careens and then flips onto its side. Her head bangs against the passenger seat, but she straightens up and hits the button on the incendiary device.

The car will blow in ten seconds.

Isa takes off her helmet and goes to release the seat belt.

It's jammed.

Isa doesn't panic. She's ready and pulls the React device out of the cigarette lighter, fits the narrow slot over the belt and pulls down. The interior blade slices the belt and she's free. Lying back, she kicks the driver's door open, gets out and crawls off the road.

The follow-car driver stands on the brake as he sees the Hummer sliding down toward him, flipped on its side and keeping on coming.

It screeches to a halt fifteen feet in front of them.

"*¡Rodéalo!*" the guy beside him yells.

But there's no room to go around it.

The road is completely blocked.

The passenger punches a number into his phone and yells to his teammate inside the delivery truck.

"*¡No lo abras! ¡De la vuelta!*"

Don't open it! Turn around!

No response.

Then the Hummer blows.

A tower of flame shoots up and he can't see anything but fire and smoke.

Gordon looks into the retina scanner.

The door slides open, and he leads the five men carrying the cash into the corridor toward the vault room.

Business as usual, but then he sees something weird.

Himself.

Pointing a .38 revolver at him.

"Easy now," Highland says. "You don't want to die for someone else's money. Have them set the boxes down and press their hands against the wall."

Gordon hesitates.

"We can do this soft or we can do this hard," Highland says. "I'd go with soft, but it's up to you."

"Drop the boxes," Gordon says. He struggles for the Spanish.

"Suelten las cajas," Jamal says.

The men set the boxes at their feet.

"Manos contra la pared," Jamal says.

The men press their hands against the wall.

Highland holds the gun on them while Jamal takes black plastic garbage bags from under his coat, opens the boxes and starts to shove the cash—tightly wrapped bundles of hundred-dollar bills—into the bags.

"There's more than we thought," he says to Highland.

"How much?" Highland asks Gordon.

Gordon doesn't answer.

Highland aims the pistol at his face. "How much?"

"Ten," Gordon says. "Million. You know they'll kill you. It's not too late. Walk away now and—"

"Shut up," Highland says. He looks at Jamal. "Three minutes."

"Got it."

Colt steps out into the kitchen and shows the cooks and dishwasher the MAC-10.

"Tranquilos," he says. "Be chill."

He smiles at them.

Jamal fills five bags.

You wouldn't think that too much money is ever a problem, but it's a problem. They'd figured on $5 mil tops—two to three bags weighing about sixty pounds. Now it's going to be five bags checking in at a buck-ten.

They're both thinking the same thing.

"You want to leave some?" Jamal asks.

"No," Highland says.

He whacks Gordon on the side of the head with the pistol barrel and the man goes down. He grabs two bags while still holding the pistol. Jamal hefts the other three, and they press past the Mexicans and make it out the door into the walk-in freezer.

They take a breath and look at each other.

"You ready?" Highland asks.

"Born ready."

They step into the kitchen.

Isa crawls into the brush and watches the follow-car people get out of the car, draw guns and make their way around the burning Hummer.

Then they disappear up the road toward the casino.

She gives it a few seconds, then steps onto the road. Then she walks not toward the extraction point but toward the front of the casino.

"Go," Highland says to Colt.

Colt runs through the kitchen and out the back door. They follow him out.

A few seconds later, Highland hears the shooting.

Colt engaging the follow-car people.

Colt crouches in the bushes on the opposite side of the parking lot and lays down fire at the people trying to get to the back door of the casino. He fires a short burst and moves, another short burst and moves so the flashes don't give away his position.

He has his watch alarm set for exactly two minutes.

Not a second more.

Anyway, plenty of time for Highland and Jamal to get out.

When the alarm dings, he fades back into the brush and starts making his way up the hill to the extraction point.

Highland and Jamal run.

Colt waits on the edge of the grow field.

His boys are in place around the periphery, sighted in on the center of the field, where the plane will land.

So now hc just waits for Highland and Jamal.

Even though they had a head start, he knew he'd beat them up the hill, what with them being old and lugging the heavy bags.

So he waits for them to show up.

Listens for the sound of the airplane engine.

But he doesn't hear it.

What he hears instead is a helicopter rotor.

WHAT HAPPENS NEXT will be known in lore and legend as the Great Castle Cash Giveaway.

Summer sees it firsthand.

Sees Highland and Jamal burst out the kitchen door and stride through the casino tossing hundred-dollar bills out of garbage bags over their shoulders.

No one stops them.

Everyone—gamblers, drinkers, security guards—is too busy scooping up hundies to bother stopping these two guys.

If it's a bet between greed and duty, take greed and give the points.

Highland made that bet.

Knew it was his out, his exit.

People are scrambling, sprawling all over the floor, fighting each other to grab the cash. No one will ever get an accurate count of how much money got thrown around the casino that night, but it had to be a couple of hundred thou.

Highland and Jamal make it across the floor into the stairwell and then head up.

By the time they reach the roof humping the bags, they're tired and out of breath. They peel the masks off their faces, and the cold, crisp night air feels great.

Isa is already there.

"You okay?" Jamal asks her.

"Fine," she says. "Why?"

Highland looks at his watch.

"Any minute," he says.

Harley lands the chopper on the roof like he's setting a baby down on an egg.

The Bell 47 is one of those bubble-and-frame jobs that looks like a grasshopper. Built for the pilot and two passengers, but they can make it work for the three on a short hop.

Highland steps under the rotor to the pilot side. Yells, "We're a lot heavier than we thought we'd be!"

"Not good!"

"Can you do it?!"

Harley thinks for a second. In 'Nam he'd load a chopper down with wounded and make it work. He wasn't leaving anyone behind. "Load up! Hurry!"

They start shoving the bags into the cockpit.

Isa climbs in, then Jamal. Highland's about to follow him when he turns and sees—

Summer standing there.

"Take me with you!" she yells. "Please!"

"Go back down! It's okay!"

She shakes her head. "Gordon knows it was me. He figured it out, tried to grab me! They'll kill me!"

"Take her!" Highland yells.

He grabs Summer by the arm and pushes her into the cockpit.

"You won't get away!" Jamal yells.

"I don't need to get away!" Highland yells. "Only the money needs to get away!"

He doesn't need to tell him to get Jewel her share.

Highland watches the chopper fade into the dark.

Then he goes back into the stairway, walks down to the main casino and simply strolls through the chaos and out the door.

Colt waits for an hour.

His uncles don't show up.

Neither does the plane.

On the plus side, neither does the cartel.

After the hour, he gives up and calls his boys in. They walk down to their bikes and head home.

Colt feels aggrieved.

"HOW DID YOU know?" Jamal asks.

"About Colt?"

They're talking via the phone, a thick glass-and-wire partition between them.

"He never asked about what his cut would be," Highland says. "So I figured he was planning on taking the whole thing."

"Isa and her partner got married," Jamal says.

"Did you go?"

"You know how I feel about Filipino food."

"What about Summer?"

"I get postcards," Jamal says. "She's on a kind of world golf tour, it seems."

"Good for her."

"Good for her."

Just as no one ever figured out how much money had been thrown around in the Great Castle Cash Giveaway, no one ever figured out who had pulled off the heist. Summer Redbird was under some suspicion, but she was gone, and the most any of the witnesses could say was that they saw guys in masks. The names of John Highland and Jamal Mobley were tossed around among the criminal cognoscenti, because it sounded just like them. But the casino didn't have a lot of interest in pursuing the loss of illegal money in the official law enforcement system, and the cartel just wrote it off as the cost of doing business.

They didn't even bother to kill Gordon Matthews, although he was fired.

Highland is quiet for a moment and then asks, "Have you seen Jewel?"

"We went to lunch the other day," Jamal says. "She misses you."

"She visits."

"Ten mil might have bought a lot of judge," Jamal says.

It's an old discussion. Highland had simply refused to use the extra millions to try to buy his way out of the bit, and the judge racked him up on three-strikes law.

So John Highland is going to die in prison.

He's okay with it.

Jewel is well taken care of, he had done what he set out to do, go out on top, and he was tired of running, he said.

At some point you accept what life gives you.

The final score is just that.

The final score.

THE SUNDAY LIST

Rhode Island
1970

EVERY SUNDAY, NICK McKENNA PICKS up the list.

Known as the "Sunday List" for the obvious reason.

You see, Rhode Island is a dry state on Sundays.

Monday through Saturday you can walk into Tillman's Package Store and buy all the booze you want, but on the Lord's Day the liquor stores are closed, and those improvident enough not to plan ahead or to drink themselves dry on Saturday are just shit out of luck.

Unless they know enough to get on the Sunday List.

Heavy partiers, serious drinkers and hard-core alcoholics in the little town know that they can call in to Tillman's, place an order, and their booze will go out the back door into Nick McKenna's Chevy Corvair for home delivery.

Cash only, though.

No accounts, no plastic.

Nothing that would leave a record.

You give Nick the money, he gives you your bottles, and what could have been a bumpy Sunday gets smoothed out.

Not everyone can get on the Sunday List, though. You have to know Tillman, or at least Barry the clerk; you have to be a local or a regular. And you have to be discreet—if some civilian calls and says he heard about the Sunday List from you, both of you are banned.

And then Sunday becomes Saharan, a long dry desert without an oasis.

If you're smart, you not only give Nick prompt payment for the booze, you also give him a healthy tip, because while it's not mandatory, it's a good idea to have the kid on your side. If you're hungover or jonesing, or you're having a party that starts at a certain time, you'd rather be at the top of his schedule as opposed to the bottom.

Generally, Nick organizes his route geographically, driving first all the way out to the port, because the hard-drinking fishermen want their bottles early, then working his way back along the coast, stopping at the affluent houses that line the beaches. Then he heads back into town and covers the upscale suburb known as the Elms, then through the poorer parts of town near the package store. After that, he heads up to the university, where the professors form a large chunk of his clientele.

This approach makes sense because of time and gas money, but if Nick knows that you have a particular need at a certain time, and you've been a good tipper, he'll alter his route to get your order to you on time. It's not that big a deal—the town is relatively small, and no place is much more than a twenty-minute drive from any other place.

Nick's side job is illegal as hell and hence risky, even though the local cops know about it and generally tolerate it as long as certain time-honored arrangements are observed. The police chief's attitude is that he'd rather have the drinkers get quietly soused at home than drive down to Connecticut to get loaded and then drive drunk on the roads.

"You might say we're performing a community service," Tillman has opined to his friend Bill Dietz, the local bank president and premier power figure in the town. What Dietz doesn't know isn't worth knowing, and who he doesn't know isn't worth knowing. Which isn't as harsh as it sounds, because he knows pretty much everyone.

Making the deliveries isn't as risky for Nick as it used to be, because he started on the Sunday List when he was seventeen and underage. Now, a year later, Rhode Island has dropped the legal drinking age to eighteen, so at least he's not a "minor in possession" and Tillman's isn't in jeopardy of contributing to the delinquency of said minor.

And really, with all the dope flowing through town, mostly marijuana and acid but also some heroin, law enforcement is less concerned with alcohol violations. People are so freaked out about drugs, Nick thinks, that they'd practically hang a medal on your chest for just drinking.

But it's still against the law to sell alcohol on Sundays, and even if the local cops turn a blind eye, the stiffer state cops might not. Then there's the liquor board and a host of other agencies who might get it into their heads to disrupt what is a pretty orderly and sensible arrangement.

So the Sunday List is kept on the Q.T.

This particular Sunday morning, Nick pulls his 1962 yellow-and-rust Corvair into the narrow parking lot, really more of a driveway, behind Tillman's Package Store and waits for Barry to come out.

Nick is in that heady summer between high school and college, that small liminal space between ending and beginning, those short golden weeks that merge childhood into adulthood and when everything seems possible.

Slight of build and baby-faced, Nick looks more the child than the man, but don't let that fool you. He is, as they say, wise beyond his years, a maturity that comes from being the son of an artist mother and a musician father. He's an adult before his time because both his parents refuse to be.

John and Jackie McKenna felt trapped by their generation, ensnared in the ideal of the suburban house, the two-point-five kids (they have three: Nick and the twin girls, Harper and Holly), and the respective roles of breadwinner and homemaker. They had always tended more toward the beatnik gestalt anyway, so when the hippie revolution came along in the mid-'60s, they jumped sort of backward into it, reverting from their forties into their twenties, and now, as the era trudges to its desultory end, are ensconced in the amber of a perpetual Summer of Love.

The McKennas are local celebrities.

John is the lead guitarist in a rock band, Stand and Deliver, that plays the beach bars; Jackie, an artist who sells an occasional oil painting when she compromises her finer artistic sensibilities to paint a landscape, an ocean scene, a portrait or something else at least vaguely recognizable.

John is raffishly handsome, sexy in the way of rock guitar players, with long black hair, a beard and a crooked grin that has beckoned more than one fan from the club floor to the back of his van, which is, of course, a VW Microbus. Jackie is also often described as handsome, rather than pretty, herself. Tall, with aquiline features, long, straight honey hair and a pair of startling green eyes, she can't help but look elegant, betraying her aristocratic New England *Mayflower* roots even when wearing the standard hippie peasant dresses or the overalls in which she paints.

The McKennas live in a rambling Colonial-era farmhouse out on the western edge of town with a decrepit barn Nick's dad uses for rehearsals and where his mom has her studio, but the large house itself is more of a commune. Musicians and artists wander in and out, crashing on couches or the living room floor, and when Nick comes down from the little fort he's created in one dormer on the second floor, he never knows whom he's going to find in the kitchen.

Often, his mom will be up, presiding over a communal pancake breakfast, which, too often for Nick's tastes, might include an impromptu poetry reading or an especially annoying idiot in a headband playing an Irish folk song on a recorder.

Nick's current bête noire is someone called, seriously, "Baba," who is sleeping in one of the upstairs bedrooms while he builds a yurt near the little pond on the back acreage.

"His name can't really be Baba," Nick said to Jackie one morning as they looked out the kitchen window at Baba sitting in a lotus position on the grass, wearing only a loincloth and the bandanna that tied back his long brown hair. "I'll bet it's really 'Jeffrey' or 'Albert.'"

"His name is whatever he chooses it to be," Jackie said. "We are what we discover ourselves to be."

Nick figured she learned this bit from Baba.

Jackie went on. "*You* can choose your own name, if you like. We called you Nicholas because, well, we had to pick *something* to fill out the forms. But if you'd like to create your own identity . . ."

"Nick is fine," Nick said. He looked out the window as Baba lifted himself into some kind of yoga pose, Cat Shitting on Grass or Goat Humping an Inner Tube or whatever. "What is he, some kind of guru?"

"He *is* a guru," Jackie said. "He's starting an ashram."

Baba even has a name for it, the Institute for Astral Analysis, which Nick refers to as the Institute for Asshole Analysis, because all Baba really seems to do is contemplate his various bodily orifices.

One time, Baba came up to Nick and said, apropos of nothing, "Today I performed Salutation to the Sun for seven straight hours."

"Why?" Nick asked.

Baba has already gathered a few followers, a handful of reedy hippies who sleep in makeshift tents while they spend their days working on Baba's yurt (which is more than Baba manages to do), chanting some shit, listening to their master's interminable lectures and smoking massive amounts of grass, which Nick figures probably helps with the lectures.

They're incredibly annoying, and if Nick has to hear one more of them strum a guitar and whine "Blowing in the Wind" he might blow his own *brains* into the wind.

Nick is not a hippie.

To his parents' dismay, he's what is described as a "townie," with relatively short hair, shirts that aren't tie-dyed and jeans that aren't holey. He prefers beer to grass and wouldn't think of doing acid, having seen the casualties of which wandering around the acreage having deep conversations with woodchucks, and he goes into town at night to play street hockey with fishermen's kids and other townies.

"Does he have to start the ashram *here*?" Nick asked.

"He's not starting it here," Jackie said. "He's starting it in California. He's just raising the money."

"By meditating?" Nick asked.

"Baba is imagining it into being," Jackie said. "You can't actualize what you can't visualize."

Nick would like to imagine or visualize a few things into being. College tuition and textbooks, for instance. Instead, he puts in twenty to thirty hours a week at Mike's Pizza as well as delivering the Sunday List.

Even with in-state tuition, going to the nearby state university is going to cost about $4,000 a year, and Nick knows that John and Jackie are going to be of little, if any, help.

John makes decent money in the summer but rarely gets a gig the rest of the year and spends those fallow months working on an album that is never going to be an album, and Jackie's rare painting sales wouldn't pay the tuition on a single course. She had enough money from her trust fund to buy the farm, and enough to buy groceries and dope, but that's about it.

So in terms of paying for college, Nick is on his own.

Which is fine with Nick, because he does pretty *well* on his own.

And he puts his money in the bank.

Has since he started picking up odd jobs as a twelve-year-old.

Jackie had objected to the savings account, as she feels that banks are a capitalist institution.

"What do you want me to do?" Nick asked. "Leave it under the mattress? Bury it in a soup can out back? Besides, it earns interest in the bank."

"Interest is evil," Jackie said. "It is just money creating more money."

Exactly, Nick thought. That's what he likes about it. Because he works for his money, he loves the idea of his money working, too. He thinks this is one of the best ideas ever.

When he said this to his mother, Jackie said, "If that's what you want to do, go ahead. I object on ethical and aesthetic grounds, but you can do what you want."

"Actually, I can't," Nick said. "I'm a minor. The people at the bank said I have to have a responsible adult open it with me."

Lacking said responsible adult, his mother would have to do.

So they went in and opened a joint savings account, a phrase his father found hysterical. "I've done a lot of things on account of a joint, but saving sure as shit wasn't one of them."

Was for Nick, though.

He's going to live at home instead of in the dorms, the farm being just three miles from campus, so that will save a lot of money, and he got a small scholarship package from the university. So with that, his pizza job and the Sunday List he almost has enough saved to get him through his freshman year. Will by summer's end, anyway.

His intention to major in business disappoints Jackie. "I thought you'd choose something more creative," she said. "Something that wouldn't rob you of your freedom and individuality."

Nick thinks there's a little too *much* damn freedom and individuality around his house. His parents feel free to sleep with a variety of partners, to do a similarly staggering variety of drugs, and, well, to do just about anything.

Take the incident at the nude beach, for example.

There's this beach in town down at the end of a little dirt road. If you turn left onto the sand, it's pretty much your normal beach, but if you turn right it's a nudist beach.

Nick went down there one time with Molly, a girl he was dating, and started to go to the left, but Molly was curious and wanted to go to the right. So they walked down to where the naked sunbathers were, and there was Jackie, stretched out in all her glory on a blanket with another equally bare woman.

Ms. Fisher.

Nick's eighth grade English teacher and the subject of many an adolescent sexual fantasy.

Walking back from the beach, Molly said to him, "You should think about majoring in psychology. I mean, you're going to need all the therapy you can get."

The nude beach inspired a mercifully brief obsession with nude volleyball games back at the farm, with a lot of body parts bouncing and jiggling that shouldn't have been seen doing either, but it came to an abrupt end when John took an overhand slam right in the package and declared an end to volleyball of any kind, nude or otherwise.

And as regards freedom, his parents have left Nick and his siblings free to live a semi-feral existence.

The twins are thirteen, generally speak only to each other, and spend a lot of their time at the pond catching turtles, painting their shells with butterfly and flower images and then releasing them back into the wild. They also tend to a menagerie of injured birds, stray dogs and cats, and a goat named Captain Kidd who appeared from nowhere, decided to take up permanent residence, and has become a kind of one-beast recycling plant for the garbage that comes out of the house. When Captain Kidd isn't scarfing trash he's mostly licking his own genitals, to the ceaseless amusement of the twins, and provoking Jackie's comment that it's too bad *all* males can't do that and save women the trouble.

Except for the communal breakfasts, mealtimes at the farm are pretty haphazard and catch-as-you-can. Nick used to help by bringing misorders back from the pizza place, but Jackie has put a crimp on that now that she's on a Baba-inspired vegetarian kick. A couple of months ago, she made an alfalfa-sprout sandwich for Nick's school lunch.

"There's nothing *in* this sandwich," Nick said, opening the bread.

"There are alfalfa sprouts," Jackie said.

"There's nothing *in* this sandwich," Nick said. "Couldn't we go back to bologna or something?"

"Meat is murder," Jackie said.

Nick found his dad committing homicide in the barn that night, a bag from Burger King at his feet. "I'm a rocker," John said. "I need meat. Don't tell your mother."

Nick jutted his chin at the bag. "You'd better burn the evidence."

Anyway, Nick started to buy his lunch at the school cafeteria, usually a hamburger floating in a vat of grease. The seventy-five-cent cost annoyed him because it came out of his Sunday List money and because, well, Nick is cheap.

And now it's summer, and he has to bank as much money as he possibly can.

Summer is vital to everyone.

Economically, the town is a four-legged stool that now has only two and a half legs and is therefore teetering.

The four legs used to be tourism, fishing, the university and the textile factories.

The tourist industry is strong, but it only lasts from June to September. The merchants who rely on the beach-going summer people always say that they have ten weeks a year to make their money.

The population swells by a factor of ten from Memorial Day to Labor Day. Some are summer people who own houses here but flee to Florida for the long, cold gray winters; others rent cottages by the beaches at incredibly inflated weekly rates.

Whoever they are, they spend money at the grocery stores, the restaurants and bars, the gas stations, the surf shops and Tillman's Package Store.

But when they go, the money goes with them.

The university year almost exactly complements the tourist season, so it picks up some of the slack.

So far, so good.

But what once were factories are now empty shells since the textile industry moved to the warmer climate and cheaper labor down south, a migration that threw a lot of people in the town out of work.

And the fishing is in rough shape. Between the sharp rise in fuel costs, government regulations, and Russian factory ships cruising just behind the maritime limit, sending their boats to devastate the populations of cod, haddock and tuna, the once thriving fishing port is spiraling down the shitter.

It hardly pays to go out for the fish that are still there—fewer and fewer boats do it—and guys who would once crew those boats now spend more time in bars wondering what the hell happened to their lives.

Bill Dietz put it succinctly at a town council meeting. "Some of you think the factories are Jesus Christ. But I'm telling you, unlike our Savior, they're not coming back. The fish are all headed for Minsk or wherever, and they're not going to resurrect and swim back, either."

The town is fat in the summer, but winters are marginal.

Hard to balance the stool sometimes.

Tillman feels it, the slide.

He's not naive, he knows that despair is good for business. That's the funny thing about alcohol—people want it most when they're very down or very up. Summers, more people are up; winters, more are down.

But his business, like the town, is on a downward trajectory.

He still sells as much booze, but it's different booze.

Less Walker, more Seagram's.

Less French wine, more Californian.

Less imported beer, more cheap domestic.

Not so much in the summer—the tourists have money (as Dietz puts it, "The tourists have ten-dollar bills, the locals have unpaid bills") that they're willing to spend on premium product; they'd be embarrassed to serve cheap shit at their parties. But the locals? Not all of them by any means, but some of them—shit, more and more of them—are opting to cut back, both in quantity and quality.

No, not "opting," that's a misnomer implying choice.

So the Sunday List never used to be that important to Tillman. It was more of a service to loyal customers than a profit center. But more and more he needs the money just to keep the store open.

This morning, Nick gets out of the car and meets Barry, who has the Sunday List in his hand, and asks, "Any specials?"

"Just the regulars," Barry says.

Nick peruses the list. "You have the order ready?"

"What do you think?"

"Let's load up, then."

They're carrying the stuff to his car when Nick hears the phone ring. Barry answers it, starts nodding and saying "uh-huh" as he scribbles on the list. He hangs up and looks pointedly at Nick.

"No," Nick says.

"Yup."

"I thought I was going to skate this week."

"You thought wrong," Barry says. "That *was* Mr. Faherty."

"Goddamn it," Nick says.

Terry Faherty is a royal pain in the ass. Summer person, some kind of stockbroker from New York, has a freakin' mansion on the shore and more money than God ever thought about having. He always calls in late, then complains that they got his order wrong, always busts Nick's balls, tells horrible jokes and, worst of all, tips like he's a senior citizen on a fixed income.

He's a cheap, cheap bastard.

And then there's *Mrs.* Faherty.

A whole other story.

"Big order, too," Barry says. "Sounds like they're having quite a party."

Nick walks over to look at the immense order. Expensive scotch, French wines, cases of imported beers. "This is bullshit. He couldn't have forgotten this. He just likes to get special service."

"The hell you care?"

"He's not local," Nick says.

Like most of the natives, Nick has a love-hate relationship with the tourists and the summer people. On the one hand, they keep the locals alive with their money; on the other hand, they keep the locals alive with their goddamn money.

"How'd he ever get on the list, anyway?" Nick asks.

"He's a friend of Mr. Dietz," Barry says. "They go fishing together."

That does explain it, Nick thinks. If you're Bill Dietz's friend, you're everyone's friend.

"I'll have to make two trips," Nick says. "I can't fit it all in one."

"Faherty wants it by noon."

"Of course he does," Nick says. "Don't worry, I'll make it."

Barry isn't worried.

What Nick is, he's responsible. If Nick McKenna says he's going to do a job, the job will get done, done well and on time.

Nick is a worker.

Even Bill Dietz has said so. "That Nick is a worker. I don't know where he gets it, because his people are trust-fund trash. But he's a good kid."

Now Nick drives out to the fishing port.

His first stop is at Gardiner's house. It's always a little sad to Nick, because George Gardiner is the father of a girl Nick knows in high school, and he recently gave his boat back to the bank, which makes him drink even harder.

Nick gets out of the car, grabs the bottle and walks up to the door of the little clapboard house built back in the '40s before the tourists discovered the town and started building bigger summer homes.

Mrs. Gardiner opens the door.

She looks resigned, but that's the way a lot of the fishermen's wives look these days, resigned to the reality that life isn't likely to get any better than it is today and that today isn't very good at all. "Hi, Nick."

"Hi, Mrs. Gardiner."

Over her shoulder, Nick can see Emily Gardiner sitting on the living room couch watching television, but she doesn't look over at him.

He knows she's embarrassed.

Nick hands Mrs. Gardiner the bottle of Jameson. "That will be eight dollars, please, Mrs. Gardiner."

She already has the five and three ones ready and hands the bills to him.

"Thank you," Nick says.

She nods and shuts the door.

He leaves the house feeling crappy.

Not because he didn't get a tip—he knows the Gardiners need every buck they have—but because he feels like he's done something mean to Emily.

Nick makes his next delivery, then drives over to Mrs. Haverford's, a cottage across the road from the beach. The little house is as neat as a pin, freshly painted a sky blue. Roses grow on the trellis. Nick grabs her bottle of Harveys Bristol Cream, walks to the front door and rings the bell.

Mrs. Haverford comes to the door.

She's as prim and well maintained as her house. At eighty years of age, Eleanor Haverford is tiny, a Kewpie doll of a woman, as Jackie expressed when she painted her portrait seven years ago. Always stylishly and carefully dressed, even on a Sunday morning, her makeup impeccable if a little heavy, and her smile the same as she learned in finishing school so long ago.

A widow for thirty years, she's still a regular at every local cultural event. An art show, a concert, a play of any kind, Mrs. Haverford is going to be there, and Bill Dietz has made the town's one cab company aware that she is to be picked up, taken to the event and brought home for a flat fee because no one wants her to get into the old Cadillac that still sits in the driveway and take it onto the road. Likewise, the grocery store delivers every Monday, and on Sundays, Nick faithfully appears.

"Nicholas," she says now, "did you bring my sip?"

"You know I did, Mrs. Haverford."

"Won't you come in?"

Nick goes in. He doesn't really have the time, but he doesn't want to hurt her feelings by violating what has become a weekly ritual. Every Sunday, she asks him in and offers him milk and cookies, and Nick always politely declines the former but always munches a cookie while listening to a few minutes of her memories.

"I see that you're a Toll House man," Mrs. Haverford says. "Mr. Haverford was also a Toll House man. He was always a little grumpy when I made oatmeal cookies instead. And I know that he used to sneak two Toll House cookies into his jacket pocket and take them to the office, because sometimes I would find crumbs inside his pockets and I would say, 'Winthrop, why don't you wrap them in a napkin, I know that you're taking them,' but he would always deny it. Winthrop always liked to think that he was getting away with something, the rascal. I'll bet you're a bit of a rascal yourself, Nicholas. Most Toll House men . . ."

Mrs. Haverford continues her soliloquy as she opens the bottle and says, as always, "You know, I only sip on Sunday."

This is actually true. Judy Carpenter, her cleaning lady, has told Nick that Mrs. Haverford pours out the rest of the bottle and has a standing order on the Sunday List just to get a little company.

So Nick sits and listens, even though he's in a hurry. After two more anecdotes about Winthrop's mischievous exploits, he says, "I'm afraid I have to go, Mrs. Haverford."

"You men are always so busy. Winthrop, he used to . . ." She opens her little purse, takes out a dollar and hands it to Nick. "Spend this on some nice girl. Do you have a girlfriend, Nicholas?"

"Not really," Nick says. He's too busy working to date a lot, doesn't want to spend the money or bring anyone back to his zoo of a home. Sometimes he and Molly will slip under the low boughs of this big pine tree on campus that form sort of a tent and make out a little, but that's about it.

And Nick's not about to take a chance on getting a girl pregnant. He's seen that movie—guys in town who knocked a girl up, had a quick wedding and are shoveling fish guts down at the processing plant.

Not Nick—he's going to college.

The other noncollege option is Vietnam, and Nick doesn't want to do that, either. One thing he agrees with the hippies about: this war is jacked up, and Nick doesn't want to kill or die for nothing.

He's seen that movie, too—two townies just a year ahead of him in school, guys he played street hockey with, went to 'Nam and didn't make it back.

They talk about it, he and the guys he plays street hockey with. Nights in the town park, the custodians take the nets off one of the tennis courts and put out goals so the kids can play. No skates, of course, and Rollerblades aren't a thing yet; they play in sneakers and with hard, heavy rubber balls and sticks with plastic blades. After the games, they sit around and bullshit.

About hockey, girls.

Lately more about Vietnam.

"You go to college, you get a deferment," Teddy Bailey said one night.

Like they didn't know this.

"I don't have the grades to get in," Peter DeBlasio said. "But if I get drafted, I'm going into the marines. What I heard, if you're wounded, the army doesn't risk more lives going in to get you, but the marines do."

"Go in the navy," Teddy said. "You're safer on a boat."

"I don't see myself in one of those little white hats," Peter said. "I'd look like a jerkoff."

"Yeah, but a *live* jerkoff," Teddy said, then felt bad that he'd said that.

They all did.

It got real quiet then, because they were thinking about Scott and Bobby, who used to play hockey with them right here, used to sit and bullshit just like this, and now they're dead because they didn't have the money or the grades to go three miles away to the university.

"It's okay," Nick said. "If they were here, they'd laugh."

"It's always the same," Peter said. "The rich kids get off easy, the working-class kids get screwed."

"I'm not rich," Nick said.

He knew his choices.

The fish factory.

Vietnam.

College.

I'll take Door Number Three, Nick thought.

"You should have a special girl," Mrs. Haverford is saying. "Winthrop always used to call me his 'special girl.'"

"I'll bet he did," Nick says.

She must have been something back in her day.

He says goodbye, gets into his car, goes to three more fishermen's houses and makes another five dollars in tips. He drives past Faherty's house on the way back to town, then swings into the Elms to the house of the university's chief financial officer.

Mr. O'Neill, now the happy possessor of a fifth of Walker Red, pays Nick and is kind enough to ask, "Do you have all your paperwork in, Nick?"

"Yes, sir."

"Don't forget that tuition check." Mr. O'Neill hands him a five.

"I won't, Mr. O'Neill."

"Due by August thirtieth," O'Neill says.

"I have it on my calendar," Nick says.

He does.

Nick actually has a calendar with all the vital dates marked: when to register for classes, when to send in his check for tuition and fees, when his first semester starts.

Now he pulls up at a history professor's house with two bottles of Gordon's gin and two bottles of tonic water.

It's one of Nick's least favorite stops, second only to Faherty's.

The professor's wife comes to the door, and in one glance Nick knows that this is one of those mornings after one of those nights before.

"It's Nick, our deliverer," she says. "Give us this day our daily gin, and deliver us from evil, huh, Nick?"

Nick hears Dr. Kenner yell, "Just pay the kid and let him go!"

"My role in life," Mrs. Kenner says. "To pay for my husband's vices. Well, *my* vices, too, in all candor. Do you know, Nick, that I never drank before I met my husband?"

"No, ma'am."

Please make it stop, he thinks.

It doesn't.

"You don't understand," Mrs. Kenner says, getting hostile. "If *you* were married to Ed Kenner for twenty years, you'd understand."

"Goddamn it, June! Pay the kid!"

Mrs. Kenner smiles now, like, *See what I mean?* She pays Nick—her hand trembles—and gives him a ten-dollar tip. "My way of fining my husband for yelling at me. There'll be better ways later, but this will do for the moment."

Nick thanks her and gets the hell out of there. It's not his favorite stop, but it's not the worst one he's had, either. What Nick really hates is when people leave the door unlocked and yell for him to just come in, because he never knows what he's going to come in *to.*

There was that time he walked in on Father Brown unabashedly committing an act of onanism with one hand and proffering his payment with the other without missing a beat, as it were.

"That's okay, Father," Nick said, retreating. "We'll catch you the next time. When you're not so . . . busy."

Or the time when he made a delivery to a regular customer calling from a hotel room, heard the dreaded "Just come in and leave it on the table!" and saw a married couple—married, but not to each other—on the bed actually *doing* it.

"The money is on the table," the man said. "I'm counting on your discretion, Nick."

Big tip, and Nick never told anyone. He just tried, unsuccessfully, to scrape the image from his brain.

Now he hustles back to Tillman's, where Barry has Faherty's order boxed up and ready to go.

"You have ten minutes," Barry says.

"I'll make it."

And would, too.

Except—

He's two minutes from Faherty's, on Ocean Road, when the cop pulls him over.

A town cop.

Steve Pierce.

Nick has known him forever. Pierce is one of those assholes who gets off on hassling people, especially kids. He shows up sometimes when the guys are playing hockey to see if they have any beer and likes to pull over the kids with long hair just because.

He walks up to the driver's side and gestures for Nick to roll the window down.

"Where are you going, Nicky?" Pierce asks. "Faherty having one of his Sunday parties for his rich New York buddies?"

"I wouldn't know anything about that," Nick says.

A cardinal rule of the Sunday List: you never give out a customer's name, not even to another customer, and never to a cop.

"Pop the trunk," Pierce says.

"Oh, come on, Pierce."

"That's *Officer* Pierce," Pierce says. "*Now* you can get *out* of the car and open the trunk."

Nick does. He's annoyed at Pierce, but he's really more pissed off at himself. In a hurry trying to get Faherty's order to him on time, he forgot about the arrangement.

They look at the boxes of liquor.

"And I'm sure all this is for your personal use," Pierce says.

"I'm a big drinker," Nick says.

"You gonna get smart with me now?"

"I was coming to see you later," Nick says.

"'Later'?" Pierce says. "I'm not your *last* stop, McKenna, I'm your *first*."

He looks through the boxes and takes out a fifth of Glenlivet.

An expensive bottle.

"Not that one," Nick says.

"I get my taste," Pierce says.

"Yeah, a taste, not a *gulp*."

"What, it's too good for the likes of me?" Pierce asks. "I'm just, what, Crown Royal?"

"That's the arrangement," Nick says. But he knows he messed up. "Look, okay, you can have one of the Walkers."

"No, I want this one," Pierce says.

"Give me a break this once," Nick says.

"You jamokes have been underpaying for—"

"Take that up with Mr. Tillman, but right now—"

Pierce takes the Glenlivet. "Cost of doing business. And tell Tillman not to even *think* about going to the chief on this, or my hand to God—"

Nick holds his hands up like he's surrendering.

Pierce smiles again, walks back to his patrol car and pulls out.

Nick gets into his car and drives toward Faherty's. He's seven minutes late now, which sounds like nothing but *is* something to Terry Faherty.

When Nick pulls in, the man is already standing in his driveway, his arms crossed over his bare chest, tapping his foot. In his early sixties, Terry Faherty is big, an intimidating guy with a hairy barrel chest, wide shoulders, thick legs, his belly hanging over his pink Bermuda shorts. His salt-and-pepper hair is thick and curly, his mouth wide, his lips fat.

To Nick, he is the epitome of the New York summer person: loud, demanding, rude, pushy, with more money than he knows what to do with, so he uses it to bust balls.

Faherty points at his watch. “Explain to me why your time is more valuable than my time.”

“I don’t think it is, Mr. Faherty.”

“Well, apparently you do,” Faherty says, “because you just took seven minutes of my life that I can’t get back. Time is the only thing they don’t make any more of, Nick.”

“I’m sorry, sir.”

“This isn’t like you,” Faherty says. “Are you slipping, Nick?”

“No, sir.” He doesn’t tell Faherty about getting pulled over, or that he covered for him on the illegal delivery.

It’s not Faherty’s problem.

“Let’s get going,” Faherty says.

Nick gets out, opens the trunk and decides that he’d better get ahead of this. “There’s a bottle missing. The Glenlivet.”

“Why is that?” Faherty asks. “I have an important guest who drinks Glenlivet.”

He’s not happy, and Terry Faherty is a guy who thinks that he should always be happy. And if *he’s* unhappy, *other* people are going to be unhappy.

Nick doesn’t answer the question. “As soon as I unload, I’ll go to the store and get another. Then I’ll drive straight back.”

“This is not the kind of service I’m used to getting, kid.”

“I know, sir. I’m sorry.”

“Okay, take this stuff out back.”

By out back, Faherty means by the pool. The house is a hundred yards from the freakin’ ocean, Nick thinks, and the guy has an Olympic-size pool, a pool house, a built-in barbecue and grill, the whole nine yards.

And it's no short walk to get there because the house is enormous, a big central building with two wings, all made of stone. Nick is starting to sweat by the time he carries the first box to the table set up by the pool.

Mrs. Faherty is lying out on a chaise longue.

Mrs. Faherty.

The other story.

In a black bikini.

At least twenty years younger than her husband, she has shoulder-length honey-blond hair and a figure Nick has seen only in the *Playboy* magazines he and his junior high buddies used to filch from their fathers and pass around to each other.

She sees Nick, lowers her sunglasses and gives him a seductive smile. "Hello, Nick."

There have been two objects of sexual fantasy in Nick's life.

First Ms. Fisher.

But his mother effectively killed that one off.

Then Anne Bancroft in *The Graduate.*

Even the movie poster—Mrs. Robinson's bent leg in a black stocking—will remain Nick's erotic ideal. He will always have a thing for older women, and it started with that movie.

And now, this summer, Mrs. Faherty has decided that it would be amusing to play Mrs. Robinson, to Nick's extreme discomfiture.

She lowers her voice and asks, "Aren't you going to say hello, Nick?"

"Hello, Mrs. Faherty."

"You can call me Margo."

"No, I don't think I can, Mrs. Faherty."

"You can if I insist."

Please don't, Nick thinks. Please don't. "I have to go get the other boxes, Mrs. Faherty."

"Do you have a girlfriend, Nick?" she asks.

It's a hell of a lot different from Mrs. Haverford asking him. "No."

"A handsome boy like you?" Mrs. Faherty asks. "I don't believe that."

Mr. Faherty rescues him.

Nick hears him yell, *"Nick, do you think these boxes are going to carry themselves?!"*

"I'd better get going, Mrs. Faherty."

"If that's what you want, Nick, if that's what you want." She lifts the glasses back up to her eyes. "Go."

Nick walks back to the car.

"What's with you today?" Faherty asks. "This is not the Nick McKenna I know. Was Mrs. Faherty distracting you?"

"Huh?"

"'Huh?'" Faherty says, mocking him. "Mrs. Faherty in a bikini can be very distracting."

"No, sir."

"She can't be?" Faherty asks. "Are you saying that Mrs. Faherty isn't attractive?"

"No, sir."

"Are you saying that my wife is ugly?!"

"No, Mr. Faherty!"

"So you *are* attracted to her."

Nick feels like he could throw up. "I didn't say that."

"Well, what *are* you saying?" Faherty asks. "You're either attracted to her or you're not. Which is it?"

Nick takes a deep breath. "Mrs. Faherty is a lovely lady."

"You're goddamn right she is," Faherty says. "Now, do you think you can keep your eyes off my wife long enough to do your job?"

"Yes, sir."

"Well, get to it, then."

Nick carries the next two boxes to the pool area with his neck straight like it's stuck on rebar. Out of the corner of his eye he can see Mrs. Faherty give him a little wave and hear her gently laugh at him. "Nick."

He feels his cheeks turning red. He pretends not to hear her.

"Nick." Sharper this time.

Nick sighs and turns to look at her. "Yes, Mrs. Faherty?"

"My husband is a teddy bear," she says. "A big, fat, *soft* teddy bear. Do you know what I mean?"

Right now, Nick would rather be looking at Father Brown giving himself a gift. "No, I don't, Mrs. Faherty."

"Margo."

"Margo," Nick says.

"Now, was that so hard?" Mrs. Faherty asks.

"I need to get back to—"

"Well, I want you to do what you need, Nick," she says. "I want you to do exactly what you need."

Nick goes back to the driveway. "I'll go get the Glenlivet now."

"Why are you wasting both our time telling me what you're *going* to do?" Faherty asks. "Instead of just doing what you already should have done?"

Nick drives back to Tillman's.

Tells Barry, "I need a bottle of Glenlivet."

"No, I packed it."

"I need another."

"Why?" Barry asks.

"Pierce took it."

"That's not the—"

"That's what I told him," Nick says. "You can tell him, too, if you want. Or have Tillman tell him. Just give me another bottle. Faherty is wicked pissed."

"That greedy prick Pierce," Barry says as he gets another bottle. "Wait until Christmas—he's getting coal in his stocking from us."

Nick races back to Faherty's.

The fat jerk is in his driveway waiting.

Nick hands him the bottle. "Again, I'm sorry, sir."

Faherty slaps a wad of cash in Nick's hand. "Count it."

"That's not necessary," Nick says. "I'm sure that—"

"I said count it."

It's a big order, more than three hundred dollars' worth. Nick counts the bills.

"Well?" Faherty asks.

"It's twenty short," Nick says.

"That's right," Faherty says. "That's for coming up late and short."

"I'll have to pay the difference out of my own pocket," Nick says.

"What do you want from me?" Faherty asks. "Tears? Boo-hoo-hoo. Sympathy? 'Poor Nick.'"

Mrs. Faherty walks behind them into the house. She turns her head and makes a kissing gesture with her lips.

"I'm teaching you a valuable lesson, kid," Faherty says. "Consider the twenty tuition."

Nick works up as sarcastic a tone as he can dare or manage. "Gee, thanks, Mr. Faherty."

"Think nothing of it," Faherty says. "See you next Sunday, Nick."

In your dreams, Nick thinks as he pulls out of the driveway. Although he knows that they won't scratch Faherty off the Sunday List: he's too big a customer and Tillman needs the money.

Back at the liquor store, Nick gives Barry the money and says, "It's twenty short."

"It's *your* job to collect, Nick."

"I know." Nick takes his tip money out of his jeans pocket and gives Barry two fives and a ten. "Freakin' summer people ass-wipes. I wish they'd all stay in New York."

"Take it easy, now."

"I busted my ass for virtually nothing," Nick says. "I didn't even make gas money."

"Some days are like that," Barry says. "It's still early. Go down to the beach, jump in the water, cool off. You'll feel better."

Nick doesn't go to the beach but heads back to the farm instead. Maybe I *should* screw Faherty's wife, he thinks as he drives. It would serve him right. That pleasant fantasy, a heady blend of lust and vengeance, gets him home.

Where Jackie is sitting on the front lawn in a circle with Baba and his disciples in a group meditation session. They're chanting in a language that Nick doesn't understand and thinks that they don't, either. Eyes closed, they don't notice Nick, who slips into the house and goes upstairs to take a shower.

Then he lies down on his mattress and looks through the college catalog because it's almost time to put in his request for classes.

SUMMERS ARE FUNNY—long days that somehow go too fast.

As if life is giving you this wonderful gift and taking it back at the same time, little by little, but relentlessly.

Before Nick knows it, August is here.

He's managed to pick up extra hours at Mike's and a few shifts as a dishwasher at the Holiday Inn. That plus his Sunday List money, and he has more than enough for tuition and books stowed away in the bank.

Over four thousand dollars.

On Sundays he goes to all his regulars.

One morning Nick shows up at Gardiner's, and who comes to the door but Emily, his classmate. "My mom said to tell you that we don't have the money."

He hands her the bottle of Jameson.

"No, we don't have any money," she says.

"It's on the house," Nick says.

"I can't take this."

"Yeah, you can, Emily."

She looks ashamed but grateful. "Thanks, Nick."

"You got it."

Some things stay the same—when he delivers to O'Neill's, the administrator always reminds him of when the tuition is due—but when he goes to Dr. Kenner's one morning, it's the professor, not his wife, who comes to the door.

The saturnine man says, "Only the one bottle today, Nick."

"No problem," Nick says. "I'll just take the other one back."

"Mrs. Kenner left me last night."

"I'm sorry to hear that, Dr. Kenner."

Kenner shrugs. "I have mixed feelings. This *Who's Afraid of Virginia Woolf?* thing had to stop."

Nick doesn't know what that means, but he knows that something sure as hell had to stop.

He keeps going to Faherty's, even though the man's wife continues to be a cock-teasing witch and he keeps being a cheap bastard. Margo Faherty seems to always manage to be wearing the skimpiest outfit possible when Nick arrives, and she keeps giving him that mocking smirk.

Terry Faherty gives him nothing but shit.

And never a tip.

"You want a tip, Nick?" Faherty says one Sunday. "Here's a tip: Buy real estate. They're not making any more land."

Nick thought it was time they weren't making any more of, but he doesn't say so. Who knows, maybe it's both.

"Where are you in school?" Faherty asks another time.

"I'm about to start college," Nick says. "Here at URI."

"What are you majoring in?"

"I'm thinking business."

Faherty takes this in. Then he says, "Here's your tip, Nick. Dress for the job you want, not the job you have."

That's great, Nick thinks. Thanks.

Then one morning he goes to Mrs. Haverford's with her sip but doesn't see her old Cadillac in the driveway. Instead, Judy Carpenter's little Pinto is pulled up out front. The cleaning lady comes to the door.

"Where is Mrs. Haverford?" Nick asks, feeling scared.

"Nick, Mrs. Haverford passed," Judy says. "I'm cleaning the place before her daughter puts it on the market."

"I didn't know she had a daughter," Nick says.

"Well, she wasn't *much* of a daughter," Judy says.

Nick drives away feeling sad and somehow empty.

Summer is a gift that goes away.

Before it ends, Nick writes a check for his tuition and sends it in.

ON THE LAST Monday afternoon in August, Nick gets a call at the pizza parlor from a lady at the bursar's office.

Mrs. Morelli knows Nick because her son Tony was one of his classmates. She likes Nick and knows about his situation at home, so she makes the call. "Nick, this is Elizabeth Morelli. I'm sorry to tell you this, but your tuition check didn't clear. I wanted to give you a chance to deal with it."

"What?" Nick says, shocked. There was more than enough money in the bank.

"I don't know what to tell you, Nick."

"I'll call the bank."

He doesn't call but drives right over there.

The teller looks it up and says, "There were insufficient funds."

"No, I had over four thousand dollars in there," Nick says. "So what's my balance now?"

"Uhhh, you don't have a balance," she says. "It's zero."

Nick's head is spinning. "That's not possible . . . There has to be some kind of mistake . . ."

He sees Bill Dietz in his office, gesturing for him to come in. Dazed, Nick walks into the office.

"Nick," Dietz says, "your mother came in and withdrew the money."

"How could . . . ?"

"You have a joint account," Dietz says. "Didn't she tell you she was withdrawing the funds?"

"No."

Dietz looks sympathetic. He feels bad for Nick. "Maybe you had better go talk to her."

Nick races home.

JACKIE'S NOT THERE.

Neither is Baba.

Or any of the hippies.

Nick finds his dad in the barn, fingering out a Clapton lick on his guitar.

"Where's Mom?" Nick asks.

"Gone," John says. He doesn't stop playing.

"Gone *where*?"

John doesn't look up. "I guess to California."

"You *guess*?"

"Jackie took off with Baba," John says. "To San Diego. Or San Fernando, maybe? I don't know, one of them Sans."

"She took my college money," Nick says.

"She gave it to Baba," John says. "To build his ashram."

"That was *my* money," Nick says. "I worked for it."

"She said she's putting it to a higher use," John says. "That astral awareness is more important than you becoming another capitalist wage slave. She said you'd be better off."

"She *said* that?!"

John switches to another riff.

"Don't you *care*?" Nick asks.

"About which?" John asks. "Her leaving or leaving with your money?"

"Either," Nick says. "All of it."

His dad ponders this. Then he says, "You know what? I guess I don't, man. Maybe I should, but I really don't."

Nick doesn't know what to say.

"You want some fatherly advice?" John asks.

Nick damn near laughs. "Sure."

"Don't trust anybody, son." John goes back to playing.

Nick stands there for a few seconds and then goes into the house. The twins are in the kitchen making peanut butter and honey sandwiches.

"Mom's gone," Harper says.

"Gone," says Holly.

"I heard," Nick says.

"You want a sandwich?" Holly asks.

"No, thanks," Nick says.

He's not hungry.

He feels sick to his stomach.

There's going to be no college.

It's the fish factory.

Or Vietnam.

Summer's over.

And childhood with it.

Nick's an adult now.

THERE'S NO PRIVACY in a small town.

Especially not when it concerns a family as notorious as the McKennas. The word quickly gets around that the infamous Jackie ran off with a hippie guru and drained her son's bank account to boot.

The general reaction could be pretty much summed up as "Go figure. Something was bound to happen out there, with all those goings-on." No one really feels bad for John, they figure that he had it coming, but they do feel bad for Nick. "Such a hard worker, such a good kid."

Nick just gets on with it.

Shows up for his shifts at Mike's, makes pizzas and buses tables and tries to ignore that people are talking about him. He works, but he doesn't know what he's working for anymore.

He's not even sure he's going to show up for the Sunday List.

Thinks about just getting it over with and going to enlist in the marines. And if he makes it through 'Nam, he can get on the GI Bill for college.

It's a plan.

So Friday morning, he gets up, makes himself and the twins some pancakes and decides to drive to the recruiting office.

He has a couple of stops to make, though, on the way.

First to Tillman's.

Then to the town cemetery.

It's small, so it takes him only a few minutes to find Mrs. Haverford's grave. The headstone is right beside her husband's, and Nick knows that would make her happy, being next to that rascal Winthrop.

Probably makes Winthrop happy, too.

Nick opens the little bottle of Harveys Bristol Cream and pours a trickle onto her grave.

"Here's your sip, Mrs. Haverford," Nick says. "I know you usually only drink on Sundays, but . . ." He sets the bottle down by the headstone. "I'm going away, so I'm not going to be delivering the Sunday List anymore. But this should keep you for a while, until I get back, at least."

Nick drives back into town, pulls up to the curb outside of the recruiting office and gets out.

Scared, but he knows what he needs to do.

Mr. O'Neill comes out of the diner next door. "Nick. Looking forward to your first semester?"

"I'm not going, Mr. O'Neill," Nick says. "I don't have the money."

O'Neill frowns. "No, I pulled your paperwork to check on you. You're paid up for the whole year."

"That's not possible," Nick says. "There's been some kind of mistake."

"I know my job, young man," O'Neill says. "You're paid up. I'd better see you on campus next week."

"Yeah, okay."

Nick gets back in his car.

Just sits there for a few minutes.

TWO SUNDAYS LATER. Nick pulls into the narrow driveway behind Tillman's Package Store.

Barry comes out with the list.

"Any specials?" Nick asks.

"Pretty much the regulars," Barry says. "So did you start school this week?"

"Yeah."

"How was it?"

"Good," Nick says. "It's good."

It is. It's better than good.

It's excellent.

Nick drives over to Faherty's.

Terry wants his order first thing this Sunday.

But he's not standing in the driveway when Nick pulls in, so Nick walks up to the door and rings the bell.

Margo Faherty opens the door.

"Hello, Nick." Same smirk that says she knows he has a thing for her and that it's not entirely unrequited. She's wearing an emerald-green robe that shows off her hair, and the robe is open enough to display a lot of leg. "Mr. Faherty is out back by the pool."

"Thank you, Margo." Nick smiles back at her. Like, *Yeah, you know I want you and it amuses you and we both know that it's never going to happen, so no harm, no foul, Mrs. Robinson.*

He walks back around to the pool.

Terry Faherty is lying out, his fat belly dripping from just having been in the water.

His eyes must be closed under his sunglasses, because he says, "Is that Nick?"

"Did you pay my college bill, Mr. Faherty?" Nick asks.

"What do *you* think?"

"I think you did."

"Bill Dietz came to see me," Faherty says. "Told me what happened to you. He also told me I'd probably been a real prick to you."

"I never said anything to him."

"No, he *knows* me," Faherty says. "I *am* a prick. When, of course, I'm not being a teddy bear."

He looks directly at Nick and smiles.

Nick doesn't take the bait.

"I was pretty hard on you," Faherty says. "So was *Mrs.* Faherty, if we're being honest here, am I right?"

Nick lets that slide.

"Anyway," Faherty says, "Dietz told me you were a good kid. A real worker. That was my impression, too, by the way. So . . ."

He leaves it there.

"I don't know how to thank you," Nick says.

"That kind of money, it's nothing to me," Faherty says. "It's *tip* money. You get me?"

"I get you."

"And you can thank me by doing well," Faherty says. "And being on time with my orders."

"You got it."

Nick turns to leave.

"And, Nick?" Faherty says.

Nick turns back around. "Yes, sir?"

"Keep your hands off my wife, okay?"

"You got that, too, Mr. Faherty."

He walks away hearing Faherty laughing his ass off.

Nick starts laughing, too.

Rhode Island
2021

Travis Howard pulls onto the dirt road that leads up to the beautifully restored Colonial farmhouse.

He's in that heady summer between high school and college, that small liminal space between ending and beginning, those short golden weeks that merge childhood into adulthood and when everything seems possible.

The farmhouse, now painted and looking as fresh as a Sunday morning, used to be an eyesore. Travis's mom and dad, both locals, have told him stories about the place, how it used to be some sort of hippie haven with weed and orgies and God knows what.

Not anymore.

The front lawn is clipped and the flower beds that line the house are impeccably maintained. It looks like they're doing construction work on the old barn that sits behind the house.

The new owner is something of a local celebrity—reputedly a

bestselling writer. Travis hasn't read any of his novels but did see a movie they made out of one of them.

It was pretty good.

Travis grabs the bottle of Glenlivet and gets out of the car just as the owner comes out of the house to meet him.

"Mr. McKenna?" Travis asks.

"That's me," Nick says.

"Here you go."

Nick hands him three twenties.

"It's only thirty-five, sir."

"The rest is for you."

"Oh. Thanks."

"Sure," Nick says. "You in school?"

"I'm starting at the university in the fall," Travis says.

"What are you going to major in?"

"Business," Travis says.

"I started in business there," Nick says.

"Oh yeah?"

"But then I switched to English," Nick says. "It offered more freedom."

Travis looks up at the house. "I guess it worked out, huh?"

"Yeah," Nick says, looking back at the house. "I guess it did."

He bought the farm back just two years ago, after the last movie deal. It was a wreck, but his wife said it had potential. Scary word, "potential"—it usually means big bills. But he feels lucky that he can pay them. They moved in just a few months ago. Now they're restoring the barn—he'll use part of it for his office; Beth will take the bigger part for a studio.

She's an artist, God having a sense of humor.

His parents have been gone for years. John died of cancer here, Jackie out in California. The ashram thing didn't work out, of course, and she moved up to Mendocino and opened a coffee shop/art gallery and lived pretty happily. Nick would go see her when business took him out to the West Coast.

He was with her when she died.

She didn't know who he was, but that didn't matter.

The twins, strange but true, married twins who had a construction business, and they all live in a farm complex in upstate New York, where the girls raise babies and goats and there's a pond where they can catch turtles.

"Well, I'd better get going," Travis is saying.

"Long list today?"

"Long enough," Travis says. "Summer, you know."

"Summers go by fast," Nick says.

"Right?" Travis says.

Like he knows, Nick thinks.

Like a kid knows.

He goes back into the house. Beth is in the kitchen making French toast for them. She laughs and shakes her head when she sees the bottle, because neither she nor Nick actually drinks.

"Happy now?" she asks.

"Yeah," Nick says.

He puts the bottle in a cabinet.

Maybe they'll have use for it when they have a party.

Maybe not.

Doesn't matter.

Nick just wanted to be on the Sunday List.

THE NORTH WING

THE NIGHT CHRISSY PRITCHETT KILLS Sarah Gaines isn't that much different from a lot of other nights.

Chrissy gets shit-faced at the Seaside, climbs into his car behind the wheel and tries to navigate his way home through the thick Rhode Island fog. Usually, through the grace of God and the dumb luck of drunks, he manages to maneuver his old Chevy Nova the two miles or so back into his driveway, but on this night he crosses the center line, hits Sarah's little Toyota head-on and kills her.

She was twenty years old, a 4.0 student at URI on her way to becoming a speech therapist.

Thanks to Chrissy, she never makes it.

Chrissy, as so often happens with drunk drivers, has minor injuries—a few lacerations on his face and a bruised sternum—but otherwise escapes "unscathed," as they say. He's treated and released . . . that is, into the custody of the South Kingstown police, who throw his ass into a cell.

The worst part for Doug Pritchett—well, one of the worst parts, because it's all pretty shitty—is that he gets the call and is the first to roll up on the scene. He sees the smashed Toyota and knows it's going to be bad. Looking into the car, he sees that the female occupant isn't going to make it, if she isn't gone already.

It's horrifying.

The next horrifying thing is the other car.

He recognizes it right away, even before he looks at the plate.

His cousin Chrissy's old beater, the Chevy Nova.

Doug feels his heart freakin' stop.

Right away, he puts together what happened. Fuckin' Chrissy got hammered at the Seaside and decided it would be a good idea to drive home, barely a mile from the scene. He's done it countless times before, one time telling Doug that the fog was so bad he had to open the car door and look down to follow the yellow line.

"You shouldn't drive when you're like that," Doug said.

"Gotta get home."

"Call me," Doug said.

"And you're going to do what?" Chrissy asked. "Come in your cop cruiser and pick me up?"

"If I have to," Doug said. "Yeah."

So Doug knows what happened.

Here's the other thing he knows: Chrissy is going away for a long time.

And should.

He deserves it.

Chrissy is sitting on the side of the road, his head in his hands.

Doug walks over to him as the ambulance roars up, flashers and siren on.

Chrissy looks up at Doug. "What did I do? What did I do? The other car . . ."

"There's a girl in there."

"She's okay, right?" Chrissy asks. "Tell me she's okay."

"I think she's dead."

"Oh god." Chrissy bends over and throws up. Then he starts to cry, moaning, "What did I do, what did I do?"

"Stay where you are."

Doug walks to the Toyota, where the EMTs are gently extracting the girl and starting to work on her. They know it's no good—the head trauma alone . . .

Another cop car pulls up. Steiner gets out and walks up to Doug. He looks at the Nova and asks, "Jesus, isn't that your cousin's car?"

It's a small town.

"Yup," Doug says. "He's over there puking."

"Drunk?"

Doug nods.

"Let me take this one, Doug," Steiner says. "You stand down."

"No, I can—"

"No, it's protocol," Steiner says. "You're a relative, it's cleaner this way. Go back to your car."

Doug walks back and sits in his cruiser.

Watches the EMTs place the girl's body on a gurney and lift her into the ambulance. Watches Steiner administer a Breathalyzer test, then cuff Chrissy, walk him to his vehicle and sit him in the back. Then Steiner comes over. "I'm going to take Chrissy to the e-room, get him checked out."

"What did he blow?"

"Point-one-three."

"Jesus."

"Once they check him out, I'll book him on DUI."

"Right."

"We got no choice here, Doug."

"No, we don't," Doug says. "The girl?"

"She's gone," Steiner says. "They'll pronounce at the hospital, but she's gone."

"Did they get an ID?"

"Sarah Gaines," Steiner says. "Twenty years old."

"Give me the info," Doug says. "I'll notify the family."

"No, you're done for the night," Steiner says. "I'll do it."

Worst job a cop has, going to family to tell them that their loved one isn't coming home. A lot of cops never really get over it.

Doug says, "I can do it."

"No, you can't," Steiner says. "What if they find out, later, it was your cousin who killed their daughter? Anyway, I know the parents from church. It will be better coming from me."

"I should go talk to Chrissy's mom."

"It can't wait until morning?" Steiner asks. "He's not going to make bail."

"Too small a town," Doug says. "Better she hears it from me."

A COP CAR rolling up to your house at one in the morning is terrifying.

Aunt Janine flings the door open before Doug can even ring the bell.

"Oh, Jesus and Mary," she says, "is it Chrissy?"

"Can I come in, Aunt Janine?"

"Tell me!" she says. "It's Chrissy, isn't it?! He's hurt or he's dead."

She's a tiny woman, just topping five feet. Where Chrissy gets his slight frame. A skinny, middle-aged woman in an old nightgown. Doug takes her by the shoulders and guides her into the house, an old fisherman's shack with a second bedroom tacked on.

Chrissy's room.

"He's alive," Doug says.

"Thank God," Janine says. "Then what . . . why are you here? Is he in trouble again? Another goddamn DUI? Let me get some clothes on, grab my purse . . ."

It's happened twice before.

She bailed him out both times.

"He was driving drunk," Doug says. "This time he hit someone."

"Oh my god."

"Sit down, Aunt J."

She sits in one of the wooden chairs by the kitchen table. Doug sees that her hands are shaking. He reaches out and holds them.

"The other driver," he says. "I'm afraid she passed."

Janine looks down at the table and then up at him. "Oh my god, the poor thing. Is it anyone we know?"

"Sarah Gaines."

"Oh my god. I know the family."

"It's terrible."

Then she asks, "Chrissy's going to prison, isn't he?"

Doug said, "I think we'd better prepare ourselves for that possibility."

Except it's not a possibility, Doug thinks.

It's a lock.

THE GAINES FAMILY are, what do you call it, "pillars of the community." Richard Gaines is the vice president of the bank; Susan Gaines, a member of the Junior League. They go to the Congregationalist church, they give to charities, they always show up at Sarah's soccer games.

And the Gaines name goes way back, since before the Revolution.

So does the Pritchett name, but it was different.

A definite class distinction, never spoken of but always present, exists even between old WASP families. The Gaineses are and always have been patricians, New England nobility. Doug's family are and always have been the peasants. The Gaineses were the bankers, the lawyers, the factory owners, maybe clergy; the Pritchetts were the small farmers, the fishermen, the mechanics, the handymen. The Gaineses owned the big, graceful houses on Main Street and summer cottages on the beach; the Pritchetts lived in small farmhouses out in the boonies or the fishermen's shacks near the harbor. The Gaineses went to Brown; the Pritchetts celebrated when a kid graduated high school. (It was a major step up for Doug to have made it on the police force.)

People looked up at the Gaineses, and it wasn't that they looked *down* on the Pritchetts—there was a certain respect accorded to a family who had been here for coming on four hundred years—it's just that the Pritchetts were, well, Pritchetts.

You needed a part for your car, you could probably buy it from a Pritchett, and for a few extra bucks he'd install it for you. You wanted a few dozen ears of sweet corn for your summer cookout, the person you bought it from was probably a Pritchett. You needed your driveway plowed, the guy who showed up at night smoking a cig and sipping from a Dunkin' cup was probably a Pritchett.

Not a Gaines.

Gaineses hired Pritchetts.

SARAH GAINES WAS well-liked.

For good reason, Doug thinks.

An A student in high school, a soccer and track star—pretty, funny, popular.

A good kid. A really good kid.

Chrissy? Chrissy's an oddball.

One of those kids in high school who you barely knew was there. Didn't play sports, didn't even do the drama club or the band. He was a short, skinny kid who would have been bullied, except that the would-be tormentors were mostly Doug's hockey and football teammates. They thought the world of Doug and knew that, anyway, he'd beat the shit out of anyone who picked on his cousin.

Doug was always looking after Chrissy.

After all, he was family, and the kid just couldn't seem to catch a break. His old man was a piece of crap who did an Irish goodbye when Chrissy was just four years old and sent his son a birthday card every few years, just enough to keep the hurt fresh. His mom did the best she could, but Janine had to work two jobs to keep them in Wonder Bread and SpaghettiOs, so she wasn't home much.

Chrissy, he'd come in from school, grab a book and go read.

That was until he discovered alcohol, then he'd come home from school, grab a book and a bottle, go read and drink.

Used to show up at school sometimes half in the bag, not that the teachers noticed, because he'd always sit in the back of the class and not say anything anyway.

Doug noticed.

"You can't be doing this shit," Doug told him.

"Obviously I *can* be doing this shit because I *am* doing this shit," Chrissy answered. "What's the problem? I'm passing all my classes."

"Just."

"If the minimum wasn't enough," Chrissy said, "it wouldn't be the minimum."

That described it perfectly, Doug thought. His cousin had a minimum life. He expected the least, so he wasn't disappointed.

That wasn't Doug.

He had a goal and he never deviated from it.

He wanted to be a cop.

Ever since he was a little kid and watched those shows on TV, he wanted to be a cop. When he saw a police cruiser drive by, he imagined himself behind the wheel. When he played pickup basketball at the park, sometimes there were off-duty cops there, and they were his heroes, he was thrilled just to be with them.

One of them, Brian Donohoe, a sergeant in the state police, became a kind of mentor, guiding Doug in how to prepare, what classes to take, how to conduct himself so that one day he could walk into that world.

Doug wanted to be a cop because he believed that police really helped people—when they were in car accidents, when they had a problem. The police were the good guys who kept people safe from the bad guys, and he wanted to be one of them, he wanted to do that.

So he graduated high school with good grades, went to URI, got his degree in criminal justice and caught on with the local police force.

He does his job, does it well, is a rising star.

There's word that state police have an eye on him.

And that's his dream, to get onto the state police, put in his time as a trooper and then move up to the detective bureau, work on major crimes. That would be a career, that would be a life well spent.

Chrissy? Chrissy did manage to graduate high school and then got on with his minimum life. Got a series of Pritchett-type jobs pumping gas, busing tables, clearing driveways, shoveling sidewalks, putting in storm windows—enough to put gas in his shitty car and get hammered at the Seaside.

Living with his mom, reading his books, getting drunk. No real job, no girlfriend, no dreams.

That was his life.

Until he took Sarah Gaines's.

CHRISSY MADE BAIL.

His mother put her house up.

Which is a topic of conversation between him and Doug in the weeks when they're waiting for the sentencing hearing.

"You thinking about running?" Doug asks him.

They're sitting out in the little backyard behind Aunt Janine's house, near the hummingbird feeder that she religiously keeps filled with sugar water.

"What kind of dirtbag do you think I am?" Chrissy asks. "I'm going to see my own mother thrown out in the street?"

They're quiet for a second, and then Chrissy says, "She told me maybe I should, though. Said she could go live with your mom."

"She could," Doug says. "Sure."

"I'm not going to, though," Chrissy says. "Run, I mean. I couldn't do that to her."

"You'd get caught, anyway," Doug says. "Then they'd max you out, add charges. You'd do more time. Better to face the music."

"Yeah, you ain't facin' it, Doug."

Doug wants to say, *Yeah, and I didn't get behind the wheel shit-faced, either*, but he doesn't. No point in being cruel, because the music that Chrissy has to face is freakin' grim. He isn't going to do time in a county jail like the last time; he's going to prison, the ACI, the Adult Correctional Institutions.

The big time, the major leagues, where the real bad guys are.

Doug can barely stand thinking about it, can imagine what Chrissy must be feeling.

He's looking at five to fifteen.

CHRISSY PLEADS GUILTY.

On his lawyer's advice.

"You don't stand a chance of acquittal," Tom Tolbert told him. "If you make them take you to trial you'll only piss off the judge more, and she's already pretty pissed."

Tom Tolbert is the little town's best attorney, actually one of the best in the state. He's a veteran, on the last turn before retirement, and he knows whereof he speaks. And he's cutting Aunt Janine a deal on his fee. Even so, she's spent most of her meager savings paying him.

Another reason Chrissy pled guilty.

Tolbert's hourlies were already stacking up, and his mother couldn't afford the cost of a trial.

Regardless, the prosecutor, guilty plea or no, was going to ask for the max.

Bumping into Doug in the courthouse one day, Mary Beth Gilglio went right to it. “Don’t even start. We have nothing to talk about. I don’t need your cousin to plead out, because I have him dead to rights anyway. I would *love* to take him to trial. I’m going for the full fifteen.”

“I wasn’t going to start,” Doug said.

“Good,” Mary Beth said. “Because I like you, Doug. You’re good people, you have a good future. Don’t mess it up getting involved in this.”

“I am involved,” Doug said. “I was first at the scene.”

“You know what I mean.”

“Yeah, I know.”

Don’t go down with your cousin, Doug thought, by pissing people off or by looking like you’re trying to help him evade justice. You’re a police officer, and you have to do things by the book. People will respect you for that.

I did it by the book, Doug thought. I painted by the numbers.

Which Doug felt a little guilty about, a little conflicted. What I could have done is I could have driven Chrissy off the scene and then had him report the car stolen.

But I didn’t do that.

I behaved like a cop, not a cousin.

And now the kid’s life is basically over.

No, that’s not true, Doug thought.

It’s Sarah Gaines whose life is over.

But Chrissy, Chrissy is totally fucked.

THE VICTIM IMPACT statements are *brutal.*

Chrissy sits there and openly weeps as first Sarah’s father and then her mother address the judge and him.

Mr. Gaines excoriates the court system, noting that this was Christopher Pritchett's third DUI, that if the system had done its job the first or even the second time, his daughter would be alive today. Then he looks right at Chrissy. "Some people say this was an accident. This was no accident, this was your choice. You chose, as you have chosen many other times, to get drunk and then get behind the wheel. You chose to kill Sarah."

He goes on to describe the person that Sarah was, the person she was going to become, someone who wanted to help children, a loving, giving soul.

Sarah's mother can't make it through her statement. Sarah was her only daughter, her only child, and now she will never have those mother-daughter moments—the wedding, grandchildren . . .

Then she breaks down.

Recovering a little, she looks directly at Chrissy and says, "You took that from me, from us . . . There's a hole in my heart . . . that will never . . ."

She breaks down again.

Her husband steps up and puts his arm around her shoulders. "I think that's all, Your Honor."

Then Chrissy gets his chance to speak.

Still freakin' crying, snot bubbles coming out of his nose, he stands up and makes himself look at Sarah's parents.

"I'm so sorry," Chrissy says. "I'm so, so sorry. I'd give anything to take it back. If I could die instead of her, I would. But I can't. I can only say I'm sorry."

Then he turns to the judge. "I'm not going to ask for mercy, Your Honor, because I don't deserve it. Anything you give me, I've got coming to me."

He drops his face and stares at the floor.

Doug feels Aunt Janine's body tense beside him. His mother, her sister, sits on the other side of her, holding her arm.

Tolbert is saying something about Chrissy having taken full responsibility and admitted what he did, thereby saving the family the horrors of a trial, and that basically he's a young man who made a terrible mistake and how it would serve no purpose to put him away for a long time, but Doug can hardly understand him, there's this buzzing in his ears and a tightness in his chest and it doesn't matter what the lawyer says, only what the judge says, and the wait is unbearable and Doug wishes that Tolbert would just shut up.

When he finally does, the judge looks down at Chrissy and says, "It's all well and good that Mr. Pritchett has taken responsibility for his actions, but with responsibility come consequences. The consequences of his actions for Sarah Gaines and her family are permanent and irreversible. A precious life has been lost and other lives shattered.

"I also have to take notice that Mr. Pritchett has had two previous offenses, one for which he was given probation, and the other for which he served thirty days in the county jail. He has been given ample chances to mend his ways and did not do so. He learned nothing, and I see nothing to indicate that he, or the community, would benefit from future leniency."

She gives Chrissy ten years.

Two weeks to get his affairs in order before he has to report.

Aunt Janine slumps in her seat and sobs.

On the way out of the courtroom Tolbert says to Doug, "He got ten, he'll do six. He'll be, what, twenty-eight? He'll still have a life."

No, he won't, Doug thinks.

Ten years, six years, one year, doesn't matter.

Chrissy won't make it in the ACI.

Five-six, a buck-thirty, no street smarts at all, he'll be a pass-around pack. Hell, he even has a girl's name. They'll rape him in his cell, in the shower, in the hallways, on the yard. He'll be a drooling, mumbling head case inside a month.

Six years, there won't be anything left of him to walk out.

• • •

DOUG GOES TO see Brian Donohoe.

They meet for coffee in a booth at Dunkin'.

"So do I have it right?" Doug asks after telling Donohoe about his fears for Chrissy.

Donohoe is six-two with linebacker shoulders and an attitude to match. "Yeah, I'm afraid so."

"Can they put him in some kind of protective custody?"

"For a week or so, maybe," Donohoe says. "But ten years? They're not going to do that. Sooner rather than later he'll go to gen pop."

The general population.

Where the worst of the worst are housed.

"What can I do?" Doug asks.

"Do you want the cruel truth?" Donohoe asks. "Forget about him."

"I can't," Doug says. "He's family."

"He killed that girl."

"I know that."

"Then stay out of this," Donohoe says. "Look, nobody blames you. This casts no shadow on your career. A year or so, I'll put in a good word with my bosses, we'll bring you in."

"I appreciate that, I really do. But—"

"There are no goddamn 'buts.'"

Doug has one freakin' idea, and it's desperate.

"What if Chrissy got assigned to the North Wing?"

Donohoe smiles and shakes his head. "That's a private club."

Doug knows.

Nobody goes to the North Wing but made guys or their close associates. They live there together like it's a social club on the outside. They bring in food, they bring in booze, they even bring in women.

And nobody touches these guys.

So if somehow Doug can get Chrissy assigned to the North Wing, he'd be protected. He'd do his time and come out relatively intact.

Doug says, "If maybe I could just talk to the warden—"

This time Donohoe laughs out loud. "You think the *warden* makes those assignments? You know who has guys placed in the North Wing?"

Doug feels stupid.

Of course he knows who makes those assignments.

Carlo.

Just a first name, that's it.

Because everyone in southern New England knows who you mean when you say that. There's only one Carlo, the guy who's run organized crime in the area for the past thirty years.

Carlo.

The scariest guy ever.

Just his name is enough to make tough guys back down, store owners put vending machines in their places of business, bar owners come up with a monthly envelope.

"Carlo would like" or "Carlo wouldn't like" aren't observations, they're commandments.

So if Carlo says he'd like Christopher Pritchett to be assigned to the North Wing, Chrissy gets assigned to the North Wing.

Except Carlo ain't going to say that.

He probably doesn't know who Chrissy is and wouldn't give a shit if he did.

Chrissy isn't a made guy or an associate. He isn't even Italian. He's just a Swamp Yankee from an old family, and the Pritchetts have no connections with the mob.

And besides, there's no way Doug can even get to talk to Carlo.

The boss did seven years in a federal lockup for conspiracy to murder, and since he got out, he talks only to his immediate family and his consigliere.

He sure as shit ain't gonna talk to Doug Pritchett.

CHRISSY'S TALKING ABOUT killing himself.

"Don't talk like that," Doug says. "Don't even think that shit."

They're out in the backyard again, because except for lawyer visits, Chrissy isn't supposed to leave his house until he reports.

"You know what's going to happen to me in there?" Chrissy asks.

"That's movies, television," Doug says.

Except he knows it's not.

It's reality.

"I don't think I can take that," Chrissy says, on the verge of tears. "I don't think I can."

"You'd rather, what, die?"

"Yeah, maybe."

"You know what that would do to your mother?" Doug asks.

"You know what it's doing to her *now*?" Chrissy asks. "She don't eat, she don't sleep unless she takes them pills . . . Neither do I. I can't sleep, I got no appetite . . ."

Doug believes him, because Chrissy looks like pounded shit.

Even thinner, if that's possible, dark circles under his eyes . . .

The kid is falling apart and the real shit hasn't even started.

"I don't want to hear any more of this suicide bullshit," Doug says. "You knock that off right now. You're going to get through this, Chrissy."

Chrissy looks down at the grass, brown now in the scorching days of August. "I can't stop thinking about what I did to that girl."

"It will get better."

But Doug doesn't believe that.

It will only get worse.

He has to do something.

DOUG FINDS GINO Battaglia at the Rocks.

Not a tough find, because Gino is one of the managers of the restaurant, which sits on a shelf of rock that stretches into the ocean.

It's an upscale place with killer views of the coast, the bay, and Newport over there across the bridge. Great views, great food, great service, you gotta have a few bucks to dine at the Rocks, and reservations during the summer tourist season can be tough to get when the place is packed with people from Connecticut and New York who have those dollars.

Most of the locals don't.

Gino's at the bar, working out one of the thousand daily details that come up managing a place like this, but Gino is very good at his job—handsome, always well-dressed, unflappable and in charge.

He started as a busboy in the place when he was fourteen years old, then worked as a waiter for years before making it to management. He knows every nook and cranny, every potential problem; he can see around the corners.

Gino and Doug went to high school together.

They weren't close friends, but they were friends, and Gino smiles when he notices Doug standing at the reception desk and waves him in.

"Long time no," Gino says. "You need a table? Is Kelli with you? Lunch rush, but I'll find you something."

"Thanks, no," Doug says. "Actually, I came to see you. You got a couple of minutes?"

"Give me about ten," Gino says. "Sit down, have a drink, I have to go in the kitchen, keep these doofs from ruining any more lobsters."

He signals the bartender to give Doug what he wants, on the house.

Doug orders a Coke.

True to his word, Gino comes back in ten minutes and sits beside Doug. "So what's up?"

"Maybe somewhere a little more private?"

"Come on."

They walk outside, along the seawall.

It's beautiful but hot.

"Remember when we were kids?" Gino asks. "We'd come down here, try to pick up city girls?"

"You had some success, as I recall," Doug says.

Gino shrugs. "Not anymore. Did I tell you I'm engaged now?"

"No," Doug says. "Melissa?"

"Who else?"

"Congratulations."

"Yeah, I'm happy," Gino says. "Next June. You and Kelli still . . . ?"

"Sure."

"When are you going to pull the trigger on that?" Gino asks.

"Saving up for a ring."

"She's a good kid."

"The best."

"So . . ."

"You heard about my cousin," Doug says.

"Yeah, I'm sorry about that," Gino says. "Chrissy, he was always . . . I mean, no offense, but . . . he's a weird guy."

"No, I know what you mean," Doug says. "Anyway, he got ten years."

"I saw that in the paper."

"He won't make it, Gino."

Gino frowns. "Why are you telling me this?"

All through junior high, all through high school, everyone knew that Gino's dad, Bobby, was Carlo's consigliere. It was an open secret.

But Doug never mentioned it to Gino. Not that he was afraid to, but because Gino was his friend and it might have hurt him.

Doug never once, not once, ever said a word about it to him, not even when he'd go to Gino's huge house and it was, well, different.

There was the house—a mansion, really. There was the restaurant. There were rumors, but Doug never asked. Never asked, even after high school, if Gino was involved somehow, if he was part of that world or simply managing the family restaurant.

Doug always figured it was none of his freakin' business.

Gino was just his friend.

But now Doug says, "I need your help."

Long silence.

Like there's been a betrayal, a breach of an unspoken code.

Because there has been.

Finally, Gino says, "That's my father, it's not me."

"I was hoping to talk to him."

"What," Gino asks, "you think my father can just squelch this? Like it's a parking ticket? Even if he could, which he can't, he wouldn't. Did you know that Sarah Gaines used to work here?"

"No."

"Yeah, one summer, a few years ago, waited tables," Gino says. "Did a good job. So there's not a lot of sympathy for your cousin in this house."

"Chrissy deserves to go to prison," Doug says. "He doesn't deserve what's going to happen to him there."

Gino points back inside, through the large window. "Third deuce down. That's the Gaineses' regular table. They don't come much anymore, though."

"I'm asking as a friend."

"For exactly what, though?"

Doug hesitates. "I need to talk to Carlo."

"Jesus Christ, Doug."

"I was hoping your father could set it up."

"He won't do that."

"He might if you asked him."

"You want me," Gino says, "to ask my father to ask Carlo to sit down with a *cop*? That he doesn't even *know*? And what are you hoping to get from this meeting that's never going to happen?"

"I want to get Chrissy assigned to the North Wing."

"And why would anyone do that?"

Doug doesn't have an answer.

THAT NIGHT HE'S sitting in the living room of the one-bedroom house he rents in Wakefield, sipping a beer and pretending to watch a Red Sox game on television but really thinking about Chrissy.

Kelli picks up on it. "You're thinking about your cousin."

"I guess."

"There's nothing more you can do, Doug."

"'More'?" Doug asks. "I haven't done anything."

"Because there's nothing you *can* do," Kelli says. "Chrissy did what he did, end of story. He has to live with it."

"He can't."

"Then that's his problem," Kelli says. "It's not yours."

She's tough. One of the things he's always loved about her. Very black-and-white. You never have to guess what Kelli is thinking.

The phone rings.

Doug picks it up.

It's Gino.

"Here's the thing," Gino says. "All the years we've known each other, you never made any *Godfather*, Al Pacino cracks. So I talked to my dad and asked. He'll see you."

"Oh, that's great."

"But this is a one-time deal," Gino says. "Eleven tomorrow morning."

"Great. Where?"

"You go to the house like a person."

"Will you be there?" Doug asks.

"I'm working."

"Gino, thanks, huh?"

"You got it."

Doug hangs up.

"Gino?" Kelli asks, giving him that raised eyebrow.

"You've known him your whole life."

"Yeah, I have," Kelli says. "Doug, what are you doing?"

Damned if I know, Doug thinks.

THE BATTAGLIA HOUSE sits on a hill atop a huge sweep of manicured green lawn. Circular driveway, a fountain with cherubs squirting water out of their mouths. Off to one side is a little grotto with the Virgin Mary cradling a dead Jesus in her lap.

Doug gets out of his car, walks up to the door and rings the bell.

He's surprised that Bobby Battaglia answers the door himself.

Further surprised that the consigliere is wearing an unbuttoned Hawaiian shirt over Bermuda shorts and sandals.

"I've been out taking a tan," Battaglia says. "Do you tan?"

"Not so much, sir."

Doug doesn't tan, he burns.

"Come on in," Battaglia says. "When was the last time you were here? High school, maybe?"

"Sounds about right."

"We'll go to the study."

Doug follows him across the huge living room and down a hallway to a smaller room with floor-to-ceiling windows that look out on the back lawn, the swimming pool, the patio, the tennis court. In the other direction, the ocean, dark blue today, edges the horizon.

Battaglia sits behind his desk and gestures Doug into a chair. "My son has a big heart toward his friends. I expect he'll grow out of it. You have ten minutes to explain to me why I should even think about helping some little dirtbag who slaughtered a former employee of mine whose parents are my customers and friends. Go."

Doug's throat feels tight. "You know what will happen to him in the ACI."

"How would I know that?"

Doug feels a little anger and, with it, a little courage. "Because *everyone* knows."

"Okay, say that I do. So what?"

"He doesn't deserve that."

"That beautiful young girl. Her whole life in front of her. You have a girlfriend, Doug?"

"I do."

"What if it had been her?"

"I'd feel the same way."

Battaglia takes this in. Then he asks, "So what is it you want me to do?"

"Arrange a meeting for me with Carlo."

"I don't know any Carlo."

"But if you did—"

"But I don't."

"But if you *did*," Doug presses, not knowing where he's finding the nerve, "you could ask him to sit down with me."

"At which point you would ask him for what?"

Doug just says it. "To get my cousin assigned to the North Wing."

"That can't happen."

"It can if Carlo says it can," Doug says. "Maybe even if *you* do, I don't know."

Battaglia stands up, walks to a window. "Come here."

Doug gets up and joins him.

"Look way down there," Battaglia says. "To the left, that little tower. You know what that is?"

"The gatehouse to the Beach Club."

"That's right," Battaglia says. "The Beach Club, the country club. You know when those old WASPs started letting Italians through that gate? Maybe ten years ago. Because they needed our money. Because now we're the contractors, the builders, the people who make things, especially money. So I go sometimes, I have a drink, maybe I jump in the water for a quick swim. They smile, they welcome me, but I know what they think of me. I know what they call me behind my back."

"I've never been invited through those gates. I doubt I ever will be." If a Pritchett is ever going to get into the Beach Club, Doug thinks, it will be to pump out the septic tanks.

"But you think that one of your family should be invited into one of *our* clubs," Battaglia says. "Why?"

"Because he won't make it otherwise."

"And what's that to me?"

Doug swallows hard. "I'm asking for mercy, Mr. Battaglia."

"What mercy did your lowlife cousin show Sarah Gaines?" Battaglia looks at his watch. "It's admirable that you stick up for family. I respect you for that. But I don't know this 'Carlo.' I'm afraid I can't help you."

"Thank you for your time," Doug says.

Battaglia nods.

Doug shows himself out.

• • •

CHRISSY FINDS HIS mother's pills.

Isn't hard, they're in the top drawer of the side table by her bed. He also finds a fifth of Bacardi in the cabinet under the kitchen sink. His mother's drink—one rum and Coke when she gets home from work.

He'd rather it were scotch or vodka, but there you go.

Ain't like this is exactly, you know, a pleasure trip.

Problem is, Chrissy doesn't know how to do it. Do you chug the booze first and then take the pills, or do you swallow the pills and then chase them with the rum? There are problems either way, Chrissy thinks. In the first case, I might get too drunk and pass out before I can take the pills, but in the second I might fall unconscious from the pills before I can get the booze down.

He decides on a combo approach.

Goes outside, sits down, and chugs half the fifth, then puts half the Valiums in his hand, pops them in his mouth, and washes them down with another belt of rum. He waits for a few minutes, then does it again.

Then he sits back to die.

Would look up at the stars, but the fog comes in too thick.

"THE HELL DID you do?!" Doug yells. "The hell did you *do,* Chrissy?!"

Chrissy wonders if he's dead and this is hell.

Except he isn't and it ain't.

He realizes that he's in a hospital bed and his cousin is looming over him, really pissed. Jesus, Chrissy thinks, I'm such a fuckup I even fucked up killing myself.

Doug explains it to him. "Aunt Janine came home early from work and found you. Nice going, asshole. She called 911. They pumped your stomach."

"Who asked them to? Not me."

"*Such* an asshole," Doug says. "How much more do you want to put your mother through?"

"*No* more," Chrissy says. "That was the point."

"Yeah," Doug says, "she'd rather visit you at the cemetery than the joint."

"Yeah, maybe."

"Fuck you."

"I can't do it, Doug," Chrissy says. "I can't do it."

"Yeah, you can," Doug says. "You're *going* to do it. First guy who comes at you, you stick your thumbs in his eyes and rip them out."

Except he knows that's not going to work. It's not going to be one guy—they'll come at him in a gang, two of them will hold him down and then they'll take turns. After that, one of them will pimp him, put him on the block and rent him out.

Thumbs in his eyes.

Right.

The court puts Chrissy on a seventy-two-hour psychiatric hold.

The system doesn't want him hurting himself.

BATTAGLIA SITS DOWN with Carlo over plates of *pasta aglio e olio* at a restaurant on Federal Hill across from the boss's office.

It's the specialty of the house.

Doug Pritchett is a topic of discussion, because any time Carlo's name comes up, from anybody for any reason, Carlo wants to hear about it.

That old saying "you never know" doesn't apply in this world.

You always have to know.

"So this guy is *who*?" Carlo asks.

"A local cop," Battaglia says.

"A captain? A lieutenant?"

"A patrolman," Battaglia says.

Carlo sets his fork down. “Too much garlic today.”

Because, a patrolman?

Come on.

DOUG GOES TO the ATM.

Third time today, because the machine lets him take out only $300 at a time. There isn’t going to be a fourth time, because this one pretty much cleans out his account.

All his savings.

He and Kelli were saving up for the down payment on a house. They’re on a four-year plan—two years to get married, two more to buy a house. It’s going to be five now, and he’s not looking forward to telling Kelli. Turns out he doesn’t have to, because when he walks through the door after his shift, she’s waiting for him.

“The bank called me today,” she says. “At work.”

She’s a lab tech at the hospital.

“They wanted to report ‘irregular activity,’” she says. “The woman asked me if I made three withdrawals at the ATM.”

“What did you tell her?”

“That I hadn’t, but I’d check with my boyfriend,” Kelli says. “So that’s what I’m doing. I’m checking with my boyfriend. Because he apparently didn’t think maybe he should have talked to me first.”

“I knew you’d say no.”

“Damn right I would have said no,” Kelli says. “Did you give it to him already?”

“Not yet.”

“‘Yet’?” Kelli asks. “Are you seriously going to help him run? You’re a police officer—if this ever got out, you’d be fired. *You* might even go to jail.”

“I don’t know what else to do!”

“Accept it!”

"He's family!"

"And I'm not?!" Kelli asks. "Because that's what you're telling me here, that your loser cousin is more important to you than me."

"That's not true."

"Then put the money back."

"I can't."

"Then give it to me," Kelli says. "I'll put it back."

She puts her hand out, palm up.

Doug turns and walks out the door.

HE PUTS THE roll of bills in Chrissy's hand.

"What's this?" Chrissy asks.

"Get in the car," Doug says. "I'm going to drive you to Maine. You disappear in the woods up there, go to Canada, I don't know."

"What about my mom?" Chrissy asks. "The house?"

"She'd rather lose her house than her son."

"But she'd never see me again."

"At least she'd know you're alive," Doug says.

"So you think I'm going to get killed in there."

Doug says, "You tried to off yourself at the *thought* of being in there." He imagines Chrissy hanging from the cell ceiling.

"Yeah, well, I'm over that," Chrissy says. "I've been lifting weights."

Jesus, it's pathetic, Doug thinks. "You been lifting for a week? Some of those guys have been pumping iron for twenty years. Plus they got, what, a hundred pounds on you? Get in the goddamn car."

"'It ain't the size of the dog in the fight,'" Chrissy says, "'it's the size of the fight in the dog.'"

"Right. Car. Now."

"No."

"What do you mean, 'no'?"

"I mean I'm not getting in the car," Chrissy says. "I'm not going to Maine, I'm not going to Canada. I'm not going to let you wreck your career, I'm not going to let my mom lose her house. I'm going to do my time, what happens happens."

"Chrissy—"

"End o' story, cousin."

DOUG TOSSES THE cash on the bed.

Kelli looks at it and says, "Thank you for changing your mind."

"Don't thank me, thank Chrissy."

"He said no?"

"He did." Doug steps into the bathroom, turns on the shower. "He's going to do his bit. 'What happens happens.'"

Kelli gets up and leans against the bathroom doorframe as Doug gets undressed. The water always takes a few minutes to heat up. She says, "I'm impressed."

"That's nice," Doug says. "You can say that at his funeral."

He steps into the shower.

"I'm not the bad guy here, Doug," Kelli says. "Don't try to make me feel guilty."

"The money is back," Doug says. "Leave it be now, okay, Kelli? This goddamn water heater, I swear."

"I'll go to the bank tomorrow over lunch," Kelli says.

She goes back to the bedroom.

Which is good, because Doug doesn't want her to hear him cry.

BATTAGLIA'S EATING BY himself at the diner, looking at the newspaper, when Tom Tolbert walks past his booth.

"Tom."

"Hey, Bobby. Long time."

"Have a seat."

Tolbert slides in across from him. The waitress, Sally, sees him and brings over his black coffee.

The lawyer has had breakfast here about every morning for thirty years.

"So what's new?" Battaglia asks.

"Same old, same old. You?"

"Every day is a new joy."

They've known each other forever. Tolbert has represented any number of Battaglia's associates. Some he got off, some he got less, some he couldn't help at all and just made sure they didn't say anything untoward under oath.

"Hey," Battaglia says, "you represented that Pritchett kid, right? The vehicular homicide?"

"Because they're an old family," Tolbert says. "The mother is good people. And I like the cousin."

"What's his name—Doug?"

"That's right."

Sally brings his usual: two eggs over easy, bacon *and* sausage, home fries and a stack of pancakes.

"You want an angioplasty with that?" Battaglia asks.

"I had the bypass," Tolbert says. "I'm good for ten years. I mean, it's *all* going to get me. The scotch, the cigars, the fried food. Everything you love kills you, right? Next, they'll figure out how sex is lethal."

"There's the AIDS."

"What I mean."

Tolbert digs into his food.

"The cousin," Battaglia says, "isn't he a cop?"

Tolbert nods. "Town cop. At least for now."

"What do you mean?"

Tolbert looks up from his plate. Why does Battaglia care? he wonders. But he says, "Word is the state police have their eye on him."

"So he's good, then."

"Smart, hardworking, a straight-arrow Eagle Scout," Tolbert says. "Just their type. Watch, they'll snatch him up in the next year or so. Why?"

"It's just interesting," Battaglia says, "how the one cousin is a citizen and the other is a convict."

"No telling about these things," Tolbert says. "You don't have a cousin you wish you didn't?"

"More than one."

"So there you go." Tolbert holds up his cup, signaling Sally for a refill. "You ready for this one? I have a client, robbed a liquor store up in Woonsocket. Cop picks him up a block away, hauls him back to the store and asks the clerk, 'Is this the guilty son of a bitch who robbed you?' Clerk says it is. My guy gets all indignant and says, 'He can't identify me, I was wearing a mask!'"

Battaglia chuckles and shakes his head. "What are you going to do?"

"Plead him out."

"No, I meant 'what are you going to do?'" Because stupid is stupid, Battaglia knows, and there's nothing you *can* do. It should be embroidered on the state flag, WHAT ARE YOU GOING TO DO?

Sally arrives with the coffeepot.

Battaglia asks her for the check.

BATTAGLIA SITS DOWN with Carlo.

Same Federal Hill joint, same dish.

"You remember that cop I was telling you about?" Battaglia asks. "The one with the cousin about to go in?"

"No."

Battaglia refreshes his memory.

"So what about him?" Carlo asks.

"The word is that the state police are going to pick him up."

Carlo takes a piece of bread from the basket, dips it in the little plate of olive oil. "Well, maybe now we got something to talk about."

DOUG ANSWERS THE home phone.

Hears "Doug Pritchett?"

"Who's asking?"

"I'm calling on behalf of Mr. Battaglia."

"*Which* Mr. Battaglia?" Doug asks.

"The elder."

Doug knows he should hang up the freakin' phone, that this is the kind of call that changes your life.

Problem is, it could change Chrissy's, too.

So he says, "Yeah?"

"He's asking for a courtesy."

"What kind of courtesy?"

"He'd like you to run a license plate," the guy says, "for a name and an address. You think you could do that?"

Again, Doug knows he should hang up.

And that would be that.

But he doesn't. Instead, he says, "Go ahead."

"You got something to write with?"

"I think I can remember it."

The guy gives him the license plate.

Now Doug hangs up.

"Who was that?" Kelli asks from the bedroom.

"One of those sales calls."

"Come to bed."

"I gotta go do something."

• • •

IT'S A TEN-MINUTE drive to the station.

The whole ten minutes, Doug tells himself to turn around, go home, don't do this thing. That it's wrong. More than wrong—criminal. His mind runs wild with the thought of what they want with the name and address.

Are they going to kill someone, and are you making yourself an accomplice in a murder? If a body shows up in the next week or so, it could be on you.

He keeps driving.

You can't do this, he tells himself.

You can't.

But he keeps driving, pulls into the parking lot and sits there for a good five minutes, trying to decide what to do. Or, more importantly, what *not* to do.

He gets out of the car and goes in.

DOUG PUTS THE license plate through the system.

It takes all of two minutes to come up with the name and address of the owner.

It's a 1986 Mercedes.

Registered to . . .

Robert Battaglia.

UNINVITED, DOUG PULLS into the Battaglia driveway and gets out. Walks past the fountain, past the dead Jesus and his grieving mother.

Battaglia is out by the pool.

Lying on a chaise longue, working on his tan. Looks up at Doug and asks, "What brings you here?"

"What was that about?"

"It was a test," Battaglia says. "To see if you'd do it."

Doug doesn't say anything.

"You passed," Battaglia says.

Did I? Doug asks himself.

"Don't ever come here uninvited again," Battaglia says. "And you're never going to be invited. If you see my son, you nod, say hello and move on."

"I don't understand."

"You're tagged for the state police," Battaglia says. "As a local cop, you're not interesting enough to get Carlo's attention. A state cop is something different. You still want your cousin in the North Wing, right?"

"Yes."

"So you get the state job," Battaglia says. "Every once in a while we need a favor. Don't worry, we're never going to ask you to finger someone for a hit, or reveal the whereabouts of a witness, take evidence from the locker, anything like that. But if you hear about a certain investigation with certain names attached, you give us a heads-up."

"You'd own me."

"Kid, we own you *now*," Battaglia says. "We got you on tape running that plate for us. It's not serious enough they'd bother to charge you, but they *would* fire you and you couldn't get another cop job in East Dog Shit, Arkansas."

"You promise my cousin goes to the North Wing."

"It's a done deal," Battaglia says. "Now I can't promise some old lifer won't make your cousin his new bride, but at least it would be one guy instead of fifty."

"What if I don't get the state job?"

"If I was you, I'd get it," Battaglia says. "You don't, I'm going to have to think it was your way of squirreling out of this, and then I'd have to take the appropriate countermeasures. Your cousin goes to gen pop, you go to the unemployment line. So, do we have an understanding?"

"Yeah."

"Win-win," Battaglia says. "Now get out of here."

Doug turns to leave.

"And, kid?" Battaglia calls. "Don't take it too hard. You're not the first, you're not the only, and you sure as shit won't be the last."

TWO DAYS LATER. Doug drives Chrissy to the ACI to surrender.

The scene at the house was awful—Aunt Janine bawling, Chrissy trying to hold it together . . . brutal.

Now Doug says, "You do what they tell you. You don't talk to anybody, you don't try to make friends, you just do what the guards say and keep your mouth shut. When you get to the North Wing, one of those guys will show you the ropes, take you under his wing."

"Okay." Chrissy is freakin' shaking.

"It's going to be all right," Doug says. "You have friends there. Protection."

"Why?"

"Why what?"

"Why do I have friends there?" Chrissy asks. "Why do I have protection? What did you do, Doug? What did you give them?"

"That's nothing for you to worry about."

"I didn't want you to do that, Doug!"

"There's a lot of things none of us wanted," Doug says. "You do your time, you get out, you live your life. We both do."

Except I'm never getting out, Doug thinks.

Life without the possibility of parole.

DOUG GETS THE state job.

It takes another two years, but the offer comes and he takes it.

It's another year and a half before he gets a phone call asking him to put his ear to the ground about an investigation involving certain people. Doug does—it turns out the investigation concerns certain *other* people, but it's good information. Sometimes it's as useful to know what's not happening as what is.

There are other things as the years go on: license plate runs, the possible existence of a wiretap, a confirmation whether someone is in the witness protection program, but not the location or the new identity because Battaglia is smart enough to know how far he can push.

The requests are few and far between, but Doug feels terrible every time he does one.

He feels dirty.

There's suspicion around him, too, this thin cloud of doubt. He makes it into the detective division but never gets assigned to OC cases involving the mob. He gets other organized crime cases, against street gangs, motorcycle gang dope dealing, that sort of thing, but not the top cases against the Mafia.

Doug doesn't ask why.

He knows why.

He could have figured it out on his own, but one day Brian Donohoe comes close to putting it right out there.

"You know," Donohoe says, "some people here have always wondered . . . hell, to be honest with you, *I've* always wondered . . . how your cousin got assigned to the North Wing."

Doug doesn't answer him, just shrugs.

But he knows that Donohoe, his hero and mentor, suspects the truth, and Doug feels ashamed, like he's let him down.

Because he has.

And Doug figures it's partly Donohoe who keeps him away from the mob cases.

But he still has the job, he spends the three months' salary on the ring, he and Kelli get married, they buy that house.

And if she ever suspects anything, she never says it, never asks.

But the question lies there in bed between them.

Doug, he feels like he's lost part of his soul.

But he finds he can live without it.

Maybe like people who lose an arm or something. They miss it, they know it's gone, but they get used to it, they go on living.

Chrissy?

Chrissy does all right in the North Wing. He doesn't become a full member of the club, of course, but the guys there tolerate him, look after him, even invite him to Sunday pasta and gravy every once in a while. One of the old guys does make a move on him, but it's more of an invitation than a demand, and Chrissy manages to put him off.

Everyone else leaves him alone.

The word is that Carlo has a special interest in the kid.

So they put out the word: Christopher Pritchett is protected.

Untouchable.

You try something with the kid and you're going to have a problem with people you don't want a problem with.

So Chrissy does quiet time.

Even gets a job in the library, so he's around books.

Goes to the AA meetings and stays away from the homemade hooch and smuggled booze that's everywhere on the North Wing.

His mom visits regularly, brings him cookies, which Chrissy makes sure to share with the other guys on the wing.

The years go by, as years do, without any help from anyone.

Doug and Kelli have their first child, a daughter they name Allison.

The Gaineses' pain doesn't fade with the years—there's this constant dull ache, sometimes sharpened when they look at Sarah's photo on the mantel or go into her room, which stays exactly the way she left it.

One day Doug and Kelli are in Stop & Shop, wheeling Allison through the grocery store in a baby carriage, when they come face-to-face with Mrs. Gaines.

She looks at them, then at the baby carriage, then back at them.

"She's beautiful," Mrs. Gaines says.

"Thank you," says Kelli.

Doug can't say anything.

Mrs. Gaines walks around them.

Five years into Chrissy's sentence, Carlo passes.

It doesn't make any difference to Chrissy—a deal is a deal and it still holds—but the New England mob falls into a period of relative chaos in which no one really steps up to take the big chair.

Battaglia doesn't want the promotion, not with all the RICO shit going on. He figures he has more money than he can ever spend and Gino is well taken care of with the Rocks and the new restaurant he's opening, so he sits back and lets the other guys take the risks.

The deal stays the same for Doug, though.

If anything, the demands pick up. With Carlo gone and no one clearly in charge, the guys are insecure, paranoid, and they want more information.

So now about once a month he drives to a parking lot somewhere—at the beach, the mall, wherever—gets into another car and tells what he's heard, what the detectives are working on, who's doing what.

Like one night, "They're writing a warrant for a wire on the Zebra Lounge," a strip club in Providence owned by one of the guys where a lot of cash passes through. Or another time, "No, the car you thought was doing surveillance isn't one of ours."

That sort of thing.

Life goes on.

Chrissy serves seven of his ten years.

Doug is there to pick him up when he gets out.

His cousin has changed. Of course he's changed—it's been seven years, everyone changes. But Chrissy has done those years in the joint, so the changes are deeper than normal time would inflict. Like most guys in there he's been pumping iron, so while he's not exactly bulked up, he's heavier than he used to be, and stronger. His hair has thinned, though, and he has that prison pallor, those circles under the eyes, that long stare.

He's awkward getting into Doug's car.

Seven years since he's opened a car door and slid in.

"It's great to have you back, Chrissy," Doug says.

"Great to be out. And it's 'Chris' now."

"Got it."

"And, Doug?" Chris asks. "What you did for me? Thanks, huh?"

Doug takes him home.

Aunt Janine holds on to him like she's never going to let him go and sobs into his neck. "My son is home, my son is home."

But Chris doesn't stay.

He can't.

Doug gets it.

It's a small town, and everywhere Chris goes he's going to be that kid who killed Sarah Gaines. And he knows, too, that sooner rather than later he's going to bump into her mother or father, or both, and he doesn't think he can face them.

And then there are the memories.

Chris doesn't want to be on that road, to drive past the spot where he killed the girl. He's never forgiven himself, tells Doug that he doesn't think he ever will.

So Aunt Janine sells the house, and she and Chris move down to North Carolina, where most of the jobs have gone anyway. The state lets him relocate—if you can have a fuckup like Christopher Pritchett go somewhere else, why wouldn't you?

Chris gets a job in a warehouse and keeps the cork in the bottle.

Lives a quiet life.

Does his job, reads his books, watches TV at night with his mom.

No real friends, no girl, obviously no wife, no kids.

He doesn't think he deserves any of that.

IT'S NOT LONG after Chris moves south that Doug goes in to work and Brian Donohoe stops him and tells him to step into his office.

Doug knows right away that it's over.

Donohoe presses a button on a tape recorder, and Doug hears himself say, "*They're writing a warrant for a wire on the Zebra Lounge . . .*"

"That's just a sample," Donohoe says. "We flipped this guy years ago."

Doug doesn't say anything.

There's nothing to say.

"Was it worth it?" Donohoe asks.

Doug can't look at him. Can't meet his eyes.

This was his hero.

Still is.

"No, don't answer that," Donohoe says. "Don't say anything. Wait for your lawyer."

Tolbert tells him the same thing—keep his mouth shut.

The lawyer does most of his best work outside the courtroom. He tells Doug that the only thing the state police hate more than a dirty cop is a scandal. They have a pristine, incorruptible reputation to defend. As furious as the state cops are, as much as they want to fuck Doug, they want this buried more.

So if Doug pleads guilty, spares the state the cost and embarrassment of a trial and all those headlines, the prosecutor will go easy.

Doug takes the deal.

Seven years, he'll do five.

But a cop going into the ACI? It's a problem.

Doug has made cases against the Latin Kings, the Hells Angels, all kinds of very bad people who'll be delighted to see him come through those gates, who will try to make sure that he never walks out again.

Five years? they think.

He'll be lucky if he makes it five weeks.

They're sharpening the shivs already.

They shouldn't have bothered, though.

Because Doug gets assigned to the North Wing.

TRUE STORY

– True story. You know Lenny, right?
– Lenny the Barber or Lenny No Socks?
– Lenny No Socks.
– You kidding? I've known him since he *wore* socks.
– So anyway, Lenny gets this job, a house construction out on the shore, two-point-two million dollars.
– Nice.
– Right? Guy from New York—
– Of course.
– Of course. Hedge fund guy, investment banker, whatever. Comes up here on vacation, loves the place, buys this lot overlooking the ocean, just up from the lighthouse. Access to the beach—well, it's not beach right there, it's rocks, but still—
– If you want to fish.
– Yeah, if you want to fish. Stripers, bluefish, whatever. Beautiful view of Scarborough, Narragansett, Newport. Here's the beauty part: it borders a park, so no one is ever going to build right next to you. So New York guy buys the lot, gets an architect to draw up plans for a freakin' *castle*. Money no object.

– Just for the summer, which lasts, what, ten weeks?
– Eleven now. Global warming. Three floors, huge deck off the ground floor, big wide balconies on the top two—
– You can probably see Massachusetts.
– Yeah, if you want to. Then this, like, turret thing on the top, what do you call it—
– A gondola.
– I don't think so. That's a boat, right? You row it around freakin' Venice or something.
– I think you use a pole.
– A pole? How do you row with a pole?
– I dunno. Do I look like, what, a gondolist?
– Hey, Donna, as long as you have that pot, how about warming this up for me? Maybe *you* know, you're smart, what do you call that thing, looks like a turret, on top of a house sometimes . . . A cupola? I got your cupola right here—a cupola coffee.
– Hey, just a cupola guys talkin'.
– This guy, honey, he tops me every time.
– First liar doesn't stand a chance.
– Thanks, Donna.
– You ever been to Venice?
– I've never been to the old country at all.
– Neither have I. Must have been two other guys.
– Anyway, New York gets his plans drawn up, goes shopping for a contractor. Interviews everyone in freakin' Rhode Island, decides on Lenny No Socks. You know how Lenny got his name, right?
– I don't, in fact.
– He goes to a meeting with Carlo and them. Bobby—
– Bobby Bats or Bobby Five Fishes?
– Bobby Bats. Since when is Bobby Five with Carlo?

– I dunno.

– Yeah, you're right, you don't know. Because the answer is never. Bobby Five is a freakin' lowlife. Degenerate gambler. He couldn't get in the same zip code with Carlo. Anyway, they're at the table at Angelo's, Bobby *Bats* looks down, sees that Lenny isn't wearing any socks. Says, "Lenny, why aren't you wearing socks?" Lenny says, "I'm not wearing socks?" Bobby says, "No. How come?" Lenny says, "I dunno, I left the house in a hurry." Bobby, he won't let it go. Says, "I mean, it's a little disrespectful, isn't it? Coming to a sit-down with the boss, a nice place, with no socks on." But Carlo, he looks at Bobby, says, "The fuck do I care Lenny has no socks on?" After that, it was "Lenny No Socks." True story.

– I remember when Bobby Five bet on urinals.

– What?

– Yeah, we're at the Bruins game, we gotta take a piss, we're about to walk into the men's, Bobby Five says, "I'll bet you a grand there'll be an even number of urinals open."

– See, this is what I mean. Degenerate gambler.

– So Louie—

– Louie Cacciatore or Louie Doughnuts?

– Louie Doughnuts.

– Another degenerate.

– Right? So Louie, he takes the bet. Mind you, Bobby Five has already laid three g's on the Bruins giving one. We walk in, guess how many urinals are open.

– I gotta guess?

– Zero. All full. So now a debate starts whether zero is an odd or even number.

– Even.

– Why do you say that?

– It comes before one. One is an odd number. So zero has to be an even number, because they take turns. Even, odd, even, odd.
– Try telling that to Louie. You know how he got *his* name.
– You kiddin'? Look at him. I'm surprised he could fit through the men's room door.
– You'd think that, right, because he's a fat fuck? But that's not it. Louie is running a card game in the back room of this body shop. Cop comes in—
– Someone didn't get the word.
– Right? Cop—new to plainclothes—walks in to bust the place. Going to get on the scoreboard, right? Louie is sitting at the table with a carton of a dozen Dunkin', assorted—glazed, jelly, chocolate, chocolate glazed—
– You can't beat their chocolate glazed.
– No, you cannot. Louie holds the box up to the cop and asks, "Doughnut?" Everybody just cracks the fuck up. Even the cop. True story.
– So what happens?
– Louie, he tells the cop to call his sergeant. Sergeant straightens him out. Cop gets a doughnut and an ass-chewing from his sergeant, Louie gets a nickname.
– I meant with the urinal bet. What happened with the zero thing?
– Next day, these two mopes go up to Brown, find the mathematics department and go in to talk to a professor. I shit you not. Can you picture it? Poor guy with his tweed jacket, elbow patches, pipe—
– How do you know? Were you there?
– Who's telling the story here? He's sitting grading papers, thinking about coeds, whatever, when *Guys and Dolls* squeezes through his door and shuts it behind them.

"Professor," Bobby says, "we just want to know this and then we'll get out of your hair. Is zero an odd number or an even number?" Professor says, "Even." Louie says, "Bullshit," accuses Bobby of greasing the professor. Professor says, "No, it's true." Something about being able to multiply or divide by two, I dunno. Bobby tries to tip him a hundred, but the professor won't take the money. Louie pays up. Good thing, too, because the three g's Bobby put on the Bs? They lost by two goals.

– You know why they lost? Because Bobby bet on them. If Bobby bet the moon was in the sky, I'd look for it in the basement.
– What were they meeting about?
– Who?
– Lenny and Carlo and them.
– You and me? Lenny was bidding on a state job, wanted to know the competitors' bids so he could slide in just under.
– Did he?
– Like Mookie Betts. Carlo and them get the concrete, the subs on the drywalling, the windows, and Lenny makes out like a bandit. How do you think he bought that boat?
– What boat?
– Come on, you haven't heard the story about Lenny's boat?
– I guess not.
– Lenny takes his state job money and buys this fishing boat, a fifty-one-foot Lindell, used, but still—
– Must have set him back a pretty penny.
– Taxpayer money. I figure you and me got a piece of that boat, the overcharges, the cheap substitute materials, all the shit that just grew legs and walked off that state job. Anyhows, first trip, maiden voyage as it were, Lenny takes the boat out with Joe—

– Carpenter Joe or Painter Joe?

– Painter Joe. Carpenter Joe won't go near the water since . . . you know.

– No, I don't know.

– You never heard that story?

– If I heard that story, I would have said "I know." But I said "I don't know," so no, I never heard this story. I have a feeling I'm about to, though.

– Carpenter Joe does some carpentry work—

– Go figure.

– On this nice house over in Newport.

– A lot of nice houses in Newport.

– You wanna hear the story or you wanna keep interrupting me?

– Go ahead.

– It's mostly finish work—

– My lips are sealed.

– Jesus Christ. It's mostly finish work, so Carpenter Joe is watching a lot of expensive shit being moved into this place. Builds some cabinetry, which the lady of the house fills with a lot of jewelry. Diamond bracelets, rings, watches, you know. About three weeks after they move in, the owners go on vacation, Bermuda or someplace, doesn't matter. They come home, the place has been *sacked*. Bracelets, rings, watches—gonzo. And here's the thing—they don't have insurance on the shit. Why not, you might ask?

– I wasn't going to say a word.

– Because hubby, he has better insurance. You think you're in good hands with Allstate? You're in better hands with Bobby Bats. See, this guy is a stockbroker, gave Bats an inside tip that paid off big time. So he calls his good neighbor Bobby. Bats asks him a few pertinent questions: Who was the contractor? Who were the subs? Hubby gives him Joe's name and it's an aha. Few days later, Carpenter Joe gets a call from Bats: "Hey, you wanna go fishing?" Carpenter Joe is thrilled. Come on, going out on Bobby Bats's boat? He's creaming himself. Out they go, beautiful day, not a cloud in the sky, they go out through the harbor onto the open ocean—Joe, Bats, and two guys from Bats's crew, Jimmy G and Tony Fiera. Carpenter Joe is drinking a beer, baiting up, having a wonderful time. Bats says real casual-like, "Joe, you did some work on that Connelly house in Newport, didn't you?"

– Clouds appear in the sky.

– Joe says he did. "Did you hear they got robbed?" Bats asks. Joe, he says no, he hasn't heard, that's a shame. And Bats knows right away he's lying, he's guilty as shit, just from the look on his face. Says, "No, you didn't have to hear, because you were in on it. Who did you tip off, Joe? Who did the job?" Joe pleads ignorance and innocence.

– A classic pairing.

– Bats says, "You're going to tell me. Up to you whether it's the easy way or the hard way."

– Another classic.

– Joe, he swears he don't know nothing. Jimmy and Tony grab him, tip him headfirst, tie a rope around his ankles, while Bats is saying, "Joe, you hear they've spotted sharks in the area? Great whites." He takes a knife and slices the soles of Joe's feet. Not deep, but enough to bleed. Then they throw him overboard, rope tied to the railing. Joe, he can't swim so good, he's out there flailing, Bats saying, "Better not to thrash around, Joe, it attracts their attention." Joe goes under. They wait a minute, haul him up. Bats asks again, "Who did the job?" Joe, he don't wanna give it up because turns out it's his cousin Eddie and some buddy of his. Down he goes again, under the water.

– Literally shark bait.

– It takes three rounds. The dumb bastard damn near drowns, but finally he gives up his cousin. You know what Bats does next? Keeps fishing. They bandage Joe up, dry him off, keep going like nothing happened. No hard feelings. That night, Bats has his guys go find this Eddie, and lucky for him he still has the stolen shit.

– Where was he going to fence it?

– Right? Because he's Joe's cousin, he gets off with a slap on the wrist. Well, two broken wrists, but not bad given the circumstances. Joe, he just gets a lecture from Bats. "We want you to make a living, but when you're setting up a job, just check with us first. All we ask." But Carpenter Joe, he won't go near the water now. He won't go to the beach, he won't go to a pool, he won't even take a bath. He won't *drink* water.

– So it's Painter Joe, not Carpenter Joe, who goes out on the boat with Lenny No Socks.

– Correct. And they take two women that they are not connected to by, shall we say, the bonds of matrimony.

– More of a commercial relationship.

– There you go. They go out fishing—

– They didn't go fishing.

– They did a little fishing. But yeah, more screwin' and a lot of drinking. A *lot* of drinking. Sun goes down, Lenny ain't back in port, ain't even in the harbor, decides it's too risky to try to bring the boat in, given his condition, plus he wants more time with the working girls. So he calls his wife, tells her that the port is fogged in, they're going to anchor for the night.

– Sound decision.

– You would think. But Lenny hooks the boat to what he thinks are mooring buoys, except they're lobster pot buoys. It's some kind of Native rights thing, the Narragansett tribe or one of them has rights to lobster just outside the harbor.

– I thought they had casinos.

– They do have casinos, but they also have lobster pots and they got them marked with buoys, which our dumb friend Lenny ties up to to spend the night. Thusly secure, the happy campers go below for more martinis and monkey business, after which they pass out to await the rosy dawn.

– Except . . .

– Ex*cept* the wind comes up. Blows the boat along past the harbor wall right up on the beach at Jerusalem in front of those houses there. I mean, the bow is up on the sand like it's been valet parked. So soft a landing it don't even wake up our sleeping partygoers. Finally, long about daybreak, Lenny gets up, goes topside to find that his boat is now some sort of amphibious landing craft. He is beached and ain't goin' nowhere because the tide has gone out.

– As tides will do.

– As tides will do. Plus, people start coming out of those beach houses to gawk and point and laugh—

– As people will do.

– Human nature, and there's Lenny and Joe with two semi-clad hookers whining, "How are we gonna get off the boat?!" which is the least of Lenny's problems because who shows up but the Coast Guard, who see a fifty-one-foot boat on the sand with someone else's lobster pots bobbing behind it, and they have some questions, and Lenny, he's trying to say that he's not a lobster thief, that he really *is* that stupid to hook up to lobster buoys and could maybe the Coast Guard tow him out, and they're like, "The fuck we look like, an auto body shop? You gotta get a commercial guy to come out," which is going to take at least two days because there's a hurricane coming in that is also maybe going to pound Lenny's boat into pieces, and to make matters worse—

– Worse?

– The Coast Guard captain has to fill out a report, and when he asks how many people are on board, Lenny says, "Two," because he'd rather the boat get split in half by the storm than in divorce court, so he says, "Two," and the captain looks around and says, "I see four." "No, you don't," Lenny says, "you see two." Lenny, he's one of them guys who always keeps a hundred-dollar bill in his wallet, which he now takes out and repeats, "Two." The captain asks, "Are you trying to bribe me, sir?" Lenny says, "Look, it's not like they're illegal immigrants I'm smuggling into the country or something. They're just friends that I would prefer my wife not find out about. Do you have a wife?" The captain does not. "Do you own a home?" Lenny asks. "Because if you need some work done . . ." "I rent," the guy says. Lenny's getting so frustrated, so he says, "But you eat, right? Please tell me that you eat." "I eat," the captain says. Lenny says, "So, look, you, your crew—what are there, four of you? Your wives, girlfriends, whatever . . ." Then he mentions this restaurant owned by a friend of ours. "You go there, you say my name, there'll be no tab. Dinner, wine, dessert, coffee, them little mints, whatever. Now how many people do you see on this boat?" "I see two," the captain says, "but you still gotta do something about the lobster pots." "What if," Lenny says, "and I'm just saying, what if the storm blew them in?" "I guess that's possible," the captain says. So Lenny unhooks the pots, helps the two girls onto the beach, calls a cab and they leave the boat there. Lenny phones his insurance company, tells them that he was caught in a storm—which is sort of true—and that he's lucky to be alive. Somehow made it to shore, phew, close call. Lenny goes home, tells the wife that he and Joe had a miraculous escape from death, light a candle to Saint Anthony and the Virgin Mary, he's safe and home in the arms of his beloved. The hurricane does come, does pound the shit out of the boat, the insurance company pays, Lenny takes the cash, sells what's left of the thing and says he never wants another damn boat long as he lives. Everybody lives happily ever after, right? Except—

– There's always an "except."
– Two weeks later, Lenny's wife is at the hairdresser. Guess who's in the chair beside her?
– One of the girls from the boat.
– See, there you go again, topping me.
– You told me to guess. I guessed.
– One of the girls from the boat, who goes on and on about this crazy experience she and her girlfriend had on this party boat with these guys and they were blown onto the beach. Lenny's wife—
– Gina?
– I think so. She puts two and two together—
– Appropriately.
– And figures, how many boats could get washed up onshore like that? And she is wicked pissed. Leaves the hairdresser's and goes straight to one of Lenny's jobs, he was building a house over in Narragansett for Jerry O'Brien.
– Irish Jerry?

– No, *Polish* Jerry O'Brien. Jesus. Hey, honey, you got any corn muffins back there? I'd take a corn muffin, lightly toasted, butter.

– You don't want jelly?

– No, I don't want jelly. If I wanted jelly I would have said jelly.

– Because strawberry jelly with a corn muffin is delicious.

– There's only one kind of jelly. Grape jelly.

– Strawberry, raspberry, blackberry, all the berries . . .

– Can I ask you a question?

– Okay.

– When you were a kid, did your mother make you peanut butter and jelly sandwiches?

– She did.

– And what kind of jelly did she use?

– That's two questions.

– Indulge me.

– Grape.

– End of story. You know about Irish Jerry and that strip club job.

– Which strip club?

– The Spotted Tiger.

– That don't make any sense. Tigers don't have spots. Leopards have spots, cheetahs have spots, your kid's dog Spot has spots. Tigers have *stripes.*

– What are you, Animal Planet now? You know who has a piece of that club? Bobby Bats. You wanna go straighten him out about spots and stripes, whatever?

– Pass.

– Goddamn right, pass. So anyway, Irish Jerry owes twelve k, vig growing every day, to Fat Tommy.

– You know, we sure got lots of "Fats" in this thing of ours.

Fat Tommy, Fat Vinny, Fat Leo—

– Fat Pat.
– Fat Pat, my personal favorite Fat. We got any "Skinnys," though?
– Used to. There was Skinny Jimmy—he went on the, whatchamacallit, the Atkins, I dunno. Got hit by a train.
– Ouch.
– I guess they didn't see him. Back to the topic at hand, Irish Jerry owes Fat Tommy, and Tommy is always at him, like, "Where's my money?" "Get me my money." "You got my money?" So Jerry, he gets fed up, decides to hit this strip club. Breaks in through the back door around four in the morning, cracks the safe and makes off with twenty grand. In dollar bills.
– Twenty thousand dollar bills?
– He stuffs them into burlap bags, walks into Tommy's office, plops them on his desk and says, "Here's your fucking money, you fat fuck."
– But that takes serious balls, hitting a place Bobby Bats has an interest in.
– But Jerry, he didn't know that.
– How could he not know that?
– He's Irish. So now Fat Tommy is pissed off. He goes to Bobby Bats and says, "Guess who gave me two bags with thirteen thousand dollar bills? Irish Jerry." Bobby Bats says, "You got thirteen k of my money? Give it." Tommy says, "But it's payment to me on what Jerry owed me." Bobby says, "But it's money stolen from *me*, so I should get it back." What's Fat Tommy going to do, tell Bobby Bats to go fuck himself? So he gives him the money. Then he goes back to Jerry, tells him what happened and demands that Jerry pay him again. Jerry says, "I paid you once,

I ain't payin' you twice." "You paid me with stolen money," Tommy says. "What the fuck difference does that make?" Jerry says. "If you kept your big mouth shut, you'd still *have* your money. Serves you right for ratting me out, you lard-ass piece-of-shit snitch."

– Honestly? I can see both sides. WWJJD?

– "*JJ*"?

– What Would Judge Judy Do?

– But now, of course, Irish Jerry has a big problem in the form of Bobby Bats. He thinks about running, but where can you go with seven thousand one-dollar bills?

– A strip club?

– So Jerry goes to Bats with the seven thousand, says he's really sorry, he didn't know Bats had an interest in the club and that he'll never do it again. "Fuckin' A, you won't," Bats says. "You're not gonna do *any*thing again."

– I would have shit my pants. What did Jerry do?

– He shit his pants.

– No shit.

– No—*shit.* Bats, he's so disgusted, he throws Jerry out of his office.

– So Irish Jerry saves his own life by shitting himself.

– More to it than that. See, Bats has an angle.

– Of course he does, he's Bats.

– He has the stolen money back, but his partners in the strip club don't know that. And they're not going to know that unless Bats puts a hit out on Irish Jerry—then the story is going to come out. So Bats keeps all the money and doesn't tell his partners he got it back. "They should've had a better lock on the door," right, and anyway, they had insurance. So Jerry pays off his debt *and* gets a pass on the Spotted Tiger job.

– Luck of the Irish.

– The only loser in the whole thing is Fat Pat.

– You mean Fat Tommy.

– What did I say?

– Fat Pat.

– No, Fat *Tommy.* He can't tell anyone that Bats took the money from him, and he can't go back on Irish Jerry because that would bring up questions better left unasked. So he just has to eat it.

– Eating is not a problem for Fat Tommy. Or Fat Pat. *Any* of the Fats, for that matter.

– So where was I?

– I dunno. Something about Irish Jerry and Lenny No Socks's wife.

– Right. So Gina goes over to the worksite at Irish Jerry's.

– Who's Gina?

– Lenny's wife. What you said.

– You know, I think it's Celia.

– Whatever. Let's Call Her Celia gets there, she is pissed, she has spent the whole drive getting madder and madder, so by the time she gets out of the car, she is ready—and I am not speaking metaphorically here—to kill someone. And a construction site, of course, is full of lethal weapons.

– That was a good movie.

– That was a good *several* movies. First one was the best, though. *Lethal Weapon One.*

– Well, they just called it *Lethal Weapon.* Because they didn't know there was going to be a second one. Like World War One.

– What now?
– World War One, they didn't call it "World War One." They just called it the "World War" because they didn't know there was going to be a World War Two.
– Mr. History Channel here.
– So it's like *Lethal Weapon.* They didn't know there was going to be a *Two*, *Three* and *Four*, so it was just *Lethal Weapon.*
– Hey, Donna, decaf for my friend here from now on, okay?
– Anyway, I liked *Two.* Joe Pesci. And the first didn't have that, I dunno, je ne sais quoi.
– Je ne say *what*?
– It's French. I'm taking a French course.
– Are you going to France?
– Ginny's been after me for years, take her to Paris, take her to Paris. Our twenty-fifth is coming up, so I thought, what the fuck. I mean, you never know, right?
– You never know. So the worksite at Irish Jerry's is full of— I'm taking a risk here—lethal weapons. You got hammers, crowbars, nail guns, a freakin' arsenal there. She grabs one of them nail guns and starts yelling, "Where is my husband, where is that no-good son of a bitch?!" The work crew just stares at her, they're, like, frozen, then Lenny No Socks comes out of the house, sees her and says, "Sweetie, what are you doing here?" Let's Call Her Celia holds up the nail gun and says, "What am I doing here? What I'm doing here is I'm going to put a tenpenny nail through each of your balls, you lying, cheating, no-good bastard." One of the crew—you know Georgie Pass the Ball?
– I know Georgie *Big* Balls.
– This is a different guy. Used to play basketball at the Y, real ball hog, would never pass, so guys were always yelling,

"Georgie, pass the ball!" Anyway, Georgie Pass the Ball, he says to Gina—

- Celia.
- Celia, he says, "Actually, those are roofing nails."
- Not helpful.
- Celia . . . Celia?
- Celia.
- Celia didn't think so, either. She turns on Georgie, says, "Really, Georgie? Roofing nails? How about I roof your tongue to the roof of your big mouth?" Georgie rolls over the retaining wall and hides. Celia turns back to Lenny, starts advancing on him, nail gun pointed right at his package. Lenny's backing up, asking, "Is this about the boat?" "Why do you think it's about the boat, Lenny?" Celia asks him. "Why do you think it's about the boat? What did you do on the boat?" "Because I can explain," Lenny says. "You can explain, motherfucker?" Celia asks. "Go ahead, explain." "I don't know what you heard," Lenny says, "but it's not true." "If you don't know what I heard," Celia says, "how do you know it's not true?"
- Reasonable question. Rookie mistake on Lenny's part.
- "Because I haven't done *any*thing," Lenny says. "So what*ever* you heard can't be true."
- Not bad. Blanket denial. Been known to work.
- "You and your idiot friend Joe had two sluts on your boat," Celia says. "Who said that?" Lenny asks. "Your whore," Celia says. "I was sitting next to her at the beauty parlor—" "Your hair looks great, by the way," Lenny says, "did you do something different with it?" "—and she told the whole place how you fucked her on your boat, and then how you were such a dope that you ran the boat up on the beach. Sound familiar?" "Must have been a different boat," Lenny says.

"Different boat with a Joe and a Lenny on it?" "Very common names," Lenny says. "Yeah?" Celia says. "Is Lenny No Socks a very common name? Because she specifically referred to a Lenny No Socks." Now she has him up against the wall.

– Well, yeah.

– No, actually up against the wall of the house. Trapped. Nail gun pressed against his *braciòle.*

– I'm sweating here.

– And Lenny, he goes the other way with it. "I asked *you* to come on the boat. You turned me down."

– He went on the offensive.

– "You know I get seasick," Celia says. "I never wanted that boat, I wanted to use the money for a little house on the lake." "You want a house on the lake, baby?" Lenny asks. "We'll get a house on the lake. We'll go right now, drive over there, look at houses, call a Realtor. Come on."

– Genius. Grace under pressure.

– Celia asks, "Can we call Jeff Kelly?" "Anyone you want, sweetheart." "Because he's a great Realtor," Celia says. "He's great in the sack, too. I do him every Tuesday and Thursday afternoon when you're at work. Right in our bed."

– She went for the balls anyway.

– Lenny sucks it up, though, plays for the tie. Says, "So we're even." "Not quite," Celia says, and she shoots him in the foot. "*Now* we're even."

– Sicilian women.

– Later, she tells him she was lying about Mike Kelly, but Lenny, he's not sure.

– Did she get the house by the lake?

– Fuckin' A, she did. Lenny said it was cheaper than a divorce. So Gloria—

– No, Celia.

– No, *Gloria.*
– Who's Gloria?
– *My* wife. You were at the wedding.
– Your fourth.
– Third, but thanks for keeping track. Gloria tells me she had lunch with Celia and asked her why she shot him in the foot and not the balls, and Celia said she wanted a lake house, and besides, Lenny was great in bed, even the whore in the beauty parlor said so.
– Still, getting a nail in the foot . . .
– Okay, here's a question: Which hurts worse, a nail in the foot or your wife doing another guy?
– Apples and oranges—different kinds of pain.
– Pain is pain.
– No, there are three distinct and different kinds of pain—you got your physical pain, your mental pain and your emotional pain.
– What is this, science? You read this in a book?
– No, these are my own thoughts. You want to hear them or not?
– Please, proceed.
– Physical pain is simple—the nail in the foot. It hurts, but most of the time it goes away. Mental pain is like aggravation, a problem, like how do I pay off Fat Tommy, how do I make it good with Bobby Bats. Painful, but also temporary. Emotional pain, that's like your feelings and shit. That pain sticks. It don't go away.
– Time heals all wounds.
– The hell it does.
– No, sooner or later you die, you don't feel nothin'.
– I guess you weren't paying attention in catechism. Burning in hell for all eternity, that kind of thing?

– No, I paid attention. You got your heaven, you got your hell, your purgatory and your limbo, whatever the fuck that is, I never did understand. The nuns didn't, either, they just pretended they did. Trust me.
– Whenever they didn't know the answer, they just said it was a "mystery." Like that old lady on TV.
– What old lady on TV?
– The one that goes around from town to town, everywhere she goes, there's a murder, she solves the mystery. What mystery? Haven't they figured out yet she's the one doing the murders? You got an old lady serial killer here.
– You remember Mystery Mike?
– Mike Bouchard, the bookie?
– Mike *Mullen*, the burglar. Aka Mystery Mike. He's a burglar, but not a very good burglar. He breaks into this house, gets away with some costume jewelry and a TV set, leaves fingerprints everywhere.
– He didn't wear gloves?
– Didn't you hear me say he wasn't a very good burglar? He gets popped, takes a bench trial, swears up and down he was never in that house, never ever, unh-uh, never, not me. Judge asks him, "Sir, if you were never in that house, how do you explain your fingerprints being in the house?" Mike shrugs and says, "It's a *mystery*, Your Honor."
– He should have been a nun. Donna, how about a little more coffee here? Then after that don't give me any more, even if I beg. Are you sure Gloria is only your third wife?
– I think I would know.
– Because I could have sworn there was—
– Who? You mean Angela? I don't count that one. I mean, we went to Vegas, we had a good time, too many dirty

martinis, before you know it we're standing in front of Elvis tying the knot. Burning burning love, right? It lasted, what, two weeks?

– Hot fires burn fast.

– She was something, though. A real firecracker. Temper like her old man.

– Who's her old man?

– Peter DiPrete.

– Drywall Peter DiPrete or Ball Peen Peter DiPrete?

– Ball Peen Peter. Drywall is her cousin, sad to say.

– Worst thing ever he did.

– The worst. I mean, boosting a dead guy's watch. At the viewing?

– On the other hand—so to speak—why bury a guy with his watch? What, Stevie had a dentist appointment he couldn't be late for?

– Stevie, may he rest, he loved that watch. Won it in that game Marco used to run. Inside straight. Always said it was his lucky watch.

– Couldn't have been that lucky. I mean, he's dead.

– Ball Peen, he smacked Drywall around something good for snatching that watch. Said it brought shame on the family. An *infamia.* Made him give it back to Stevie's widow.

– She didn't know Ball Peen made her a widow?

– I guess not. Anyway, she pawned it.

– Ball Peen Peter. A legend.

– All of it true.

– You think? I mean you really think he—

– I don't think. I *know.*

– You don't know.

– Okay.

– Really? Thanks, Donna. And I *know* you didn't give me decaf, no matter what this guy here says. Okay, good, thanks. So, you *do* know?

– You and me? Timmy Shoes told me. He was there.

– Timmy Shoes worked with Ball Peen Peter?

– He did a lot of work with Peter.

– I didn't know.

– You *still* don't know.

– Right. Sure. So . . .

– So it's all true. Ball Peen, Timmy and Bobby Bats—he was a kid then, on the come—pick up John Mallenfont outside freakin' jai alai one night, shove him in the trunk, take him to a warehouse in Woonsocket, tie him to a chair.

– Refresh my memory, what had Mallenfont done?

– You mean *other* than knock up Carlo's niece, then throw her a beating? That's not enough, you think?

– No, that would be sufficient.

– Timmy said Peter picked up the ball peen, showed it to Mallenfont—who was sobbing and pissing his pants, by the way—then started on his toes and worked his way up. Said it took an hour or more, talk about your physical pain. When Peter was done, they threw what was left of Mallenfont in a burlap sack, weighted it, drove down and threw it in the bay. A legend is born—Ball Peen Peter.

– So DNA being what it is, I assume you kept Angela well away from the toolbox.

– And the kitchen, not that that was a challenge.

– And Carlo gave the green light on the Mallenfont thing.

– Didn't have to. If Carlo even *thought* of something, Peter went out and did it.

– But it wasn't Peter, it was Bobby, got the boost after that.

– Bobby had the brains. Peter, the muscle. Tough, sure, but

not that bright. He knew it, he was content where he was. Listen—Angela, for all her fine qualities, was no Rose Scholar, either.

– Whatever happened to Shoes?
– People still wear them, I think.
– No, Timmy Shoes.
– He got the Alzheimer's.
– That's a shame.
– I dunno. If you did a lot of work with Ball Peen Peter, maybe there are things you're better off not remembering.
– You make a point.
– Anyway, he's in one of them places now.
– Gonna happen to all of us.
– Not me, I own a gun. Anyway, this thing of ours, old age ain't always the issue.
– You know where I *don't* want to die? The joint. Gotta be the worst. Those old-timers got those heavy RICO bits, they knew they were going to die in there. That's freakin' *grim*.
– Why so many of them ratted. Not like it used to be. Not like old John Petrillo.
– Johnny Petrillo's dad?
– The same. Old John, he took a life bit for that job he did on Danny Mac, kept his mouth shut. Not *one word*, not to his lawyer, not to the court, nothin'. Sentencing, the judge asked him if he had anything to say, he just stared. Didn't even shake his head. He died in there, the cancer.
– Like I said, grim.
– The priest? Comes to give John the last rites, asks him if he wants to make his confession. John looks up at him and says, "*Now? Now* I'm going to confess?" Balls o' steel to the end. The son, though, whole different story.

– Johnny "Says Everything Twice" Petrillo. "Hi, guys! Hi, guys! How's it going? How's it going?" It takes a freakin' hour to get directions from him. "You go to the corner, you go to the corner, you turn left, you turn left." Like, how many freakin' lefts am I supposed to turn? One? Two? Sometimes I just want to whack him 'longside the head, knock the logjam loose.
– You remember him on that truck job, the load of coats out of New Hampshire? "Hands up! Hands up! This is a stickup! This is a stickup! No mistakes, no one gets hurt! No mistakes, no one gets hurt!" The guys we were *robbing* got bored.
– Remember the driver said, "Look, guy, I gotta be somewhere . . ."
– And Johnny's wedding? Took freakin' forever. "I, John, I, John, take you, Barbara, take you, Barbara . . ." Priest snapped, said, "Jesus Christ, just get on with it."
– No, he didn't.
– It makes a better story, though. But as weddings go, not as bad as Bats's daughter's. You heard about that one?
– I don't think so.
– I was there. Big Italian wedding, the whole lasagna. Full Mass, reception at Giocomo's. Thing must have run a hundred k, easy.
– Bats has the money.
– That's the thing. Bats is going to pay the caterer in cash—
– Of course he is.
– Of course. Uncle Sam was not invited to this wedding. Bats has the thirty g's shoved in his coat pocket, which he hangs up in the hallway. Perfectly safe at Giocomo's, right?
– What idiot is going to rob Giocomo's? Suicide.

– *No* idiot. The groom is Renny LeClerc—
– What was he, a freakin' goalie?
– French family from Woonsocket. The kid was, I dunno, a teacher or something, totally unconnected.
– I'm surprised Bats let that happen.
– Hey—love—what are you gonna do? Anyway, Bats goes to pay the caterer, money is not in the pocket.
– Oh, shit.
– Bats is embarrassed as hell. Every wiseguy in New England is there, it's the freakin' Appalachian meeting with place cards. The caterer—Maggiano, I think . . .
– He's good, my cousin used him.
– . . . is telling him it's okay, he knows Bats is good for it, don't worry about a thing. Happiness to the bride and groom. But Bats, he's furious, he's livid. Plus he's out thirty g's, which even for Bats is a fair piece of change. But he lets it go for the time being, doesn't say nothin', puts a smile on his face . . . cut the cake, throw the bouquet, happy couple leaves for the honeymoon. Hooray. But Bats, he goes back to the hallway . . .
– Scene of the crime.
– . . . and notices a surveillance camera.
– I'm surprised he lets *that* happen.
– Goes to the manager, gets him to show him the tape, and guess who he sees taking the cash out of his coat pocket? The father of the groom.
– Now you're just lying.
– True story.
– This is a very awkward situation.
– What's Bats going to do? Have his son-in-law's father clipped? Would have put a real crimp on the honeymoon.
– What *did* he do?

– He waits a few weeks, lets things settle down, the kids come back from the Bahamas, wherever. Then Bats goes to the in-law's place of work—he owns a couple of dry-cleaning shops—gets him alone and asks, "Is business bad? Are people not getting their clothes cleaned anymore?" This LeClerc says no, business is fine, steady. "Then why," Bats asks, "did you feel the need to steal from me? And don't deny it, because I got you on camera. This is your one fucking chance to be a man, tell me the truth." Guy starts crying, blubbering, he needs money because he had a thing on the side and now he's being blackmailed. "Why didn't you come to me?" Bats asks. "I didn't know you that well," LeClerc says. "But you knew me well enough to steal from me?" Bats asks. "I'll pay you back," LeClerc says. "I promise, I'll find a way. I'll pay you back." "No, you won't," Bats says. "I'll get my money. What's this *buchiach*'s name?" And this is where it gets interesting.

– I was already pretty interested.

– The side piece isn't a woman, it's a guy.

– LeClerc's a *finòcchio*? He has a wife and a kid, for Chrissake.

– Big world out there, my friend. Who knows. Anyway, he breaks down some more, finally admits to Bats that he was getting it off with this young guy, gives Bats his name. You ready for this? "Lance."

– You're just making shit up now.

– No—true story. He's one of them dancers, the strip shows women go to. Was banging LeClerc in his apartment and taping it all. We get his address, Bats and me go over to pay him a visit.

– Wait a second. You were in on this?

– How do you think I know the story?

– How come you didn't call me?

– Two-man job, Bats wanted to do it personally. So we knock on the door—one of them second-floor walk-ups, making Bats even more annoyed—Lance opens it up, knows he's in deep shit right away when I stick a .45 in his nose. Lance about pisses his pants.

– Well, yes.

– "Take it easy," Bats tells him. "We're not going to hurt you unless you make us. Sit down." Lance plops on the couch. His eyes are freakin' bugging. "First things first," Bats says. "I don't give a fuck you're gay—live and let live—but you are going to keep your mouth shut about Gil LeClerc and you are never going to threaten him again. Do we have this mutual understanding?" Turns out we do. "Next and last thing," Bats says. "You're going to give me the money he paid you. Go get it." "I don't have it," Lance says. "What do you mean you don't have it?" "I spent it," Lance says. "You spent thirty g's in three weeks?" Bats asks. "On what?"

– Coke.

– You did it again, stepped on my line. Yes, coke. Lance and his buddies partied hardy, shoved thirty large in snow up their noses. Turns out he was going to go back to LeClerc for more money, bleed him dry until he was tapped out. "Well, I hope you had a good time," Bats says, "because now I'm going to have to ask my friend here to put two in your head, which he will do if I ask, won't you, friend?" I nodded.

– And you would have.

– And I would have. Lance goes through the usual routine—"Please, please, I'll do anything," blah, blah, blah . . . Bats says, "What you need to do right now is think. Think of what you can do, or what you might have, that would be worth thirty k to me. I'd think real hard if I was you."

– A lot of pressure, you about to cancel his reservation.
– I didn't think the kid had nothin'. But then, out of the blue, like it dropped from the sky . . .
– What?
– LeClerc wasn't his only mark. He was also doing the dirty with, wait for it . . .
– I'm waiting patiently.
– A judge. Superior court.
– Get out.
– My hand to God. I can barely look at Bats when the kid says this, right, I don't want to tip Lance he's holding an ace.
– Was this doof trying to blackmail the judge, too?
– No, just getting cash and prizes. So Bats says, "Well, maybe we have something to work with here." Week later, I find His Honor on the street, ask him if we could have a quick cup of coffee. He tells me to see his clerk, make an appointment. I tell him he don't want his clerk in on this and ask him if he knows a guy named Lance. Two minutes later, we're in a booth, I pull out the little tape thingy, put the volume on low and hit play. The judge listens for a few seconds, turns white, shuts it off. "What do you want?" Bats hasn't been greedy with it—
– He's too smart.
– An evidentiary ruling here, a sentencing hearing there. Still, it pays off.
– Freakin' Bobby Bats. Things always work out for him.
– The way it is with bosses.
– So what about Lenny No Socks?

– What *about* Lenny No Socks?
– You started to tell me a story about him.
– A story.
– About a house? New York guy?
– Right. So Lenny builds the guy's house. A castle. Takes over a year. New York guy checks it out. Loves it. It's perfect. Except—
– Always an "except."
– Remember I told you the adjacent property was a park?
– Vaguely. Seems like a long time ago now.
– Well, it was a park. Some old lady died, the park is undeveloped land and she wanted it to stay that way, so she set up the foundation so that nothing is built on it "in perpetuity."
– Good for New York guy.
– You would think, huh? Except—
– Here we go.
– The guy who runs the foundation comes out, starts taking measurements. And you ain't gonna believe this—they built the house five feet onto the park.
– The hell?
– Five feet of this freakin' mansion is on the park's land.
– How can that happen? Between the Realtor, the surveyor, the architect, the inspector—
– And the contractor, Lenny. They all missed it. But New York guy blames it on Lenny. "You put my house in the wrong place!" Lenny shows him the plan. "I put it right where the architect said to put it." New York guy says he should have double-checked. Lenny says *he* should have double-checked. They're at loggerheads. New York guy goes to the foundation manager to see if they can work

something out, can the foundation sell him those five feet.

– "Money no object."

– "Money no object." Foundation guy says he'd like to but he can't. "What do you mean you can't?" New York guy asks. It's all in the bequest or the beheath or whatever the fuck you call it, nothing can be built on that land, and moreover, the foundation can't sell any of it, not an inch, never mind five feet. Tells New York guy he has to either cut the five feet off his house or move the house back five feet.

– How you going to cut five feet off a house? With a chain saw?

– And it's more than losing the sunroom, I dunno, whatever. Whether you give the house this bris or you move it, you're talking huge bucks, never mind the structural damage, because Lenny put a foundation under that thing like the Germans at Normandy.

– *Private Ryan*, another good movie. Those first five minutes? I mean, come on.

– Lenny poured a lot of concrete because—

– Carlo and them had the contract.

– There you go. At first, New York guy says fuck the foundation, let them sue me, except his lawyer on the thing explains to him he's going to lose, plus he could get hit with punitive damages. New York guy comes back to Lenny and says there must be something he can do. "Like what?" Lenny asks. "Like you must know someone, maybe with the state." Implying that Lenny is connected.

– He is.

– But New York guy has no right to make that assumption. Italian American building contractor in Rhode Island? It's one of them stereotypes.

– Politically incorrect.

– New York guy pushes it. "Come on, you must know someone who can straighten this out."

– He said that, "straighten this out"?

– He also said, "You must know somebody who could lean on somebody at the foundation."

– These civilians watch these movies . . . What's he think, an offer they can't refuse, this foundation is going to bend over?

– So Lenny, he don't want to go to Carlo and them with this—he already went to them with that state bid—so he decides he's going to take a shot at this himself.

– A shot at what?

– Being a wiseguy. So he sets up a meeting with this foundation guy, this old-school WASP, his family came over on the *Mayflower* type. Somebody Bradford, it don't matter. They go to lunch at the Beach Club—

– Did Lenny wear socks?

– The fuck do I know. So they sit down over swordfish or something and have a conversation during which Lenny asks him can they come to some sort of arrangement. Bradford says he'd like to oblige, but, as he told New York, his hands are legally tied, he can't make any alterations—

– What is he, a tailor?

– In the old lady's will. Lenny takes another tack. Goes all Tom Hagen. Implies that he has some suck with the state and how it would be a shame if an inspector found some kind of dangerous liability on the park property—maybe, God forbid, someone fell through a decrepit railing and plunged down the bluff to his death on the rocks below—and decided it had to be closed. And you know what this bow-tied, suspender-wearing citizen says?

– The suspense is killing me.

– He don't blink an eye. Very calmly, very politely, he tells Lenny that the days when—and I quote—a "nongovernmental organization" can exert pressure on a state to that extent are long gone. And, by the way, the railings are just fine, but thanks for asking.
– A "nongovernmental organization"? Is that what we are?
– Apparently.
– I kind of like that, actually. What did Lenny say?
– What *could* he say? The guy was right. You and me? These are facts we gotta face. We're not what we were.
– No, we are not.
– And Lenny, he was never even what we *used* to be. What's he gonna do? Leave a horse head in the guy's bed?
– You know I never bought that bit? I mean, you know how hard it must be to cut off a horse's head? How heavy it's gotta be? Then to carry it into the house and up the stairs with no one seeing or hearing anything, the guy not waking up? I never bought it.
– Great movie, though.
– The best. So, *One* or *Two*?
– The eternal question. Gun to my head, gotta go with *One*.
– Because . . .
– Because the lines everyone remembers are from *One*. "Sleeps with the fishes," "Leave the gun, take the cannoli" . . .
– Yeah, but *Two*, "I know it was you, Fredo. You broke my heart"? And De Niro? I mean, come on.
– Great actor, no question. Anyway, Lenny, he trudges back to New York guy, says sorry, no luck. He did his best, but the house has to be moved. New York guy says fine, do it. Lenny says he knows how to build a house, he don't know how to take one apart and move it, and besides, does

New York guy know how much money it's going to cost? "What's that to me?" New York guy says. "I'm not paying for it." "Who is?" Lenny asks. "You are," New York says. "You built it in the wrong place." Lenny says, "Get the Realtor to pay for it, the surveyor, I dunno, but it ain't going to be me. Just pay me the rest of my money and I'm out of here." New York guy says, "Are you fucking kidding me, cowboy? I'm not paying you one dime. In fact, I'm suing you." So now Lenny is out about three hundred k and he's looking at a lawsuit that could put him on the hook for seven zeros, which, of course, Lenny don't have. He's staring down bankruptcy, maybe his wife leaving him . . .

– What does she want? She has the lake house.

– Not if New York guy takes it because her husband built a house on somebody else's land. So Lenny goes to the old playbook, calls his insurance company. Sure they'll pay—to policy limits, which would still leave Lenny a few hundred k short. He's fucked.

– If he loses the suit.

– Defense costs, he loses anyway. Plus he's out the money for the house construction, so he's totally fucked. Unless—

– There's always an "unless."

– He can get the real wiseguys to step in. So *now* he goes to Carlo and them.

– Should have done that in the first place.

– He don't go to Carlo directly, he goes to Bats. Says he has this problem, lays it all out, maybe they could offer him a little help. "Like what kind of help?" Bats asks him. Like maybe they could lean on Bradford, or lean on the New York guy, get him to pay Lenny the money, sue someone else in the chain. "You want me to move the house for you, too?" Bats asks. So Lenny offers Bats a taste. Says, "Of course, Bobby, I'll kick up a percentage of whatever you can recover for me." "Why didn't you say that at first?" Bats asks. "I thought it went without saying," Lenny says. "So if we get this New York asshole to pay you, you'll kick back, say, thirty points," Bats says. "But if we stop him suing you, how does that work, how do we come up with a number on that?" Lenny says he doesn't know, maybe Bats has an idea. Bats does. He says, "That would save your company, wouldn't it?" Lenny says it would. So Bats says, "So that's worth a piece of the company, isn't it?" "How big a piece?" Lenny asks. "You going to negotiate with me now?" Bobby asks. "You come with your hand out, asking for my help, you're going to negotiate with me?" "No," Lenny says, "of course not, Bobby." "So a third of your company works for you?" Bats asks.

– What's Lenny going to say?
– He's going to say yes, which is what he says.
– So Bats goes to Carlo.
– Lays out Lenny's whole tale o' woe and what Lenny will fork over for some assistance. You know what Carlo says? "Lenny? Who's this Lenny? I don't know no Lenny." Bats tells him Lenny is the guy got them all those contracts on the state job. And Lenny has a company that has some genuine value that he would be willing to share. You know what Carlo says? "Lenny? Who's this Lenny? I don't know no Lenny." Because Carlo ain't going to go to war with the powers that be over a guy who isn't even made. "Them WASPs," he says, "these foundation types, they're a mob of their own. We don't need no trouble with them." And he ain't gonna get involved with potential lawsuits, because lawsuits mean courts and courts are never good. Lenny No Socks is on his own.

– So what does Lenny do?

– He hires a lawyer to sue New York guy.

– Goes on the offensive again. Who'd he get?

– You ever meet Frank O'Malley?

– At a wake, I think.

– You'd remember him. Big round face like a frying pan, red nose from the Jameson's. O'Malley looks at the case, tells Lenny he'll handle it, and here's how he handles it: he heads right to Bats.

– To Bats? Why?

– To warn him, make him aware of certain realities of the civil litigation process. To wit, if Lenny sues, he'll have to open up his books, including his billings on the state job, which could cause embarrassment—not to mention possible indictments—of certain people.

– Like Bats and Carlo. Jesus.

– Right? Bats summons Lenny to a meeting, tells him to shut this lawsuit down. Lenny says he can't do that, it will mean he'll lose his business, he'll go bankrupt, lose his house, the whole nine yards. Bats says okay, he'll take one more stab, he'll go visit New York guy, see if he can get him to see reason. Lenny is so grateful: "Thank you, Bobby, thank you."

– So Bats goes to New York guy.

– He does.

– And?

– And it didn't go well. Which is what brings us here today. Donna, sweetheart, the check when you have a second? We should probably head out, it's a little bit of a drive. Did you bring . . .

– In my car. Clean, untraceable.

– Why I like working with the pros.

– Back atcha.

– Oh, thanks, Donna.

– I'll get it. My turn.

– No, this is business.

– What, are you going to write it off? At least let me leave the tip.

– What do you do, fifteen?

– No, I usually do twenty.

– Bill Gates here.

– So finish the story. The house, did it get moved?

– Six feet to the left. Cost a freaking fortune.

– And now he's not even going to get to enjoy it.

– What do you mean? Don't forget your coat there.

– Thanks, I was going to. I meant New York guy, he's gotta go. That's what we're doing, right?

– Not New York guy. Lenny.

– How is that?

– Bats did sit down with New York guy and they worked it out. You do the math. What New York guy was going to spend on legal costs, Bats charges less. And no books get opened. So they work it out, Lenny No Socks has gotta go.

– Ain't it always the way.

– True story.

THE LUNCH BREAK

DAVE-UH!"

No response.

"Dave-uh!"

Dave the Love God—the aforementioned "Dave-uh" in West Coast Gen Z female dialect—pretends not to hear.

"DAVE-UH!"

Dave gives up and walks from the living room into the bedroom of the suite at La Valencia Hotel in La Jolla where Brittany McVeigh is sitting up in bed, her copper hair disheveled, her face twisted into a grimace of discontent.

"What?" she asks. "Did you finally hear me the third time-uh?"

"I heard you the first time-uh," Dave says. "I was ignoring you the first two times. Uh."

"Where is my room service order?"

"I don't know."

"It's your job to know-uh."

"No," Dave says. "It's my job to make sure that you show up at the set on time—not drunk, high or hungover—ready to work. It's my job to make sure you don't disappear on a drug- or alcohol-fueled bender. It's my job to protect you from your imaginary stalker. I'm not your butler, I'm your bodyguard."

"You're my jailer," Brittany says.

"Really?" Dave asks. "If you'd ever seen a jail cell . . . Oh, that's right, you have. Several of them."

This is true—Brittany has served several brief stretches for DUIs and probation violations. Not to mention three trips to rehabs that were every bit as luxurious as La Valencia.

"You're mean," she says. "I want somebody else."

Dave looks at his watch. "You're in luck. Boone's shift starts in an hour."

"Boone is boring-uh."

"Boone is steady," Dave says. "You'll have him for eight hours, then Tide is on."

"Is he that Samoan guy?"

"He is."

"He never says anything."

"Tide is stoic."

Also true—the three-hundred-pound Samoan doesn't say much, but he especially doesn't say much to Brittany, because he can't stand her.

Neither can Boone, for that matter.

Or Dave, who is now silently cursing Boone Daniels out for getting him into this job.

It started at the Lunch Break.

The surfing day is unofficially divided into five major sessions, to wit:

The Dawn Patrol.

The Gentlemen's Hour.

The Lunch Break.

The Sundowner.

Night Surfing.

The Dawn Patrol is that (obviously) early-morning session for surfers who have jobs (contrary to stereotype, most do). The Gentlemen's Hour is mostly for the rich and retired who paddle out to their respective breaks after the working guys have paddled in. The Lunch Hour is exactly what it sounds like—instead of hitting the brown bag, Mickey D's or In-N-Out Burger, the working guys hit the waves for a quick session and usually grab a burrito or something for the drive back to the J-O-B. The Sundowner is, again, self-explanatory, occurring after work at dusk, and often features one of the most beautiful sights in California, when surfers typically sit on their boards to face the setting sun and watch it go down. Night Surfing happens—yeah, you're ahead of me—in the hours of darkness, albeit sometimes lit by the moon, and is one of the dumbest and funnest things you can do.

But it's the Lunch Break we're concerned with here.

Dave was sitting out on a relatively flat summer sea, waiting for waves that probably weren't going to happen, with the Pacific Beach Dawn Patrol crew, who had come back down for the noon session. Boone, High Tide, Johnny Banzai, Hang Twelve, Downward-Facing Doug, Free Billy, and Sunny Day were all out there.

Boone, a former San Diego cop, makes his living as a private investigator. Well, barely, because he does the investigating gigs to just support his surfing jones, which is what he spends the bulk of his time doing.

Ben Carruthers, aka "Cheerful," the local real estate billionaire and certified curmudgeon who has for some reason made it his quixotic quest to manage Boone's finances, once asked him, "How much money do you make surfing?"

"None," Boone said, a little surprised that the normally pragmatic Cheerful would waste precious time asking a question the answer to which was so obvious.

"Wrong," Cheerful said. "It's *minus* none, because every minute you're riding a wave is a minute you're not making money."

So, suitably chastened, Boone took the job when Alan Burke, the lawyer who is his biggest single client, called him.

"Have you heard of Brittany McVeigh?" Burke asked.

"The movie star?" Boone asked.

"The very same," Burke said. "She's going to be shooting scenes for a film in San Diego, and one of the insurance companies I represent has written the completion guarantee policy."

Sometimes film studios take out an insurance policy on one of their stars in case for some reason they can't complete the project. An accident, an illness or, in Brittany's case, the kind of incredibly irresponsible, destructive, self-absorbed behavior for which she has become renowned in the tabloids and on the internet and TV entertainment shows. In fact, Burke told Boone, the banks wouldn't fund the film unless the studio took out just such a policy.

"The insurance people want someone to babysit her," Alan said. "To make sure she shows up on the set in shape to work. Also, she's on probation from her last DUI and has to submit to random drug and alcohol tests. If she pisses positive, she goes back to jail. So she has to stay dry and not high."

"I can't watch her myself twenty-four seven," Boone said. "I'll have to bring at least two other people on."

"No problem," Burke said.

Boone decided to ask Dave the Love God and High Tide to split the gig with him. He'd used them before, on sketchy bail bond recoveries and some surveillance work.

He brought it up at the Lunch Break.

Josiah Pamavatuu—High Tide, thusly named because his weight displaces a massive volume of water (i.e., if he's in the ocean the tide is *always* high)—said, "She sounds like trouble, bruddah."

"She's about five-three, can't go more than a buck-five," Dave said. "How much trouble could she be?"

Now he knows.

Bad things come in small packages.

• • •

DAVE, BOONE AND Tide met with Brittany's agent Mel, a studio executive, and an insurance rep before Brittany's arrival in San Diego.

They had lunch at Eddie V's on La Jolla Cove.

The insurance rep, Warren Ferrar, led off. "I want to go on record that I opposed writing this policy. She's too high a risk."

"Brittany has changed," Mel said with a palpable lack of conviction. He added, "Two stays in jail on those DUIs, the rehabs, she's learned her lesson. We had a heart-to-heart—"

"Not possible," the studio exec, Eric Stoltz, said. "Between the two of you there's only about half a heart, and that's yours."

"That's not fair, Eric," Mel said.

Eric turned to Boone. "I've been opposed to casting her all along. We could have gotten Hunter Bartlett and we should have."

"Why is that?" Boone asked.

"Brittany McVeigh is the single worst human being I have ever had the misfortune of having to work with," Eric said. "A drunken, drug-addled, promiscuous little diva with no regard for anyone but herself and a level of entitlement that would put a collective blush on the faces of the British royal family. And this from a guy who works in Hollywood."

"Then why did you put her in your movie?" Boone asked.

"Box office," Mel said. "Eric is more greedy than he is outraged. So is his board of directors. The fact is that Brittany had several hits as a teenager, and while her personal life has driven her career into a ditch, the resultant publicity has lifted her name recognition to an all-time high. People will buy tickets just out of curiosity."

Eric shrugged in agreement. Like, *What are you going to do?*

"That's *if*," Ferrar said, "you can get the film finished."

"That's where you come in," Eric said to Boone.

"Doesn't she already have security?" Boone asked.

"She's fired all of them," Mel said. "Well, *I* fired the last one because he was supplying her with coke."

"And sex," Eric said.

"He was guarding her body a little too closely," Mel said.

"Brit doesn't so much need protection from other people," Eric said, "as she needs protection from herself."

Mel looked uneasy. "Well . . ."

"What aren't you saying?" Boone asked. "If there's a threat, we need to know that."

There was an uncomfortable silence. Finally, Mel said, "Brittany claims she's being stalked."

"'Claims'?" Dave asked.

"Just a pathetic bid for attention and sympathy," Eric said. "There *is* no stalker. We've had her thoroughly surveilled, her house watched, for weeks. LAPD has checked it out. Nothing. You know how some people have imaginary friends? It only stands to reason that Brittany would have imaginary enemies."

ON THE WAY out from lunch, Mel lingered behind to buttonhole Boone and Dave. "She's actually not such a bad kid. Never really had a chance. She's been working since she was four years old, her shit parents took most of the money and fought over it in the ugly divorce. Then Brit 'developed,' went from child star to teenage heartthrob to sex symbol. No wonder she sees herself as nothing more than an object of other people's desires, and she pays them back in kind."

"'Poor little rich girl'?" Dave asked.

"Something like that," Mel said. "And I'm as guilty as anybody else. I take my percentage. Anyway, try to take care of her, huh? It's her last chance."

"What do you think?" Boone asked as they walked back to their cars.

"I think it's bullshit," Dave said. "She had too much money as a kid? Boo-hoo. Her parents ripped her off? Boo-hoo. There are kids with cancer, kids starving in Sudan, I'll save my sympathy for them. But what's your take on this stalker business?"

"If a woman says she's being threatened, we should believe her," Boone said. "What do *you* think?"

"Better to assume it's something and have it be nothing than the other way around," Dave said. Sure, he thought, there are some people sick or needy enough to fake a stalker, but it's unusual. And if a guy said he had a stalker, he'd be believed; a woman says it, she's being hysterical. "Are you going to strap up for this?"

Boone has a concealed carry permit for a gun, but rarely, if ever, uses it. Dave doesn't own a piece at all. He doesn't like guns, they make him nervous. One millisecond of a mistake could result in a lifetime of tragedy.

"No," Boone says. "Not yet, anyway."

The first thing they did was go to La Valencia Hotel for a conversation with the security director, Glen Rice. Which went easier than you might expect, because over the years Boone had quietly handled a number of problems at the hotel that might otherwise have ended up in the newspapers.

"Please have the bar in her room cleaned out," Boone said, "with strict instructions to the staff not to restock. Tell your room service people not to send up any booze she orders and warn them that she'll probably ask them to get her weed. Same with the parking valets. Whatever tips she offers we'll more than match. There'll be a nice envelope for everyone."

"That won't be necessary," Rice said.

"I want to do it," Boone said. "I'll have someone stationed either in or outside of her room twenty-four seven. Her room number is not to be given out, and I'd appreciate it if the desk would call me or my people any time there's a visitor."

"I assume she'll check in under a pseudonym?" Rice asked.

"Book the room under my name," Boone said. "With my credit card."

"Of course."

"I appreciate all of this," Boone said. "And if you ever need my help, you have my number."

They met Brittany the next day.

She arrived at the movie location in a chauffeured limo.

Boone introduced himself. "Ms. McVeigh, I'm Boone Daniels. I'll be in charge of looking after you while you're here."

"'Looking after' me?" Brittany asked. "You mean keeping me from getting drunk or high and running off with some motorcycle dude or something."

"Pretty much," Boone said.

Brittany looked at him with unveiled disgust and said, "Go fuck yourself, Boone."

"Let me introduce my colleagues," Boone said. "This is Josiah, and this is Dave."

"You can go fuck yourself," Brittany said to Tide. Then she turned to Dave. "And *you* can go—"

"Fuck myself," Dave said. "Got it."

"So you're the hired goons," Brittany said. "At least you're *hot* goons. Except for the fat one. Under normal circumstances one of you would be my fuck toy for the shoot, but these aren't normal circumstances."

"Which is why we can go fuck our*selves*," Dave said.

"And funny, too," Brittany said. "Yeah, well, if I want laughs I'll go to the Comedy Store. In the meantime, you're not to talk to me any more than absolutely necessary. Try not to even *look* at me, okay? No eye contact."

She stopped because the film's director was walking over with what could only be called trepidation.

"Brittany, how nice to see you!"

"Don't even say it, Freddy, you dickwad," Brittany snapped. "I already know my fucking lines. Now where's my fucking trailer?"

Dave knew where her fucking trailer was because he and Boone had already thoroughly tossed it for contraband. As Brittany stormed off, he said, "I'm thinking that if you *did* make eye contact, you'd turn to stone."

"It amazes me," Boone said, "how someone so stunningly beautiful can simultaneously be so . . . ugly."

"Beauty is skin-deep," Dave said. "Ugly goes to the bone."

A Sprinter van pulled up bearing Brittany's entourage—her personal assistant, her dog walker, and some guy named Ugo, who described himself as a "chi consultant."

"What does a chi consultant do?" Dave asked.

"I align Ms. McVeigh's chi," Ugo said. "You don't want to encounter her if her chi is misaligned, believe me."

Dave believed him.

He turned to the dog walker. "I don't see a dog."

The walker looked at him as if he were talking about frozen yogurt on Mars. "Brittany doesn't *have* a dog."

"Then why does she have a dog *walker*?"

"She's thinking about getting one," the guy said. "You wouldn't want her to turn her little loved one over to a complete stranger, would you?"

No, I would not, Dave thought.

Boone was talking to the personal assistant, a young woman named Amber with tattoos all up and down her arms and legs. She was carrying a heavy shoulder bag.

"What's in the bag?" Boone asked.

"Stuff," Amber said.

"Weed," Boone said. "I can smell it from here."

"It's for my personal use," Amber said weakly.

"Who are you, Cheech *and* Chong?" Boone asked. "Out. Goodbye. Adios. *Hasta la vista.*"

"You're firing me?"

"There you go."

"Actually, I'm relieved," Amber said. "Working for her is hell. Do you know how many personal assistants she's had in the past six months? Eighteen. *Eighteen.* Two of them are in rehab themselves, one now has regular sessions in a sensory deprivation tank, and another is living in a cave in Arches National Park."

"That's not true," Boone said.

"Okay, it's a yurt," Amber said. "But it's still in Utah. So you're throwing me out? Thank you, thank you, *thank you.*"

Boone and Dave went to Brittany's trailer to tell her that they'd just dismissed her assistant/drug mule.

Brittany was already in full dudgeon, on the phone to Mel.

"How big is *Jason's* trailer?" she asked, referring to her co-lead, a major, established star whose name could open a film. "Is that right? Well, mine is a foot shorter! A *foot*! I'm *not* going to be disres*pect*ed like this! He's already getting top billing, now he gets a bigger trailer?! No-uh!"

"Noah?" Dave asked Boone. "Like the ark?"

Boone shrugged.

"*Do* something about it!" she yelled, then clicked off. She looked at Dave and Boone. "What do *you* want?"

Boone informed her that he had sent Amber away and that her dope would not be forthcoming.

That put her over the top.

She threw a temper tantrum.

Of epic proportions.

Yelling, screaming, crying, cursing, throwing things, breaking things . . .

"You pencil-dicked, jumped-up mall cops! You Kevin Costner

wannabes—do I look like Whitney Houston to you?! I'll cut your tiny balls off and use them for martini olives! I'll reach down your stupid mouths, grab your alleged cocks from the inside and feed them to my dog!"

"You don't have a dog," Dave said.

"I'm *GETTING ONE*, you fascist pigs!" she screamed. "A purebred Shikoku! Which costs more than you make in a year, you mental pygmies! Why don't you two queens get the fuck out of my trailer so you can go hump each other, huh?! I'll bet that's what you really want, isn't it! You know what I want?! I want my dog walker, I want my chi consultant and I want my weed!"

Boone and Dave were not impressed.

Because, dig it, if you have experienced the Pacific Ocean exorcising its rage, nothing, *nothing*, that a mere human being does is going to have the slightest effect on you.

Well, they did laugh a little, which infuriated her all the more.

"You're fired-uh!" she screamed.

Boone patiently explained that she couldn't fire-uh them because she hadn't hired-uh them, that they worked for the insurance company and were doing exactly what the company had instructed them to do.

"I'll call my *agent-uh*!" she screamed.

Boone nodded at her phone.

Brittany called Mel and put it on speaker, launched into a diatribe, then they all listened as the long-suffering agent said, "You can't fire them . . . No, you can't fire the insurance company, either. You signed a contract agreeing to supervision."

"Then I quit-uh!"

"If you do," Mel said, "not only will you forfeit your quote, you will also owe the studio two million dollars. Not to mention the bad publicity arising from your dropping out of another film. I won't be able to get you a job doing the weather in Bismarck, North Dakota, and we already know what the weather there is. It's cold. It's very cold, Brittany."

He hung up.

"I need my chi aligned!" Brittany said.

"Actually, we're going to send your whole crew away," Boone said. "Too many people around gets in the way of our taking care of you."

"You don't care about me," Brittany said. "Nobody cares about me."

"Tell us about this stalker," Boone said.

Brittany looked surprised. Then she hardened and said, "What's the use, you won't believe me anyway."

"Try us," Dave said.

She'd never actually seen the guy. Well, maybe a glimpse one night in her front yard. But she'd *sensed* him. Sensed that someone was looking at her, peeking through her windows, following her.

"Do you have any idea who it might be?" Boone asked.

She shrugged. "Look, I've fucked a lot of guys, okay? A few women, too, if that gives you pervs something to beat off to tonight. But it's probably someone random. You know how many creeps are out there? And what am I supposed to do without my trainer? You want me to look like a walrus with tits?"

"We'll take you to the gym any time you want," Dave said.

"So a bunch of fat, sweaty housewives can gawk at me?" Brittany asked. "No thanks, assholes. And I wasn't going to smoke the weed, I just wanted to, you know, smell it."

There was a knock at the door.

Actually, it was a kick. Someone was kicking the bottom of the trailer door.

Dave gestured for Brittany not to go to the door and stood in front of her as Boone opened it.

Jason Stasny stood there holding a big cardboard box full of his belongings. He looked over Dave's shoulder. "Brittany? There's a whole film crew out there waiting for us and the meter is running. Take my trailer and I'll take yours."

Brittany hesitated.

"No, seriously," Jason said. "Let's not waste any more time."

"Fine-uh," she said.

She squeezed past them out the door.

Jason looked at Dave and Boone. "You guys are her babysitters? Good luck with that."

"Thank you," Dave said.

Jason came in and set his box down.

"A foot," he said, shaking his head.

Dave and Boone headed toward the new trailer to check it out.

"You want to hump?" Dave asked.

"Maybe later," Boone said.

"Tell you this," Dave said. "If there is a stalker, he better not catch up with her, the poor bastard."

BUT FIVE DAYS into the shoot there was no sign of any stalker.

Five endless days of insults, curses, demands, escape attempts, unsuccessful bribes to the hotel bartender, equally futile attempts to score weed from the parking valets, threats, imprecations, whining, sulking petulance.

Dave was out on the line with the Dawn Patrol (sans Boone, who was on Brittany duty) when Johnny Banzai asked him what the movie star was like.

Dave thought about this for a few seconds and then said, "She's discharming."

"You mean 'disarming'?" Johnny asked.

"No," Dave said. "I mean, you know how someone's charm can be disarming? She's the opposite. You look at her and you're charmed, then she opens her mouth, and you're discharmed."

"There's no such word," Tide said.

Dave shrugged. "There is now."

Another lineup conversation concerned the "Top Ten Brittany McVeigh Moments."

"Shouldn't that be the '*Bottom* Ten Brittany McVeigh Moments'?" Hang Twelve asked. The dreadlocked neo-hippie was named Hang Twelve because he has twelve toes, fortuitously symmetrical with six on each foot.

("Otherwise it would be weird," Hang once observed.)

After considerable discussion, the crew agreed on a "Top Ten Best/Worst Brittany McVeigh Moments," to wit:

- The time Brittany complained that her toast was two degrees too hot.
- The time Brittany complained that her toast was two degrees too cold.
- The time Brittany complained that the temperature of her toast was just right but an attempt by the caterer to make her bloat with carbohydrates.
- The time Brittany responded to Boone that, no, she didn't know who Goldilocks was but whoever she was she could go fuck herself.
- The time that Brittany screamed at her hairdresser for making eye contact.
- The time Brittany screamed at her hairdresser for not looking her in the eye.
- The time Brittany broke down sobbing because her hairdresser quit.
- The time Brittany refused to come out of her trailer because vapor trails in the sky were trying to control her mind.
- The time when Boone explained that vapor trails were just vapor but that something *should* try to control her

mind if she couldn't do it herself and Brittany responded that Boone was a "stupid Meanderfall [sic]." ("What's a Meanderfall?" Hang asked. "A caveman who wanders around until he drops," Johnny said.)

– The time Brittany called Dave "an intellectually stunted steroid case with a package the size of a miniature walnut and the personality of a subterranean rock who couldn't get a date with anything but an undiscriminating gym sock." ("Actually, that's kind of funny," Sunny said.)

In the interest of fairness they tried to think of something that was good about Brittany, but the best they could come up with was that there weren't two of her.

And now Dave and Brittany are in a Mexican standoff over a room service order.

She says, "I'm *hungry*-uh!"

"What did you order-uh?" Dave asks.

"I don't remember-uh," Brittany says, aggrieved at the question.

"That's not going to help," Dave says.

"My assistant Amy—"

"Amber."

"Amber. You sure?"

"Yup."

"Well, that's a stupid name," Brittany says. "Her parents must have, like, hated her. Anyway, *Amber* usually remembers these things. *She* calls room service and *she* remembers what I wanted, but you idiots *fired* her so now nobody knows *any*thing about my fucking *food*-uh!"

The doorbell rings.

"Thank *God*-uh," Brittany says. "And no thanks to *you*-uh."

The waiter comes in and lays out her dinner.

A bowl of vegetable broth, three sprigs of kale and a pot of herbal tea.

"That's not a meal," Dave says.

"It is for me," she says. "That sleazy butt plug Freddy says I'm ten pounds overweight, which translates to twenty on the screen."

"You look fine to me."

"So gallant."

"I mean, you're beautiful," Dave says. "You know that."

Brittany looks up at him, tears in her eyes. "I'm always hungry."

Dave looks back at her. Then he says, "Come on."

Twenty minutes later they're sitting outside Jeff's in La Jolla Shores and she's wolfing a cheeseburger like she hasn't eaten in months.

Which, really, she hasn't.

"Fuck me, that's good." Then she says, "You won't tell Freddy, will you?"

Dave says, "I'll swear on a stack of Bibles that you had two grapes and an alfalfa sprout."

"They'd fire you for this."

"Promise?"

She actually smiles.

It turns in a heartbeat.

"Thanks for sabotaging me," she says. "Now I'm going to look all bloated tomorrow."

Okaaaaay, Dave thinks.

"DAVE THE LOVE God" is a play on words from his profession as a lifeguard coupled with his propensity for sleeping with a lot of women.

While he takes both callings seriously, if he's being honest, his true passion is the former.

Dave grew up in Pacific Beach. His father was a firefighter, his mother an e-room nurse, so he was raised with the idea that the best thing you could do in life was to rescue people.

San Diego is a town where kids worship lifeguards the way, in other places, they used to look at baseball players or basketball stars.

Dave's dad enrolled him at age ten in the Junior Lifeguard Program, and it was just a few weeks later when the head instructor, a famous lifeguard in his own right, informed him that his son was a prodigy.

"I've never seen a kid with his combination of lean muscle, cardio capacity and intuitive wave knowledge," the instructor said. "If he keeps at it, he could be one of the great ones."

His parents being too busy and too smart to hover over him in the current helicopter style, they had only one demand of their son's future occupation.

"Be useful," his dad told him. "Be useful to other people."

Dave heard him.

That commandment went into the very spinal fluid of the otherwise classic, hyperactive SoCal boy. Dave swam, surfed, skateboarded, played baseball, did martial arts, was in and out of the emergency room until he was on a first-name basis with most of the doctors and nurses.

But on one thing he was always focused: he was going to be a lifeguard.

He went to lifeguard camp every summer, studied for and got his EMT certification (no middle-aged tourist out boogie boarding for the first time was going to check out from a heart attack, not on Dave's beach), took classes in oceanography. When the time came, he killed the lifeguard tryouts, blowing out the speed record on the mandatory thousand-yard swim, and San Diego hired him.

Over the years, he became a legend.

No one knows—hell, Dave doesn't know—how many people he's pulled out of the ocean, rescued from riptides, pulled from the brink with timely CPR.

He was useful.

Freakin' useful to other people.

Could he surf? Oh, hell yes, probably as well as Boone Daniels—a legend in his own right—and almost as well as Sunny Day, the only professional surfer among the Dawn Patrol.

Dave loved to surf, but he loved being a lifeguard more.

His other passion?

Okay, women.

Not going to lie, no doubt about it, Dave more than earned his sobriquet of "love god," and his friends joke that he should be on the tourist brochures that the San Diego Chamber of Commerce puts out, because he's sent more visitors home happy than SeaWorld.

"What can I tell you?" Dave has said to the Dawn Patrol. "I love women."

They love him back.

When Sunny twigged him about whether he was ever going to engage in a "serious relationship," Dave dismissed the concept as somewhat oxymoronic. (And yes, Dave knows words like "oxymoronic"—despite the SoCal surfer bra demeanor, he's a bright guy who reads a lot.)

"Why should relationships be serious?" he asked her. "I thought they were supposed to be fun."

He has a point, at least about *his* relationships. The fact is that few, if any, of the women with whom Dave has had unserious relationships have ever harbored a resentment or even complained. To the contrary, most have described Dave as a "good guy" and their brief relationship as a "good time."

So Dave has a reputation.

For fun.

But don't get it twisted. If you're in trouble in the water—in fact, if you're in trouble *anywhere*—Dave the Love God is the guy you want.

And maybe, just maybe, if you're a twenty-six-year-old diva whose bottom is coming up at her fast, Dave the Love God is the guy you need.

Movie stars are movie stars for a reason.

No one has ever been able to really put a finger on exactly what it is—call it the X factor, or charisma, or star quality—but it just comes through the screen, and you can always see it.

And sometimes, just sometimes, one of those stars does something so brilliant that it stops your heart.

That makes it almost worth all their bullshit.

That's Brittany on this particular day.

Dave's not there, he has the night shift, but Boone is on the set when Brittany gives a performance that leaves everybody simply stunned.

It's a scene of heartbreak, one that calls for the actor to summon something deep from a reservoir of pain, and Brittany does just that. Not just for a minute, but for hours, through the cover shot, the two-shot, the reverse angles and the close-ups, and when they're finally done everyone is emotionally exhausted.

Especially, of course, Brittany.

But they're all looking at her differently now, with something akin to admiration, even gratitude, because they know that she's helped them achieve something special.

Freddy is awestruck.

Even Jason, who cordially loathes her, tells Boone that she has done something "surprising and extraordinary."

"She just took the movie from me," he says without rancor. "She's going to get nominated."

Yeah, maybe so, but it comes at a cost.

When Dave comes on to his shift, he relieves Tide in the hallway and rings the bell.

No answer.

Again, same thing.

Dave uses his key to let himself in.

Brittany is on her haunches on the floor.

Sobbing.

"I've been working," she says, "*forever.* As long as I can remember I've been performing. Performing, performing, performing. Putting it out there, giving them everything I have to give, everything I have inside me. And when I've given them everything, until I'm totally empty inside, until I have nothing left to give, nothing even for myself, you know what they want?"

Dave shakes his head.

"More." She looks up at him. "I need a drink."

"No, you don't. It's okay."

"You don't understand," she says. "I *need* a drink."

She wraps her arms around herself and rocks back and forth.

Dave takes her by the elbow and lifts her up. "Come on."

"Where are we going?"

"You'll see," he says. "Come on."

DAVE SETS THE surfboard down in the shallow water.

"Lie down," he tells Brittany.

"With my clothes on?" she asks.

Her face is still puffy from crying.

"What difference does it make?" Dave asks.

But she strips down to her bra and panties. "It's *like* a bathing suit."

"No one is going to care."

It's going on sunset anyway, most of the tourists are off the beach, and only a few surfers are out on the relatively flat ocean.

Dave pulls Brittany out into waist-deep water. "I can't believe all the years you've lived in California you've never surfed."

"I never had the time," she says. "I was always working."

"Well, you have the time now," Dave says. "Just lie down and hold on."

He turns the board so that it's pointed toward shore, waits for one of the small waves to come in and then pushes her into it.

Watches as she rides the white water and then walks to her. "Well?"

"Again?"

"Yeah."

He pulls her back out.

"I don't think I can stand," she says.

"No, we're not going there tonight," Dave says. "If I got you hurt, they'd have my head. And I don't want you to get hurt anyway. We're just going to have a little fun and relax."

Which is what they do.

He pushes her in, puts her on a wave, pulls her back out.

Rinse and repeat.

Brittany's having fun, he hears her laugh as she rides in. He's heard it a few thousand times from little kids on boogie boards. Hell, he's heard it from grown men and women on longboards. Heard it from himself.

His favorite saying about surfing? "Whoever has the most fun wins."

And now Brittany is having fun.

She surfs until the sun is just on the horizon.

Then Dave faces her toward the sunset. "Sit up and watch."

He holds the board as she sits up, and they watch the sun go down in a blaze of red and orange.

"It's so beautiful," Brittany says.

"Still want that drink?"

She sounds surprised as she says, "No."

"Salt water," Dave says, "heals everything."

THE CHARLATANS NOTWITHSTANDING, healing isn't a miracle.

It doesn't happen in an instant.

It takes time, and sometimes it's only partial, and other times it doesn't happen at all.

But it's Dave's belief, central to his core, that the ocean does heal.

He's seen it all his life, has experienced it himself. When he's down, depressed, angry at the world, he gets into that salt water and it does . . .

. . . something.

Dave can't explain it rationally, but he nevertheless knows that it's true.

So Brittany's brief surf session wasn't a baptism, it didn't give her a bright shiny new soul, but it gave her *some*thing. A relief from her addictions, a different way to get that relief, a sense that there was something bigger than herself, much bigger, that would embrace her and show her some grace and some beauty.

And that there was someone willing to take her there.

Who didn't want anything from her.

"CAN WE GO out?" Brittany asks.

She, Dave and Boone are sitting in her suite as the guys are about to switch for the night shift.

"I'm not due on set until noon tomorrow," she says. "So maybe a movie, a restaurant, a club? God, I'd love to go dancing, just, you know, *dance*."

Dave and Boone look at each other.

"The Belly Up?" Dave asks.

"Nick is playing there tonight," Boone says.

"Who's Nick?" Brittany asks.

"Nick Hernandez," Dave says. "A buddy of ours. Has a band called Common Sense. Sort of surf reggae, ska."

"I would just love to go, you know, *out*."

"No weed, no drinking," Boone says.

"I'll have Diet Cokes," Brittany says.

Boone runs it through Mel, Eric and Ferrar. The agent, studio exec and insurer are all against it.

"What if she drinks?" Mel asks.

"We won't let her," Boone says.

"What if she hooks up with drugs?"

"We won't let her."

"What if she takes off?"

"Again . . . ," Boone says. "Look, she needs a safety valve, a release. She's been doing great lately, she deserves a little consideration, a little fun."

"You're confident you can keep it under control," Ferrar says.

"Totally."

"And when is this going to go off?" Eric asks.

"Tonight," Boone says. "She has a late call tomorrow."

"I don't know . . ."

"I do," Boone says. "You hired me to do a job. Let me do it."

He gets a reluctant okay.

THE EVENING STARTS at Station Sushi in Solana Beach.

"Let's get this woman some food," Dave says. "No wonder she's crazier than a squirrel on crack. She's starving."

So it's Dave and Brittany, Boone and Sunny, chowing down on sashimi and California rolls, like any other double date night.

Boone asked Sunny to come along to accompany Brittany to the ladies' room. Sunny was reluctant. "A, I'm not a security guard. B, you've done nothing but tell me how horrible this person is."

"She's a little less horrible than she was," Boone said.

"'A little less horrible' doesn't sound like a great evening," Sunny said. Nevertheless, she agreed to go along because she likes Station Sushi, she likes the Belly Up and she likes Dave.

She also likes Boone.

They've been off-and-on girlfriend/boyfriend, lovers, pals, friends with benefits and friends without benefits for years, and would probably be engaged in the previously discussed serious relationship if Sunny weren't always traveling the world in search of big waves.

Right now, the benefits are in effect just before she goes up to Mavericks to try to set the women's record.

So they're settled at the table pretty comfortably after some awkward stares from the other diners, who soon, however, fade into the California cool "we've seen celebrities before" feigned indifference.

Brittany is on her best behavior, sort of like a convict freshly on parole. And she's obsessed with Sunny.

"You have a body that won't quit," Brittany says.

"Uhhh, thanks."

"I mean, what's your fat percentage?" Brittany asks. "It has to be, like, below zero, right?"

"I don't actually know."

"I'd kill for your body," Brittany says. "Long and lean, those legs. I'm all just tits and ass."

"You're beautiful," Sunny says.

"You don't have to say that," Brittany says. "Well, actually, you do, of course. Don't worry, Boone, I'm not hitting on your girlfriend. I mean, she is your girlfriend, right?"

"Our relationship is sort of undefined," Sunny says.

"Then you're an even bigger loser than I thought, Boone," Brittany says. She turns back to Sunny. "Leave him. Come be with me. I'm joking. But not really. Pass the sashimi, please."

It's the first time Dave has heard her say "please," but he doesn't make a thing of it.

Stuffed on sushi, they walk (Brittany describes it as a "waddle") the few blocks over to the Belly Up, on Cedros Avenue a block east of the PCH.

Tide is waiting out front, and he's already had a talk with the club's security staff.

They're on it. Brittany is far from the first celebrity they've had at the club, and they know how to handle it without being either lax or heavy-handed. Besides, SoCal crowds are pretty used to seeing famous people and tend not to get crazy about it.

The bigger concern is the phantom stalker.

"Did you brief them on it?" Boone asks, and immediately realizes that it's a dumb question.

Of course Tide did.

He's Tide.

Again, the club's staff is not without experience with crazies, and the crazies always have a similar look. It's hard to describe, one of those "know it when you see it" things, but it's a certain jerky way of walking, a sideways look in the eyes, and it's almost always a man.

There are women stalkers—the "boil the bunny" thing—but they're rare.

Tide leads them in.

The club is packed because Common Sense always sells out. The opening band is still on, a straight-up reggae band, and the crowd is jumping to it.

"They're good!" Brittany yells.

"They are!" Dave yells back. "But wait until you hear Nick!"

A few people notice Brittany, stare for a second and then turn away. No one gawks, no one comes over for an autograph or a selfie. There just seems to be an unspoken understanding that she's there for the same reason they are, to hear the music and have a good time, and that they should just let her do that.

Boone looks up at the mezzanine to the left of the stage—a small area with reserved seating—and sees that Johnny Banzai is up there keeping a weather eye on the crowd.

Boone puts his earpiece in and activates the little mike tucked inside the front of his shirt. "All good?"

"Copacetic," Johnny says.

Boone relaxes a little and turns his attention to Sunny, who's watching Brittany dance.

With abandon.

Sunny Day can't dance.

As athletic as she is—elite, world class—when she tries to dance, which is rarely, she resembles that horrible statue of a surfer that graces the sidewalk near Cardiff State Beach and is locally known as *The Kook.*

Brittany can dance.

And she's having a wonderful time doing it.

Sweaty and out of breath when the music stops, she grins up at Dave.

"You want a drink, so to speak?" he asks.

"A Diet Coke, please?" she asks.

There's that "please" again, Dave thinks. He starts to go, but Boone says he'll do it. He takes orders from each of them—none of them is consuming alcohol tonight—and walks off to the bar.

Common Sense comes on.

Money can't buy you time,
And time is what you need the most,
Not a sugar daddy coast to coast.

Brittany starts dancing again.

Pure joy.

Dave watches Nicky come to the front of the stage and sing right to Brittany.

The money felt good in your hands for a while,
But it wears off like the latest style,
And when you're all alone you put yourself on trial,
But what you need you can get with your smile.
She looks so good that takes itself,
In a world so much harder than it looks to the touch,
But I don't need that much,
Sunshine in my cup,
I don't need that much . . .

Brittany shouts into Dave's ear. "Maybe I don't need that much!"

"What?!"

"Maybe I don't need that much," she yells, "sunshine in my cup!"

They don't stay too late because Brittany still has to shoot the next day. But walking to the car she's ebullient, looking younger than she has.

"Is that the most fun you've had in a while?" Sunny asks.

"That might be," Brittany says, "the most fun I've had in my *life*!"

The fun stops when she and Dave get back to her room.

It's been trashed.

The pillows and mattress on her bed slashed, likewise the chair cushions. Big X's have been carved in the wallpaper, glasses and cups smashed on the floor. The smell is awful—someone defecated on the carpet.

"Stay right here," Dave says.

He walks into the bathroom.

Lipstick on the mirror reads SORRY I MISSED YOU BITCH.

Dave walks back out and takes her arm. "Come on, we're getting out of here."

He takes her to his place.

• • •

"IT'S NOT WHAT I expected," Brittany says.

"What did you expect?" Dave asks.

His place is modest, a little one-bedroom two blocks from the water. He bought it ten years ago, when an average person could still afford a place in Pacific Beach.

"I dunno," she says. "Some sort of bachelor pad sex pit. I've heard about your reputation."

"Lies and distortions."

"I don't think so."

But the place is immaculate. Everything neat and put away, very spare, a couple of Hokusai prints of the ocean on the walls.

"You must have a good cleaning person," Brittany says.

"I do," Dave says. "Me."

She raises an eyebrow.

"You okay?" Dave asks.

"Maybe you believe me now," she says. "About the stalker."

"I believe you," Dave says. "Try to get some sleep. You take the bedroom. I'll stay out here on the couch."

"I don't think I can sleep," she says. "Maybe I'll just watch some TV."

"I don't own one."

"You don't?" she asks. "Like, what do you *do*? Sex, I guess."

Dave shrugs. "It's better than TV."

"Depends on the sex," Brittany says. "Depends on the TV. Dave-uh, I'm scared."

"Of course you are," Dave says. "But you're safe. The stalker doesn't know you're here, and anyway, Boone, Tide and Johnny are out in the street. No one will get past them."

"You guys are good friends, huh?"

"Brothers," Dave says. It's true. You take on the ocean together, year after year, you put your lives in each other's hands, what you are is family. "Get some sleep, okay?"

She goes into the bedroom.

Dave looks in on her half an hour later.

She's out cold, hugging a pillow.

THEY ALL MEET at the hotel first thing after dropping Brittany off at the location, where Tide stays close as a bodyguard.

Sitting with Glen Rice, who is freaking *infuriated*, they go over the security tapes.

Front door.

Back door.

Lobby.

The hallway on Brittany's floor.

Collectively, they tell the story.

The stalker parked away from the hotel and walked up. Strolled right through the lobby and went to Brittany's floor and right to the room. Used a burglar's shimmy to let himself in. Came out twenty minutes later, took the elevator down and walked out.

All between 9:02 and 9:28.

"How did he know what room she was in?" Boone asks.

"Someone on the staff leaked it?" Dave asks.

"No," the security director says.

"You're right," Dave says. "If one of them leaked it, we'd have had paparazzi here."

"None of my staff leaked it," Rice says, jaws clenched.

"He could have been, well, stalking," Boone says. "Watching her come in and out. Watched the elevator to see what floor she'd get off on, work it from there."

"We'd have made him," Dave says. "Another question—how did he know she was going to be out?"

"He was watching from outside the hotel," Boone says. "The cameras wouldn't pick him up. The stalker was staking out the hotel, saw us leave, and took his shot. Occam's razor—the simplest explanation is usually the case."

"Can you zoom in on his face?" Johnny asks.

Rice gives him a close-up.

The stalker is tall and skinny. White guy with a thin face and a prominent hooked nose.

"I think I know this asshole," Johnny says. "Let me go back to the shop and run him."

Good as his word, Johnny goes back to the San Diego Police Department headquarters, where he's a homicide detective.

They're at the Sundowner grabbing breakfast when Johnny shows up and slides into the booth.

"I knew I knew him," he says. "Benny Franco, low-rent B&E guy with a sheet like a kite tail."

"For what?"

"Burglaries, mostly," Johnny says. "Here's what's weird, though. Record a mile long, but none of it for stalking, harassment, sexual assault . . ."

Which they all know is unusual. Stalkers almost always have a record for that kind of thing.

"Can we talk to him?" Boone asks.

"If we can find him," Johnny says. "Benny's a loser, but he's not an idiot. He had to know that the hotel had video surveillance. Most likely he's in the wind."

Turns out he is kind of an idiot, though.

They find him at the address he gave his PO, in a second-floor room at an SRO just outside the Gaslamp.

He's half asleep when he opens the door and sees Johnny's shield.

"Uh-oh," Benny says.

"Uh-oh, indeed," Johnny says.

Benny looks at Boone. "Who's he?"

"A friend of mine," Johnny says. "If you want him to leave, he'll leave, but if he does, we go right after him. I put the bracelets on you and we go straight to the house."

"What'd *I* do?" Benny asks.

"We have you on tape breaking into a room at the Valencia Hotel and coming out twenty minutes later, having vandalized the place and left a terroristic threat," Johnny says. "Which is normally way below my pay grade, but I have a special interest here. I'll fuck you, Benny, and I'll keep fucking you. I'll have the charges stacked up like pancakes on a fat man's buffet plate, and I'll make sure you serve them consecutively. I'll see that you get the shittiest jobs in the joint, and I'll show up at every parole hearing to tell them what a sick twist you are, a real danger to society. By the time you get out, you'll be too old to stalk an arthritic snail. *Or* . . ."

Benny is shaken. "Or what?"

"You talk to me," Johnny says. "You tell me everything."

Benny talks.

He does tell Johnny everything. About how he's always been obsessed with Brittany McVeigh, how he's seen every one of her movies multiple times, sitting in the back row jerking off. How he found out where she lives, would hang around outside her house, peeping through her windows, just hoping to get a glimpse of her. How, when she came down to San Diego, he just couldn't help himself . . .

While he talks, Johnny searches the little room, gives it a thorough toss. When Benny finishes, Johnny asks, "How did you know where to find her?"

"I figured they'd put her up in one of the best hotels," Benny says. "So I started with the Valencia, and sure enough . . ."

"Last night . . ."

"I was watching from down the street and saw her go out with all her bodyguards," Benny says.

"How did you know which room?"

"It faces the street," Benny says. "I'd see her go in and then watch to see a light come on. It wasn't hard to figure out from there."

"If you love her," Johnny asks, "why did you trash the place, take a dump on the floor, leave her that message?"

"Because I knew she'd never give a guy like me a chance," Benny says. "Stuck-up *bitch*."

"You have a phone, Benny?"

"Yeah."

"Gimme."

"You can't do that."

"Okay, stand up, turn around." Johnny reaches for his cuffs.

Benny hands him a cell phone.

Johnny scrolls through the phone and then hands it back. "Don't go anywhere."

"What about the charges?" Benny asks.

"I'll see what I can work out," Johnny says. "In the meantime, you go anywhere near Brittany McVeigh, I'll do exactly what I said I'd do."

"I won't. I promise."

ON THE STAIRS down, Johnny asks Boone, "What didn't we see in that room?"

"Pictures of Brittany," Boone says.

Stalkers almost always have them. Torn from magazines, taken off the net, whatever.

Jerk-off material.

"There were no pictures on his phone, either," Johnny says. "What I did see were several calls to and from a 310 number."

"West L.A."

"So I'm given to understand," Johnny says. "I'll run them."

On the way out, they see Dave sitting in his parked car.

• • •

IT DOESN'T TAKE long for Benny to run.

Maybe twelve minutes.

He walks out of his building and heads west.

Dave gives him a little room, then gets out of his car and follows him.

To Santa Fe Depot.

When Benny gets on the train, Dave is right behind him.

The ride gives him plenty of time to think it through.

Benny didn't go there to attack her; he went there to terrorize her.

Who knew Brittany was going out last night? Dave asks himself. Me, Boone, Tide, Sunny, all of whom we can pretty safely rule out. The Belly Up people, but someone at the club knowing the stalker? *Way* too much of a coincidence.

Who else?

Her agent Mel, the insurance guy Ferrar, and Eric what's-his-name. Stoltz. The insurance guy has no motive. In fact, the opposite—it's in his company's financial interest to see that Brittany completes the movie. That leaves Mel and Stoltz.

Get off the grassy knoll, he tells himself.

Boone's right—the simplest explanation is usually the answer, and the simplest explanation is that Benny Franco is the lone gunman here.

A few quirks for a stalker, but stalkers are . . .

. . . quirky.

Dave looks out the window at the California coastline that he loves so much. Through Camp Pendleton, then San Clemente and Dana Point, before the track turns inland at San Juan Capistrano. Then up the long, flat, dull plain toward L.A.

Irvine . . . Santa Ana . . . Anaheim . . .

Long Beach . . . Carson . . .

Benny doesn't move. In fact, it looks like he's asleep.

Finally, the conductor announces, "Los Angeles Union Station, ten minutes!"

Dave sees Benny stir.

Sure enough, he gets off at Union Station.

Dave follows him off the train and down the concourse into the station, famous as the location of so many movie scenes.

He watches Benny stand there for a few seconds, looking around. Then someone comes up to him, slips him an envelope and quickly walks away.

Down the grassy knoll, Dave thinks.

BRITTANY FALLS APART.

Her day on the set is a nightmare, a catastrophe, a total fallback to her old self.

"Brittany being Brittany," as the director observes during one of the many breaks forced by her blowing her lines, objecting to the lighting, screaming at ambient sounds, screeching at her makeup person.

Or just breaking down crying.

It's a disaster.

Freddy gets on the horn with Mel, who patches in Eric, who patches in Ferrar, and they decide to hold an emergency meeting the next day in San Diego, the agenda of which will be whether to make the best of it and struggle through, to shut down production completely, or to replace Brittany and reshoot all her scenes.

Which will effectively be the end of her career.

They decide to meet over lunch.

• • •

DAVE TAKES A cab up to the house in the Hollywood Hills.

Great view of the city and the smog.

That's not what gets his attention, though.

What gets his attention is when the wooden gate slides open and a pearl-gray Mercedes comes out.

What gets his attention is the woman behind the wheel.

Hunter Bartlett.

"HUNTER BARTLETT CAN be ready tomorrow," Eric Stoltz says.

The film is shooting at the shore that day, so the meeting happens at Jake's on the Beach, which, true to its name, sits virtually on the sand at Del Mar.

"You've talked to her already?" Mel asks. "Who authorized that?"

"As the head of the studio," Eric says, "I authorized that. I have a film to protect here, Mel."

"I can live with Hunter," Fred says.

"A little compassion here?" Mel asks. "That stalker that we all said didn't exist apparently existed. Brittany is terrorized. Give her a little break."

"She's had break after break," Eric says. "I told you that casting her was a mistake."

"You signed off on it," Mel says.

"And it was a mistake," says Eric. "Now I'm going to rectify it. Let me call Hunter."

"Can't you just roll over and tell her?" Boone asks.

"What?!"

"Jesus, Daniels," Mel says.

"You are sleeping with her, right?" Boone asks.

"That's none of your—"

"I think it is," Boone says. "I think it's everyone's business here."

He takes his phone out and holds up Dave's photo of Stoltz handing the envelope to Benny Franco. "You've always hated Brittany and you wanted your girlfriend for this role. So you hired this loser to stalk Brittany and drive her over the edge."

"That's outrageous," Stoltz says.

"I agree," says Boone.

"And it's a lie."

"We have thirteen phone calls," Boone says, "stretching over the past two months, between one of your phones and Benny Franco. He's in custody now, squawking like a parrot on speed. Five grand, Stoltz? You're not only a dick, you're a cheap dick."

"He's lying," Stoltz says. "That will never hold up in court."

"It won't have to," Boone says. "Because what you're going to do is resign. Today. Go away and do whatever."

"And if I don't?"

"Then this goes public and it's over for you anyway," Boone says. "Walk away now and you still have a chance for a career."

Stoltz stares at him for a second and then says, "Okay."

"No, *now*," Boone says. "Walk away *now*."

Stoltz wipes his mouth with a napkin, gets up and walks out.

There's a long silence.

Then Mel says, "Just when you think the town can't surprise you."

Ferrar says, "This still leaves open the question of whether or not we retain Ms. McVeigh."

Fred says, "She's a mess."

But Mel isn't looking at him. He's looking over his shoulder at Brittany walking up to them.

"You're right, Fred, I was a mess yesterday," she says. "But I'm not a mess today, and I'm ready to work whenever you boys are finished with your lunch."

"I don't think that we can take that chance," Ferrar says.

"Oh, I think you will," Brittany says. "Dave told me everything. So you go and tell whoever Eric's successor is that if I'm dropped from this film I'll sue everyone involved. I'll *own* the studio. And, Fred, get that stupid air freshener out of your Maserati, because I don't want that stink when I drive it. Now why don't you pay the check, leave a *big* freakin' tip for the server, and let's get back to work."

She turns to Boone and smiles. "I won't need you anymore. You're fired, Boone."

He smiles back. "Promise?"

She tells Dave about it over dinner at Boone's place on Crystal Pier. He's grilling yellowtail to make tacos for them and Sunny.

It's a sundown tradition of his.

Because everything tastes better on a tortilla.

"You're growing up," Dave tells her.

It comes off as patronizing as it sounds.

Sunny winces a little, even as Boone slides a piece of tuna into a tortilla and hands it to her.

"Am I, Dave?" Brittany asks. "What about *you*? When are you going to grow up, quit the Peter Pan 'Lost Boys' act, this whole immature 'Dave the Love God' bit, and try being a real adult?"

Sunny applauds.

Boone asks, "You want a taco, Dave?"

"Uhhhh . . . yeah . . ."

Brittany is holding her stare on him.

Smiling, but serious as a midnight phone call.

Dave doesn't flinch, he knows how to take a wave on the head. "You're right, Brit."

"I know I'm right," she says. "That's not the question. The question is, what are you going to do about it?"

A red sun kisses the horizon.

BRITTANY STAYS AT his place again that night.

Even though the hotel is perfectly safe for her—everywhere is safe now—she stays with Dave, and this time he doesn't sleep on the couch.

An early riser, he stays in bed and watches her sleep.

Stalker, he thinks.

He looks at the red hair splayed on the pillow, listens to her soft breathing that occasionally breaks into a snore. He smells her scent, and he knows.

Knows that the long ride he's been on is over.

That it's time to paddle over to a different break.

One that's scarier than hell, but shit, he thinks, you're Dave the Lifeguard, and this time the life you save is your own.

She's not really asleep.

She lies there enjoying him looking at her, listening to her, smelling her. Let him, she thinks, let him fall in love with me.

Let me fall in love with him.

ONE MONTH LATER, the crew is out there on the Lunch Break.

"An entire generation of female tourists," Johnny says, "are in mourning. I hear there's black crepe draped in towns all across the Midwest."

"The end of an era," Boone says.

"Unlamented," Sunny says.

Boone looks inside, toward the sand, where Dave pushes Brittany's board into the small wave.

She gets up on her knees.

"She'll be standing soon," Tide says.

Boone nods. "Dave the—Dave is a good teacher."

Hang Twelve asks, "Dave isn't the Love God anymore?"

"*Nooooooo*," Boone says. "Dave's a one-man dog now."

"Wait a second," Hang asks, jaw agape. "Dave's *gay*?!"

"Figure of speech."

"Oh." Hang thinks for a second and then asks, "Is Dave going to move to Hollywood now?"

"No."

"Well, is she going to move here?"

Boone shrugs.

"They'll figure it out," Sunny says. "They're grown-ups."

Dave watches Brit get to her knees and then shakily stand up. "Yes! *Yes!* Way to be!"

He runs in and meets her as she hops off the board.

"That was so cool!" Brittany says.

He hugs her and she holds on to him tight.

Two soaked, salty, sweaty bodies stand in the midday sun.

The Lunch Break.

COLLISION

LIFE CAN BE VIEWED AS a series of collisions.

In fact, some scientists would say that all of life, all of existence, is a series of billions upon billions of collisions between atoms.

We don't really know.

What we *do* know is that our human lives have collisions.

Collisions between who we want to be and who we are. Collisions between what we want and what we don't. Between dreams and reality. Between wants and needs, good and bad, right and wrong.

We think we have one life, but we have several.

We're sons, fathers, husbands, lovers, brothers, daughters, mothers, wives, sisters, friends, citizens, employers, employees.

We think we live in one world, but we live in many.

Those worlds can collide.

BRAD McALISTER RARELY feels nerves.

He feels them now.

"The Zegna or the Hermès?" he asks his wife, holding up the two ties.

"The Hermès," Rachel says decisively, as if there were no question.

Rachel usually is decisive, and she picked out the rest of his wardrobe for the important dinner: the navy-blue Brioni suit, pale blue Turnbull and Asser shirt and now the gray print Hermès tie.

"Expensive but not flashy" is the way she put it.

Her husband is an attractive man.

Mid-thirties, full head of black hair, six-two, solidly built. He played club rugby at Stanford when he was getting his MBA and now hits the gym five mornings a week before work.

It's more than that, though.

Brad is attractive to her from the inside out. Kind, thoughtful, gentle, funny, considerate—and a great dad who, when working from home, never shuts his office door in case Wyatt wants to play. He stops whatever he's doing and plays with his kid.

"I can always stay up late or get up early," he's said, "and finish work, but I can never replace that time with my son."

Men, Rachel thinks now, looking at him, don't always know what's really sexy.

McAlister looks back at his wife and thinks how lucky he is.

For one thing, she's gorgeous.

Black hair cut just over the shoulder, a Roman nose over wide lips, a petite frame that is nevertheless shapely.

And those eyes.

Those green eyes.

He thought she was "hot" when he first saw her walking across Lasuen Mall on campus in jeans, tennis shoes and a peasant blouse, and she looks terrific now, ten years later, in a red holiday dress that fits perfectly—not too tight and yet not at all matronly.

"Do I look like a soccer mom?" she asks McAlister, checking herself out in the mirror.

"Like a *hot* soccer mom," McAlister says.

"Good answer."

Because she is a soccer mom—five-year-old Wyatt has just

started playing in the local kiddie league and she does drive one of *those* vans.

Something else that McAlister is grateful for: Wyatt.

Before he met Rachel, McAlister didn't know that he could love anyone that much, and then Wyatt was born and he discovered a depth of love beyond his imagination.

When he found out that Rachel was pregnant, McAlister made two promises to himself: one, that the next eighteen years were primarily about the kid; two, that he was going to enjoy every minute of it.

And he has.

McAlister enjoyed the sleepless nights, cuddling the baby against his chest; he enjoyed the feedings; he even enjoyed changing the diapers. He was thrilled when Wyatt first sat up, thrilled when he first crawled, beyond thrilled when he took his first steps.

And these were moments that he and Rachel shared.

It brought them even closer.

I have this great little family, he thinks.

And this great life.

Which might be about to get even better.

"What do you think is going to happen at dinner?" he asks Rachel.

"Only something good, right?"

McAlister thinks so, too. Why else would the top brass at corporate fly out from New York and make a point to invite not just him but the whole family to dinner? Someplace quite nice, they told him, and spare no expense, please. It couldn't be just to hand him his Christmas bonus.

Although he's expecting a big one, based on his performance.

Whatever Brad McAlister has decided to do, he's done well.

Above expectations.

Something *his* father taught *him*.

"Be there when the rest of them arrive in the morning," his dad had said, "and still be there when they leave at night."

McAlister grew up in a middle-class neighborhood in Glendale, California, just outside of Los Angeles. His father was an administrator in the public works department; his mother, a high school mathematics teacher.

Normal middle-class people who loved each other and just wanted to raise a family together.

McAlister loved and respected them, but he wanted something more.

He was ambitious.

He studied his ass off in high school and got a full-ride scholarship to UCLA. Excelled there and got into the prestigious Stanford MBA program. Graduated near the top of his class and was immediately recruited by the Sterling Group, a corporation that owned the most prestigious hotels and resorts in the world.

It had an interesting philosophy about training its executives.

From the bottom up.

McAlister did time in the kitchen, in the laundry, at security, behind the check-in desk. Working crazy hours, he learned every detail about how to run a luxury resort. Corporate noticed, marked him as an up-and-comer, sent him on visits to observe their best hotels around the world, then made him an assistant manager at his current hotel, the Sterling Sands, one of the gems in the hospitality corporation's worldwide necklace, this one set on the strand of beaches that line the Southern California Golden Coast.

He wasn't assistant manager for long, because Brad McAlister had unmistakable, undeniable drive, talent and work ethic.

Now he runs the hotel.

They live in a nice house in a suburban neighborhood of Laguna Niguel. Wyatt goes to an excellent public school.

Life is good.

No, life is great.

And now corporate has asked him and his family to dinner.

He looks across the room at Rachel and thinks, once again, how lucky he is.

Rachel comes from chaos.

Her English professor father was a disappointed novelist who blamed his self-perceived failure on the fact that he had sacrificed his creative life to the trap of marriage and fatherhood. He took it out on his wife and daughter in periodic and unpredictable rages that usually erupted at the dinner table.

Her mother retaliated by becoming a quiet alcoholic who spent hours at the piano ignoring her child while butchering Chopin nocturnes, and occasionally repairing to the kitchen after one of her husband's tantrums to break every plate on the edge of the sink.

Rachel responded by staying in her room and creating fantasies of her own future marriage with a calm, dependable mate, herself becoming a sweet and attentive mother.

Children of chaos tend to go in one of two diametrically opposed directions: either they dive into the maelstrom themselves, or they seek order.

Rachel sought order.

She pledged a sorority at Stanford and majored in French literature and philosophy, but not because she anticipated an academic career. She did not anticipate a career at all; she anticipated marriage.

When she met McAlister, he seemed a perfect choice. Handsome, charming, smart, funny, ambitious, thoughtful and kind. There was nothing mercurial about him, no volcano smoldering in his soul, no sullen moodiness.

He was three years older than her and came from middle-class parents who were wonderfully normal and boring and seemed to love their son and each other.

Rachel did what she was supposed to do regarding the relationship. The first two dates were good, so she applied the expected "third-date rule" and slept with him after the dinner and movie, and that was good, too.

She fell in love.

Truly, deeply, genuinely in love.

Rachel and McAlister did what they were supposed to do. They got their degrees, they got engaged, they got married. (Even her now divorced parents managed to make it through both the rehearsal dinner and the reception without disgracing themselves or her.)

The newlyweds had a common understanding of how life was supposed to be. He would have a successful career, she would teach high school French for the first few years, "they" would get pregnant and she would be a stay-at-home mom.

That's what they did.

Rachel loves it.

Loves her kid, her husband, her life.

Loves being the stereotypical suburban mom—the preschool and kindergarten days, the playdates, socializing with the other mothers, comparing notes, making meals, being bright, attractive and interesting to her husband when he comes home from work.

"I think it's going to be a promotion," McAlister says now.

"I think so, too," she says. "But to what?"

"The property in Beverly Hills could use some help," he says. "The manager there is up in years, I hear he's thinking about retiring."

"That would be a big jump."

McAlister nods.

He doesn't want to talk about it too much and jinx it.

He's nervous.

Wyatt walks into the room.

He's dressed himself—a blue button-down shirt, untucked, over khaki slacks and his best tennis shoes.

Looking at McAlister, he says, "I need a tie, Mommy."

"Oh, I don't think so, honey."

"Daddy has a tie on."

Rachel looks at McAlister and smiles. Well, if *Daddy* has a tie on . . . "Okay."

"Does he *have* a tie?" McAlister asks.

"From kindergarten graduation," Rachel says. "I think I can dig it out."

Rachel goes to find the tie.

Studying McAlister, Wyatt starts to tuck in his shirt.

"Let me help you with that," McAlister says, stepping over to him. "It's easier if you loosen your belt and slide your pants down a little first."

McAlister does it for him, then cinches the belt again. "There. You look good, kiddo."

"It's a business dinner," Wyatt says seriously.

McALISTER ORDERS ANOTHER bottle for the table.

A Grand Siècle No. 23.

Six hundred dollars, give or take.

It's unlike him—he's usually more abstemious, with drink, money and food—but what the hell, he thinks.

He's celebrating.

It's not a done deal yet, but it sure feels like it, because the people in from corporate seem to be in a celebratory mood, and the compliments they're paying him flow as fast as the Champagne.

Sterling's CEO, Colin Gerard, a slim, sophisticated Brit transplanted to New York by the corporation, is especially effusive. "How *did* you steal that chef away from a Michelin-starred Manhattan bistro?"

"I offered him the 'California bonus,'" McAlister says. "The sunshine, the warmth, the ocean just outside the hotel. It sells itself."

"And the occupation rate," Gerard says. "Up eighteen percent."

"Twenty-two, actually," McAlister says.

It's immodest of him, but he's feeling pretty good right now. The food, the wine, the adulation.

Then there's Stacy.

Tall, slender, stylish in thigh-high boots and a green holiday dress that subtly accentuates her figure. A junior executive clearly on a quick climb up the corporate ladder, she came in from New York with Gerard, the big boss, and she's been subtly flirting with McAlister all through the evening.

If McAlister hasn't noticed, Rachel has. But she hides her annoyance. This dinner is too important to let anything so trivial get in the way. She knows her man—he may flirt a little, especially if he's had a little wine, but when push comes to shove . . . well, it won't.

She leans over to look at Wyatt's coloring. Whenever they go out to dinner someplace nice, she brings something for him to do—a coloring book, a puzzle, a little game—so he doesn't get bored and bratty. It's not fair to the child or to the other diners.

The bosses have noticed, too. Remarked what a well-behaved child he is. It all counts. She knows they invited the family for a reason.

Then Gerard says, "And may I ask, Brad, why you ordered such an expensive bottle of wine?"

It's a moment, and McAlister knows it.

He rolls the dice. "Well, I'm celebrating."

"Celebrating what?"

McAlister makes a bold move. "My promotion."

The bosses laugh, Gerard most of all. They exchange nods.

Then Gerard asks, "And what do you think that promotion should be?"

McAlister says, "I think I should get Beverly Hills."

"You're wrong," Gerard says.

McAlister feels his high spirits sink.

Then Gerard says, "We're wondering if you'd be amenable to taking on a new challenge. To wit, the overall supervision of six of our prime properties in the west."

He names the property in Beverly Hills, but also those in Las Vegas, Cabo, Santa Fe, Scottsdale and Jackson Hole.

"They could each use a little . . . refreshment," Gerard says. "Let's call it the 'McAlister Touch.' Your salary would be commensurate with the added responsibilities, and of course there would be performance incentives. What do you think?"

"I'm stunned," McAlister says. His mind is whirling—he'd expected some kind of promotion, but not this. This is rarefied atmosphere, thin air, and he's feeling it.

"Well, we didn't mean to *stun* you," Gerard says, getting a quiet laugh from the table. "Listen, we are absolutely confident that you're the man—no sexism intended, Stacy—for the job. Think about it, sleep on it, but, Brad, don't let me get on a plane tomorrow without an answer."

McAlister already knows what the answer is going to be but is too smart to blurt it out now and cheapen the salary offer. He knows that he'll have to talk to Rachel about this because there will doubtless be considerable travel involved, but he also knows that she'll be thrilled.

Rachel is by no means materialistic, but the money involved here is tantalizing. And if I do a good job on these six properties, he thinks, who knows where it could lead? His mind flashes to properties in Manhattan, London, Zurich, Cinque Terre and Monaco.

It could be generational wealth; it could mean that not only his and Rachel's but Wyatt's future would be ensured.

And he knows that he will do a good job.

No, he'll do a *great* job.

It's what he does.

Gerard pushes back from the table and stands up. "It's been a long day and I'm feeling the time change. And I think you have a sleepy little boy there. Breakfast in the morning, Brad? Say, eight A.M.? When you can deliver what I hope will be good news?"

They stand around for a minute saying their good nights.

Stacy quietly pulls McAlister aside. "So, Brad, how married are you?"

"Very married."

She sighs. "Ahh, lucky Mrs. McAlister. Well, if you ever change your mind . . ."

"I'm flattered, Stacy, really," McAlister says. "But I won't."

THE AIR OUTSIDE is crisp.

Which is good, because McAlister's brain is not. The wine, the adulation, Stacy's perfume, the incredible job offer—they've all gone to his head.

"Maybe I should drive," Rachel says as they walk to their car.

"Probably," McAlister says.

She's also overwhelmed by the offer. "Brad . . ."

"I know, huh?"

"It's wonderful," she says. "You've earned it."

"I hope so."

"What did she say to you?"

"Who?"

"'Who,'" Rachel says. "The lovely Stacy."

"Just that she hoped I'd take the job," McAlister says.

"I'll bet she does."

"Rache—"

"Mommy, I'm tired."

"I'll carry him," McAlister says. He hefts Wyatt onto his shoulder.

When they're almost to the car, McAlister stops to dig in his pocket for his keys.

"I'll take him," Rachel says.

McAlister hands Wyatt over to her, and she starts walking across the exit of the parking lot to the car.

The vehicle comes out of nowhere.

Way too fast.

McAlister hears the engine, then the squeal of brakes.

His heart stops as he lunges and pushes Rachel and Wyatt out of the way of the car.

It missed hitting them by inches.

McAlister stands in front of the car, a Dodge Charger.

The driver blasts his horn.

Enraged, McAlister doesn't move.

The horn blasts again.

McAlister yells, "You could have killed my wife and kid!"

"Get the fuck out of my way!" the driver yells.

McAlister doesn't move. "You damn near ran them over!"

Rachel says, "Brad, it's all right. Let's just go."

But McAlister doesn't move.

"Brad, *please*."

The driver puts the car in park and gets out. Big guy, heavy-set. Has probably had a couple of drinks, too. "You gonna get out of my way?"

"You could have killed them, asshole."

"They look okay to me."

"Apologize to them."

"Brad—"

"Apologize."

"Go fuck yourself," the guy says, stepping up. "In fact, why don't you put the brat to bed, and then you can fuck her?"

It happens so fast.

One instant, one second, one flash of temper—

—and it destroys your life.

McAlister throws a punch, a right cross.

He's no boxer, it's an amateur punch, but it hits the guy just right on the corner of the jaw, and he's out even before he falls backward and his head strikes the edge of the curb.

A sickening thud.

McAlister regrets the punch right away.

The guy's legs twitch spasmodically.

Rachel turns Wyatt's face away, into her shoulder.

A few people come out of the restaurant.

"Call 911!" McAlister shouts to Rachel. "Get an ambulance."

He stands there looking down at the guy.

He's not moving now.

"Oh god, oh god," McAlister murmurs. "What have I done? What have I done? Please, get up, get up."

The cops arrive just before the ambulance. One goes to the still body, the other to McAlister. He asks, "What happened here?"

"I hit him," McAlister says. "He fell."

The cops arrest McAlister.

IT TAKES THE man two days to die.

Suffering from "brain bleed," Sean Cameron lies on life support for two full days before his wife and parents make the agonizing decision to take him off and let him go.

It's agonizing for McAlister and Rachel, too.

For two days, McAlister—out on bail—sits and wonders if he killed a man, if he took someone's life.

Rachel is strong, Rachel is tough.

She knows that her husband is ashamed.

Scared.

Devastated.

She takes a deep breath and then tells herself, *This is the way it is now.* This is the new norm. You will support him, you will help him get through this.

The news comes.

Cameron is dead.

McAlister is arrested again, this time on a charge of homicide.

It's so surreal.

This is all new to them. It's terrifying.

The months before the trial are filled with stress.

McAlister loses his job—the Sterling corporation cites the morals clause in his contract and cuts him loose without as much as a severance check. The legal bills are immense. The defense bar is a profitable industry, and the hourly fees are draining their hard-earned savings like a leak that can't be plugged.

Neither of them really sleeps.

Wyatt picks up on their anxiety. He's a sensitive kid, he knows something is going on. One night he wets the bed.

McAlister wants to put an end to it.

His lawyer, Scott Monroe, comes to him with a plea deal.

"It's ultimately up to the judge, of course," Monroe says, "but in exchange for a guilty plea, they'll knock it down to voluntary manslaughter. You could get eleven, six, or three years and a ten-thousand-dollar fine. The judge will go for far less. Given your lack of a criminal record, your standing in the community, your sincere statement of regret, your not costing the state the expense of a jury trial, probation is a definite option."

If McAlister did take it to trial, on the other hand . . .

He already told the cops that he punched Cameron, never reneged on the statement, and half a dozen witnesses saw him standing over the body.

"There's no realistic chance of an acquittal," Monroe says.

And there's another thing, McAlister thinks.

Rachel would be a witness, she'd have to testify.

He can't put her through that.

It's a horrific decision.

McAlister and Rachel talk it over, deep into the night.

"He said I might get probation," McAlister says, "or home confinement."

"Or four years," Rachel says. "You'll miss so many moments in Wyatt's life. Soccer, Little League, birthdays and Christmases, Father's Days and . . ."

"I won't miss anything," McAlister says. "It's going to be okay."

McAlister takes the deal.

MCALISTER SITS AT the defense table and listens to Cameron's wife, his mother, his father, his fourteen-year-old daughter, tell him what he's taken away from them.

They're regular people.

Blue-collar people.

Cameron worked as an HVAC technician. He worked hard, he loved his family. They all stress this—alternately tearfully and angrily—that their loved one wasn't some fancy resort executive in a thousand-dollar suit who thought that because he had money he had the right to take a life.

Cameron's daughter chokes out her statement between sobs. "Because my dad . . . had the nerve . . . to talk back to you . . . you hit him . . . you killed him . . . he had done *nothing* . . ."

Then she breaks down.

Her grandfather eases her away from the dais.

McAlister sees the judge watching, listening.

Finally, he asks if McAlister has anything to say before he pronounces the sentence.

McAlister stands up.

His legs feel weak, his voice shakes.

"I want to express," he says, "my sincere regret to the family. If I could take back that moment, I would. I'd give anything . . . I'm so sorry . . ."

He runs out of words.

Sits back down.

"HOW IS THIS different from a drunk driver killing an innocent person?" the judge asks in his sentencing statement. "It's not. Mr. McAlister was legally intoxicated. Voluntarily intoxicated—no one forced the liquor down his throat. And the punch that he threw wasn't *in*voluntary. The defendant doesn't suffer from some malady that causes his arm to involuntarily shoot out. He *voluntarily* threw a punch that resulted in a death."

The judge goes further.

"I am sick and tired of rich white men," he says, "thinking that they have the privilege to do anything they want and that because they *are* rich and white there will be no consequences. We have to send a message that there are consequences, and I am going to set an example and send such a message."

He finds McAlister guilty of voluntary manslaughter and gives him the max.

Eleven years.

The gavel comes down like a hammer blow to the heart.

Eleven years.

Eleven years.

McAlister can't believe what he's heard, it echoes in his brain, he hears Rachel gasp from the gallery, he feels his heart stop. At first he thinks that he misheard it. The judge couldn't have said "eleven years," he must have said "eleven months" or maybe "one year."

But not eleven years.

For one punch.

One drink too many, one stupid macho standoff, one offhand remark, one drunken punch, McAlister thinks, and my life is ruined.

He hadn't run away, he'd stayed, standing there trembling, nauseated, regretful—what have I done? what have I done?—*praying* for the man to come to.

But that hadn't happened.

And two lives were destroyed.

Monroe says that he'll appeal.

Feel free, says the judge. Appeal away, knock yourself out.

He does give McAlister thirty days to get his affairs in order before reporting to prison.

Folsom.

THE SWING GOES back and forth.

Like the pendulum in one of those old clocks. Ticktock ticktock, reminding McAlister that time is running.

Out.

Wyatt is laughing.

Hands gripped on the swing chains, he yells, "Higher, Daddy! Higher!"

McAlister pushes him higher, dreading the end of the ride when he'll have to let the swing stop.

And break his son's heart.

Because how do you tell a little boy, a *five-year-old* boy, that his daddy is going away tomorrow and isn't coming back for years? A day to a kid that age is forever. What are five years going to feel like? And that's if they're lucky and McAlister gets parole. It could be eleven years. How do you tell a kid that?

How do you tell a kid that?

How does he take it in?

How does he understand it?

"Higher, Daddy! Higher!"

McAlister stops the swing. Steps around, picks Wyatt up, then sits down on the swing with the boy on his lap.

"Wyatt, tomorrow Daddy has to go away."

"For how long?" Wyatt asks. "How many *Blueys*?"

It's Wyatt's way of telling time, by how many episodes of the television show he's allowed to watch.

"A lot, I'm afraid," McAlister says.

He feels the tension in the boy's little body, hears the tears welling up in his voice. "Why, Daddy?"

"Daddy did something wrong."

"What did you do?"

Now McAlister feels his own tears and has to shove them back down into his chest. "I hurt someone."

"When you hit that man?" Wyatt asks.

"Yes."

"Did the man die?"

McAlister feels his heart crack. "Yes. He did."

"And now you have to go to time-out?" Wyatt asks.

"Something like that."

Wyatt shakes his head. "No. Good daddies don't hurt anyone. You're a *good* daddy."

The boy turns into him, buries his face into his chest and sobs.

McAlister holds his shaking body.

HE READS HIM a story at bedtime.

"The Bear and the Two Friends."

God, McAlister thinks, the *last* story I'll ever read him, because by the time I get out, Wyatt won't want that anymore.

He's grateful when the boy falls asleep.

McAlister goes into the bedroom that he shares with his wife.

Rachel is sitting up in the bed, reading. "Is he out?"

McAlister nods.

She's wearing a white silk robe, sexy but not overtly so. It's always been a signal, one of those codes that married couples have, that she wants to have sex. The way her black hair just touches the robe's shoulder has always stirred him.

It doesn't now.

It only deepens his depression.

She feels it. "Are you too sad to make love?"

"I don't know."

"We should."

"Because it's the last time?" he asks.

"For a while."

"A long while."

"All the more reason," she says. She gets to her knees and hugs him. "Something for both of us to hang on to."

Her hand is insistent.

Then her lips, her tongue, her mouth.

Then her.

When he comes, she cries.

Then she holds him tightly.

• • •

IN THE MORNING, before dawn, McAlister walks quietly into Wyatt's room.

Bends down and kisses the sleeping boy on the cheek.

Wyatt wakes up, reaches his arms high and holds McAlister around the neck. "Bye, Daddy."

"Bye."

"Can I come visit you?"

"Of course you can."

"I will."

"I know." He pries the boy's arms off his neck. "I love you. More than anything."

"Love *you*."

THE CAR WAITS outside.

McAlister hired it. He didn't want Rachel driving him to the prison.

She walks to the door with him.

Wraps her arms around him. "I love you."

"Love you back."

"Take care of yourself."

"You, too."

"I'll visit as soon as I can."

He feels her tears on his neck and pulls himself away.

PRISONS ARE THE saddest places in the world.

Prisons and children's cancer wards.

The difference is that in the children's wards there's hope.

What there is in prison is violence.

The threat of violence and actual violence.

The threat of violence comes first from the system itself—tall chain-link fences topped with barbed wire, walkways and towers patrolled by guards with M-14 rifles who *will* kill you if you try to escape.

There's also the threat of the guards beating the shit out of you if you piss them off, rebel, act like a fool. Or maybe they just fucking feel like it or don't like you, and don't get it twisted—the threat of that violence gets actualized a lot. It just tends to happen in the few areas that aren't monitored by security cameras.

There's violence going the other way, too. The inmates hate the guards and many would attack them if they could. Some have over the years. The guards put up with a lot of shit—literally, because some inmates will throw their feces and cups of urine through the bars.

The guards are scared, uptight, outnumbered—and that makes them violent.

Add to that the threat of violence from inmate to inmate—the threats of rape, beatings, stabbings and murders are constant, ever present, a perpetual reminder that your life is on a tenterhook and can end at any moment from any*where*: the guy who wants to fuck you, the guy whom you've offended, the guy who just takes a disliking to you.

And that's nothing stacked up to the racial violence, the gang violence.

If you think the guards run prisons, you haven't been inside one.

The *gangs* run the prisons, and the gangs are organized by race.

And they're always at war or about to be at war; if they're not actually killing each other, they're thinking about killing each other. They don't make peace, they make truces—temporary, pragmatic, cynical.

The gangs are organized by race first and then by, yeah, violence.

When you join, they beat you in, just to see if you'll stand up to them and can take it. If you try to leave the gang, the best you can expect is a ferocious beating, but more likely a stabbing, or they might set you on fire in your cell.

Violence.

Prisons are the saddest places in the world because they hold the saddest people. People who know that they've fucked up their lives, fucked up their families, hurt other people. Many know that *this is their life* now, that they're *never getting out*, that they're going to die in this hell, that there is literally no hope. Many are addicts and alcoholics, some are sociopaths or psychopaths. Many are mentally ill, or if they weren't when they came in, they will be after a few years.

Because prison is designed to make a person crazy.

The crowding, the noise, the anxiety, the fear, the confinement, the tedium, the violence, the hopelessness—prison produces both mass and individual psychosis.

It makes a human inhuman.

This is the world that Brad McAlister enters.

He's been designated a level 4 prisoner.

They put him in with the most violent.

THE CLICHÉ IS the sound of the cell door clanging shut.

For McAlister it comes earlier—the sound of a door sliding *open*.

The door to the cell block.

Unit 1, the most populated block at Folsom, more than 1,200 men locked up on five tiers. Walking down that hall is like going into a canyon of desperation and despair.

Hell opening up.

The noise, the chaos, men screaming at him from their cells, jeering, laughing, taunting, threatening, catcalling, running metal cups across the bars.

"Hey, fish, you're mine!"

"Bitch come smelling nice and wearing something pretty!"

"Welcome to hell, newbie!"

McAlister has already been stripped, searched, prodded, deloused and showered. He's bent over and cupped his balls, spread his ass cheeks. Put his clothes and belongings in a plastic bag that was taken away—like my old life, he thought—and given new clothes: a blue denim work shirt, blue sweatpants, white socks, white sneakers.

Now he shuffles in a line onto the block, holding another plastic bag with a toothbrush, a small bar of soap and a small towel.

He feels like an alien in a strange world. He knows that he stands out. The Latino guy in front of him looks like he's been here before. His head is on a slow swivel, scanning.

The guy behind McAlister, also Latino, seems almost happy to be back. Smiling, nodding at people yelling down at him.

Then McAlister sees what he can't believe he's seeing. It's unreal. Three guys, dressed in inmate blue, come out of nowhere and jump the guy in front of him. Blades flash again and again, stabbing the man until he crumples to the floor.

"Wall! Wall!"

Guards come running.

One slams McAlister into the wall.

McAlister does what the guy behind him, now next to him, does. Pushes his face flat against the wall and raises his arms above his head.

Shouting, whistles, alarms go off.

Hooting, hollering, and is it . . .

Yeah, *cheering* from the tiers.

McAlister risks a glance sideways and down and sees the man lying in a pool of blood that's spreading across the floor.

The guy next to him says, "That's Jorge. *Was*, anyway. Snitched for a lighter sentence. Stupid. They were waiting for him."

McAlister's in shock.

"Well," the guy says, "he *did* get out earlier."

"They did it right out in the open," McAlister says.

"They're lifers. They don't give a fuck."

They stand against the wall until a crew picks up the body. Inmates come in and mop up the blood.

UP METAL STAIRS to the third tier.

The guard stops him at a cell.

This door is already open.

A little hell inside a bigger hell, McAlister thinks.

The cells at Folsom were built to hold a single prisoner, but overcrowding—130 percent of capacity—has forced them to double up. So there's a bed and a single mattress on the floor.

The man sitting on the bed looks up from the book he's reading. He's maybe fifty, short-cropped gray hair, five-ten, looks muscular under the loose-fitting shirt.

"Oh shit, no," he says.

"Oh shit, yes," the guard says.

He nudges McAlister into the cell.

There's the bed, the mattress, an open metal toilet, a metal sink, two small counters and two chairs.

The guard walks away.

The man looks at McAlister and sighs. "Okay, here are the rules. I'm the bed, you're the mattress. You never sit on my bed, you never touch it. You don't speak to me unless I speak to you first. I like it quiet in the mornings. You have to piss in the night, you aim along the side of the bowl so the noise doesn't wake me up. When you jerk off, you do it quietly with your back to me. I don't need to see or hear that shit. I like my house neat and tidy, so you keep your shit tight."

"Okay."

"My name is Gentry."

"I'm—"

"I don't need to know your fucking name," Gentry says. "It's nothing to me, *you're* nothing to me. It's you or it's some other asshole, I don't give a fuck." Gentry looks him up and down and immediately makes him as a civilian. "So what did you do? Embezzlement, tax evasion, wearing white after Labor Day?"

"I killed someone."

"*Ooooh.* Tough guy."

"No."

"Well, you better *get* tough, Slick," Gentry says. "Guys like you, they get tough quick or they're everyone's girlfriend."

"I thought that was just in the movies."

"Sometimes the movies get it right." Gentry looks down at McAlister's shoes. "Don't get blood on my floor."

McAlister sees the splatters of blood on the tops of his shoes. "Jesus, I saw them k—"

"You didn't see shit," Gentry says. "And you especially didn't tell me you saw shit."

It isn't long before the cell door slides shut and the lights go out.

McAlister lies on his mattress and pulls the thin blanket over his shoulders. The noise doesn't stop.

He hears shouting, singing, howling.

Sobs, grunts like the sound of sex.

Snoring.

Gentry snores like a stalled truck.

McAlister is terrified.

The worst, scariest night of his life.

He doesn't sleep at all. Just lies there, scared that Gentry will wake up and make a move. What did he mean, "sometimes the movies get it right"? Did he mean that he's going to assault me? McAlister wonders. Make me blow him?

Worse?

And what would I do?

McAlister is no wimp, but he knows that wouldn't give him a chance against the guys he sees in here. Guys who've been pumping iron for decades, violent guys, real psychopaths.

He lies awake and knows the real meaning of despair.

Nobody sleeps the first night.

THE LIGHTS COME on.

Gentry looks down on him.

"Get up, Slick," he says. "Shower time."

McAlister pulls himself up.

"You didn't sleep, did you?" Gentry asks.

"I don't think so." "Think"? He fucking knows he didn't.

Gentry asks, "What, were you scared I was going to try to fuck you?"

"No."

"The hell you weren't," Gentry says. "Maybe you *should* be worried. You're a nice-looking guy, Slick."

McAlister doesn't say anything.

"I'm kidding," Gentry says. "No, I'm not. Well, maybe I am. I'm just fucking with you. I'll *fuck* you later."

McAlister looks down.

"Mistake, Slick," Gentry says. "Anyone says that to you, anyone says anything *like* that to you, you punch him as hard as you can in the face. And you *keep* punching until he goes down. You'll go to seg, you might be bleeding, but it won't be from the ass."

"I don't want any trouble," McAlister says. It was punching someone in the face that got him here.

"I know," Gentry says. "You 'just want to do your time.' It don't work that way, Slick. See, you're still thinking with your civilian mind. You have to start thinking with your prison mind."

They go to the shower room.

McAlister strips, hangs his clothes on a hook. Feels guys checking him out. He's used to locker rooms from his college days, but this is different. The other guys are sizing him up. Is he a potential victim or a potential threat?

He waits his turn, then gets under the nozzle. Ten seconds to get wet, fifteen to soap up, ten seconds to rinse.

The water is tepid at best and it smells bad.

McAlister thinks about his morning showers at home. The big, tiled shower, clean; the strong hot spray. Then the thick, fluffy towel to dry off, then downstairs for that first great cup of coffee and a good-morning kiss.

Stop it, he tells himself.

You have to stop thinking that way.

That life is gone.

THEY GO TO the mess hall for breakfast.

Standing in line behind Gentry, McAlister feels eyes on him.

Or maybe I'm imagining that, he thinks.

But it sure feels like it.

An inmate shovels fake eggs on his tray.

They look awful.

McAlister makes it through the line and stands there with his tray.

The tables are strictly segregated. Whites sit with whites, Blacks with Blacks, Mexicans with Mexicans. There are a lot more Blacks and Mexicans than there are whites.

Gentry gestures to him. "You sit here."

McAlister sits on the bench next to him.

"This is Slick," Gentry says to the other guys.

McAlister figures that's his name now.

The guys nod at McAlister but don't say anything to him.

He nods back.

The eggs are even worse than they look, but McAlister makes himself eat.

BLANTON CHECKS McALISTER out.

"A newjack," he says to Pettiford.

"Fresh white meat," Pettiford says.

They make an odd pair. Blanton is tall and slender, with long, graceful fingers and a handsome face. Pettiford is short and squat, just muscle on muscle, and no one would describe his face as handsome. It's marked with tattoos: 276, BGF.

Both men are Black.

"He ain't Thirteen," Blanton says, still looking at McAlister.

"Oh, hell no," Pettiford says. "That man a civilian."

"He Gentry's puppy?"

Pettiford shakes his head. "Gentry don't play that."

Blanton agrees. "Gentry don't play."

He gives McAlister a last look.

Blanton takes a little time eating his breakfast, waits for Gentry's table to get up and the new fish to pass by him. Then he says to McAlister, "Hello there, newbie."

McAlister says, "Hi."

Keeps walking.

"Don't do that," Gentry says as they walk back to the block.

"Do what?"

"You know that ice cream?" Gentry says. "I think they call it Neapolitan? Vanilla, chocolate, strawberry?"

"What about it?"

"They're separate in the carton," Gentry says. "Clean lines between them. In the same box, but separate. That's what prison is—

you got your whites, your Blacks, your Mexicans in the same box, but separate."

"What's that have to do with—"

"You gotta be one," Gentry says. "*One.* And you don't get to choose which. You're vanilla, Slick. White. You don't talk to Black. Especially not *that* Black. He's the shot caller for BGF."

"What's BGF?"

Gentry shakes his head at the abysmal ignorance. "Black Guerrilla Family, the biggest Black gang in here. And Thirteen saw you talk to them."

McAlister tries to take it all in. "Who's Thirteen?"

"Not who, *what*," Gentry says. He juts his chin toward a table of white guys looking at them. "Thirteen is AB. Aryan Brotherhood. They saw you talk to Blanton, so you already got one foot in the shit with them."

Jesus, McAlister thinks, I'm in trouble already? "What do I do?"

"I look like Yoda to you?" Gentry asks. "Figure it out yourself."

Mulligan watches McAlister and Gentry leave.

The AB shot caller turns to his second-in-command, Rogers. "Who's the new fish?"

"Guy named McAlister," Rogers says.

"He looks like a citizen."

"He whacked some guy in a bar," Rogers says. "Word is he was some kind of big-shot executive. Hotels or something. So he has some money, I'll bet."

"For now," Mulligan says.

THE INMATES GET fifteen hours a week of exercise outside, weather permitting, which it usually is in California.

McAlister follows Gentry out onto the yard.

Again, it's segregated into groups of whites, Blacks and Mexicans. Gentry walks over to a set of weight benches and says, "We got the weights, the Blacks got the basketball court—go figure—the Mexicans kick a soccer ball around over there. Then it all rotates."

Mulligan and Rogers walk over.

"You mind if we have a word with your puppy?" Mulligan asks Gentry.

"He ain't my puppy," Gentry says, and walks away.

McAlister is scared.

He should be because Mulligan is a scary dude. Same height as McAlister, but much thicker, muscled. And tattoos all over him. Celtic knots, dragons and 88s on his arms. The number 13 on the right side of his neck and a swastika on the left.

AB inked square on his forehead.

"It's good to have another white man," Mulligan says. "As you can see, we're outnumbered here."

"I can see that."

"Oh, you *can* see that," Mulligan says. "Then why were you getting friendly with Black this morning?"

"I just said hello."

"That's being friendly," Mulligan says, "and it makes us wonder if you're a race traitor."

"I—I don't know what that is."

"You—you don't?" Mulligan asks. "It's it's a white man who betrays his white brothers."

"Look, I'm not interested in—"

"Did I ask you what you're interested in?" Mulligan says. Then he smiles. "We're getting off on the wrong foot here. Real talk—you see those Browns and Blacks over there. Unless you hook up with us, they're going to make you their june bug. They already knew you're weak when you said hi to Blanton."

"What's a june bug?"

"A slave," Mulligan says. "You run their errands, you give them your commissary, you give up a lot more than that, you catch my drift. They'll fuck you in the mouth and in the ass, and if that's not enough holes, they'll make some new ones and fuck you there. They get tired of you, they sell you to the Mexicans as a *puta.* So you're either with your white brothers or you're a lame duck, and trust me, you don't want to be alone in here."

"What do I have to do?" McAlister asks.

Mulligan smiles. "You strike me as the kind of guy who has some money in the bank."

"I have a little."

"And I'll bet you have a nice little wife, too," Mulligan says.

McAlister feels a flush of anger. Feels the red come to his face and the same temper that led him to punch Cameron that night. His fists clench.

Mulligan sees it.

"It's all right, brother," Mulligan says. "I meant no disrespect. So *are* you married?"

"Yes."

"That's good," Mulligan says. "Because what you're going to do is have her put some money on my books. I'll give you the numbers, the codes. It's easy."

McAlister is scared but he asks, "Why should I give you my money?"

"You have to *buy* your way into our car," Rogers says. "There's no free ride in Thirteen."

"And then we'll get you some ink," Mulligan says. "Rogers here, he's pretty good with the buzz. You need to represent, fish."

• • •

BLANTON LOOKS OVER from the b-ball court.

"Thirteen's making its move on the newjack," he says.

"Let me see, show of hands, who gives a sloppy fuck?" Pettiford asks. He looks at his hands down by his hips. "I guess not me."

"This is why," Blanton says, "when we play chess, I win nine out of ten. I play the long game."

BACK IN HIS cell, McAlister's mind is whirling.

About what to do.

I can't have Rachel sending these guys money. She's already going to have to get a job, put Wyatt in day care. She doesn't really have the money.

And when would it stop? Are they just going to demand more and more, as long as I keep giving it to them?

And tattoos?

Prison tats, racist tats?

I have an appeal going. Even if that doesn't pan out, I'm eligible for parole in five years. It's going to be hard enough finding a job with a criminal record, never mind with swastikas on my neck.

He says, "Can I ask you something?"

Gentry is busy reading his book. His literary tastes are eccentric and specific—he likes nonfiction books about men stranded on desert islands. "No."

Nevertheless, McAlister tells him about Mulligan coming up on him and asks, "What do you think?"

"That you're fucked," Gentry says. "Everyone thinks you're weak, Slick. Because you are. You're a guppy in a shark tank. They all know they can take advantage of you, so they will."

"But maybe if I give them a little money—"

"You put money on his books, it won't stop there," Gentry says. "Pretty soon they'll have your wife delivering cash to *their* wives, you'll be buying their baby mamas' groceries, paying their rents. Next thing you know, they'll be making your wife try to smuggle in dope.

"They'll bleed you," Gentry tells him, "until they've bled you dry, then they'll turn you out, maybe to the other Aryans, then to the Mexicans and the Blacks. The only choice you have is to join the AB, become a full-fledged member.

"That's if they'll even have you," Gentry says. "You'll have to beat up some Black or Mexican first."

"*You* didn't join them," McAlister says.

"I didn't have to," Gentry says. "I'm an OG. 'Original gangster,' 'old guy,' you pick. I have a backdoor parole—the only way I ever leave here is in a coffin."

McAlister is afraid to ask, but Gentry explains. "I beat my wife to death with a claw hammer. She kept interrupting when I was trying to read. Anyway, I have respect in here."

"How did you get it?"

Gentry finally looks up from his book. "Because all these assholes know that if some tatted-up dickwad even *suggested* turning my woman into his personal ATM, I'd rip his heart out of his chest and make him eat it. Now I'm not saying you have to do *that*, but you gotta do *something*, Slick. And there is no try, only do."

Gentry goes back to his book, back to his island.

McAlister doesn't sleep again that night.

The noise, the smell, the fear, the worry.

BLANTON SITS IN his cell doing his origami.

Besides chess, it's his major hobby, and he's gotten very good at making little figures of birds out of paper. He keeps some; others he sells to the Mexicans as presents for their families when they visit.

Papel picado, the Mexicans call them.

"I'm thinking of bringing that white boy in," Blanton says.

"Into what?" asks Pettiford.

"BGF," Blanton says. "Under our wing."

"I don't know if the brothers are going to like that," Pettiford says.

Blanton hears it as a challenge. It isn't *much* of a challenge, but you gotta nip these things in the bud. "I give a fuck what they like? They need to like what I *tell* them to like."

By which he also means, *You, too.*

Pettiford backs down.

Smart move.

Blanton isn't just the BGF shot caller on the inside; he calls shots in the real world, too, behind the wheel of the gang on the streets by remote control. Man runs a drug and murder empire from the joint.

When he's not making little paper birds.

So he doesn't let little challenges go. Knows from the chessboard that if you let a pawn move around too much, pawn gets thinking it's a knight, and then you got a problem you didn't need to have.

Also knows that in a chess match, white always gets to move first.

Black always second.

McALISTER GOES THROUGH the breakfast line, comes out with his tray and walks toward Gentry's table.

Past Blanton.

"Good morning, newbie," Blanton says.

"Fuck off."

Mulligan notices. He smiles and gestures for McAlister to sit at the Thirteen table.

McAlister walks over, swings his tray like a sword and hits Mulligan square in the throat. Mulligan goes over his chair backward onto the floor, grabbing at his throat and gasping for air.

The ABs go for McAlister.

Fists, feet, elbows, punches and kicks, the Thirteen guys beat the uncouth piss out of him until the COs can come in and pull them off.

The guards pin McAlister down, handcuff him behind his back and shackle his ankles. Then they frog-march him to the infirmary, where the doctor puts some stitches into his lip and his forehead and gives him two Tylenol.

Then two other guards, both of them white, haul him down to ad-seg.

Solitary confinement.

On the way they come to a place in the hall that the cameras don't cover, and one of the guards slams his foot down on the chain that connects McAlister's ankles. His hands behind his back, McAlister topples face-first onto the hard floor.

His nose breaks.

Blood pours out.

"That's for Mulligan," the guard says, hauling McAlister up. "And do *not* bleed on my uniform, fish."

He pushes McAlister into the little cell.

It's horrible.

Six by nine feet with a metal shelf to sleep on, a metal sink and an open toilet. It reeks of dried urine, caked shit, stale sweat and desperation.

These walls have seen men go mad, men bang their heads until they bled, men find ways to hang themselves. If the walls could talk, they'd babble, they'd curse, they'd pray futile prayers to a god gone deaf.

That night, a different CO slides open the slot they use to push the meal tray through and says, "Mulligan told me to tell you that you're a body bag waiting to be filled."

MCALISTER THINKS THAT the bright side to ad-seg would be some quiet, anyway.

He's wrong.

There is no solitude in solitary.

The noise never stops.

The psychotic in the next cell never stops howling, another keeps up a running soliloquy about aliens, a third yells to McAlister how they're going to fuck him to death when he gets out.

He lies down on the shelf with a thin blanket, no pillow. It's cold and his body *hurts* from the kicks and punches. His nose is swollen and he can barely breathe. Blood is caked on his face, and he wants a shower.

McAlister thinks about Rachel.

About Wyatt.

I have to survive, he tells himself.

I have to get back to them.

But he doesn't know how.

Morning comes with an answer.

The guard who slides his breakfast through the slot is Black.

On the breakfast tray is a little white paper bird.

What the fuck? McAlister thinks.

TWO DAYS LATER he starts hearing voices in the cell.

Thinks he's going nuts already, but he swears he hears a muffled voice calling his name. He puts his ear to the door but doesn't hear it in the hall. Lies down with his ear to the floor but doesn't hear anything there, either.

Then he hears a knocking.

It sounds like it's coming from the toilet.

Oh, I'm losing it, he thinks.

But he leans over the toilet and hears the muffled voice.

"Flush the toilet."

"What?"

"Flush the toilet, man!"

McAlister flushes the toilet, then listens again.

Hears, "You McAlister, right?"

"Yeah."

"You get the bird?"

"Yeah . . ."

"That be Blanton," the voice says, "offering you his protection."

MCALISTER DOES THIRTY days in the hole.

Nothing to read, nothing to watch, nothing to listen to, nothing but time.

He probably would have lost it, but he tells himself that he doesn't have that luxury, so he wills himself to stay sane.

And strong.

His body aches like crazy, but he forces himself to do a hundred push-ups and a hundred sit-ups every day. He finds that he can back up to the shelf, plant his hands and work on his triceps. He runs in place for a hundred steps at a time until he can do a thousand without stopping.

He works his mind.

Makes lists.

Starts by trying to name all fifty states. It's surprisingly hard but he finally does it. Commits them to memory and then starts over, listing them alphabetically.

"Alabama, Alaska, Arkansas . . ."

Then he switches to US presidents.

He never does get them all—he's weak in the 1830s and '40s—but gets a lot of them, and then arranges them in chronological order.

"Washington, Adams, Jefferson, Madison, Monroe . . ."

After that he goes back to his old work—in his head. Starts going through the checklists he established for the cleaning crews, the restaurant staff, the pool attendants, the maintenance people, the security guards.

Anything to keep his mind busy, active, organized.

Because he knows now that it will take two kinds of toughness to survive in this place: physical and mental.

He'll need them both to get home to Rachel and Wyatt.

The other thing that keeps him sane is the "toilet telephone."

He learns how to do it from the guy below him, whose name turns out to be Jerome. He's a subordinate of Blanton's.

What you do is flush the toilet, then use a cup to bail the rest of the water out. Then you take the cardboard from a toilet paper roll and use it as a sort of speaking and hearing tube. Even better if you can get a Styrofoam cup and put it on top of the tube: it amplifies the sound, plus you get the bonus of not having to stick your face so far in the toilet.

It almost makes him laugh.

My life, he thinks, is literally in the toilet.

But once or twice a day, he knocks, or he hears a knock, and gets on the toilet telephone to keep up on the news.

Nicknames Jerome "CNN."

"Things tense between the BGF and Thirteen," Jerome says. *"Mexicans on the sidelines waiting to jump one way or the other."*

"Blanton be talking with the Mexicans."

"Gonna go off any day now."

"Mexicans and BGF made a pact. Thirteen shittin' bricks."

And then one day, *"You thought about Blanton's offer?"*

"I'm thinking about it."

"Don't think too long. Thirteen still want you dead."

Like I don't know that, McAlister thinks. That's not news, CNN. But he knows now that he just can't accept protection from Blanton. It would make me weak, McAlister thinks, make me a punk.

At the same time, I need protection from Thirteen.

It's a problem.

Then one day a CO comes, opens the door and takes him back to gen pop. The guard's on Thirteen's arm, so he says, "You're a dead man walking, McAlister. Thirteen's waiting for you."

IT'S REC TIME, so McAlister goes straight onto the yard.

Walks out with his chin up and his eyes slowly scanning. He doesn't turn his neck; he doesn't want to seem nervous or edgy.

In fact, he's scared as hell.

Seems like the whole yard is looking at him.

Thirteen sure as hell is.

McAlister sees Mulligan spot him from across the weights area. His bumboy Rogers starts to circulate, saying something to the others, and they all start to eye-fuck McAlister.

Then they move.

Slowly they separate into two groups, moving through the yard, through other prisoners, working their way toward McAlister from two sides.

Mulligan, he's coming straight up the middle.

So McAlister is scared, but tells himself:

Scared does you no good now.

Throw it away.

Make a plan.

Glancing far over to the ball court, he sees Blanton and his people. They're tossing the ball around but just looking.

Not moving.

"That be Blanton offering you his protection," McAlister thinks.

I should have said yes sooner.

Too late for that now. Put it out of your mind.

The Aryans are coming in two horns, to his right and left. Two or three of them, though, led by Rogers, are coming straight ahead to block McAlister from getting away. Mulligan is behind this group, staying to the rear like a general, letting his troops do the fighting.

Either the COs on the wall don't see what's happening or they don't care.

McAlister sees Gentry sitting at a picnic table.

Gentry shrugs.

McAlister presses his back against the wall to protect his spine and his kidneys. Decides he'll fight literally with his back to the wall, lash out with punches and kicks.

Yeah, fists and feet, he thinks.

These guys have blades.

He flashes back to the stabbing of Jorge.

Feels like a lifetime ago.

Put it out of your mind.

Does you no good.

He feels anger.

Rage.

Lets it come, doesn't try to suppress it. Lets the adrenaline flow through him because he's going to need it—

Mulligan grins at him.

They're almost on him.

McAlister puts his fists up.

Bring it.

Then—

The shout comes from the basketball court.

Mulligan turns around.

To see—

Dozens of BGF rushing across the yard.

Straight at Mulligan.

The war is on.

Thirteen turns to face them, to try to get back to rescue Mulligan.

McAlister forgotten.

A mass melee on the yard.

Now the COs wake up.

Whistles, sirens, guards rushing in with their batons, swinging at anything, yelling, "Down! Down!"

McAlister drops to the ground, covers his head.

Starts to choke and realizes that tear gas canisters are exploding around him, their smoke crawling across the yard.

He looks up and sees BGF swarm Mulligan, stabbing and slashing. Bent double, he manages to stagger away. Then he falls, lies fetal, clutching his stomach. Rubber bullets ping across the ground, driving the BGFs away from him.

McAlister wraps his arms around his face.

The riot lasts for only ten minutes, but the carnage is heavy. Inmates are being taken away on stretchers; others lie motionless. Some guys have blood streaming down their faces, either from inmates' clubs or from the COs' batons.

They lie on the ground for a full hour before the COs get them up, move them inside and put them in lockdown.

THEY'RE IN THEIR cells for a week.

When they're finally let back on the yard, everyone is wary, edgy, but no one wants to fight.

Especially Thirteen.

They got the worst of the fight: one guy killed, several hurt. And they're leaderless.

Mulligan took five stab wounds, one to the kidney, and he's in the infirmary.

Going to be there a long time.

Blanton comes up to McAlister. "Look at you, all alive and shit."

"I guess I owe you some thanks."

"That wasn't for you," Blanton says. "You were just a decoy. A pawn. Thirteen wanted you so bad they forgot to castle they king."

McAlister doesn't know what that means. Some sort of chess term, he guesses. He says, "I'm not going to be your june bug."

"No one asking you to be."

"I'm not putting money on your books," McAlister says, "I'm not giving you my commissary."

"I got money," Blanton says. "I got commissary."

"Then what do you want from me?"

Blanton tells him.

BGF HAS MADE an alliance with the Mexicans based on staying out of each other's way out in the real world and dealing dope inside the joint only to their own people. They'll share the white market.

It's contingent, though, on Mulligan not recovering, because the Mexicans are too worried about Thirteen if he gets back behind the wheel.

"We got the numbers," Blanton tells McAlister. "You don't have to worry about no Blacks or no Mexicans, and white is too weak to move on you with Mulligan out of action. You can do your bit here, however long it is, and walk out alive with your ass and your dignity intact. All you have to do is this one small favor."

Or . . .

"You're dead."

"HE GOING TO do it?" Pettiford asks.

"Well," Blanton says, "he motivated."

• • •

McALISTER LOOKS ACROSS the table at Rachel and Wyatt.

His heart cracks.

It took weeks to get this first visit, what with his "orientation" time, the red tape and his time in solitary.

"I tried to get here sooner," Rachel says, "but they said you were in 'ad-seg'?"

"There was a little trouble."

"Brad . . ." She sees the barely healed bruises, the swollen lip and the scabs from the cuts on his face.

And his nose.

Crooked now.

He's changed, Rachel thinks. It's not just the face—it's something inside him. There was always this trace of . . . softness . . . in Brad. She doesn't see it now, doesn't feel it.

Rachel misses it, but she realizes that it's a necessary change for him to make it in here. She glances around at the other women. They look poor, fatigued, worried. Am I going to be one of them? she wonders. Is this my life now?

"It was nothing," McAlister says. "It's over."

"Were you bad again, Daddy?" Wyatt asks.

"Daddy had to deal with some bullies," McAlister says.

"Mommy got a job."

McAlister looks at Rachel.

"I had to, Brad," she says. "We need money."

"I know."

Yeah, he knows, but he feels terrible. Providing for his family was his role, his life, his pride.

"I talked to Monroe," Rachel says.

"And . . ." He's hoping for good news about his appeal.

"He said the wheels of justice turn slowly," Rachel says.

Not when they were prosecuting me, McAlister thinks. Then

they turned pretty goddamn fast. But my appeal, not so much. "I got a job, too. In the infirmary. I'm a nurse's aide. Graveyard shift."

"Congratulations?"

He empties bedpans, changes bandages, dispenses "Skittles"—over-the-counter medications.

The nurses like and trust him.

As Blanton says, "White can go where Black can't."

Now McAlister slowly slides his hand across the table, touches his fingertips to hers. There's a no-contact rule in the visiting room, but the CO there isn't particularly watchful. Maybe out of laziness, maybe out of compassion, although McAlister doubts that.

There's no compassion here.

The CO isn't looking, but other inmates are. McAlister sees them stealing dirty glances at Rachel, up and down, checking her out like she's going to be the subject of their jerk-off fantasies later.

Even worse, he can see one or two of them looking at Wyatt the same way.

"How's school?" McAlister asks Wyatt.

"It's okay."

"Do you like your teacher?"

"She's nice."

"That's good."

As wonderful as it is to see them, the visit is awkward, even painful. What are they supposed to talk about? What's he supposed to tell them that isn't going to worry them?

Even the slight touch of Rachel hurts. Too much of a reminder of what he's lost, what he can't have.

The CO calls time.

McAlister stands up; Rachel takes the cue and does, too. She picks up Wyatt. McAlister reaches across the table, takes him from her arms and hugs him. "I love you, son."

“I love you, Daddy.”

Now the CO decides to do his job. “No contact!”

“I’m hugging my kid!”

“You want to get 115’d, McAlister?!” the CO says. “You want to go back in the hole?”

“Don’t get in trouble, Brad,” Rachel says.

He hands Wyatt back to her. Gets as close as he can to her and whispers, “I love you, Rache.”

“I love you, Brad.”

“I’ll do my time, I’ll come home to you,” McAlister says. “I promise.”

I promise.

I’ll do what I have to do.

IT’S ONE OF the nurses’ birthdays. They’re in the little office having coffee and cake, blowing out candles.

“Happy Birthday to You” and all that happy shit.

So they’re not watching McAlister as he walks down the ward to Mulligan’s bed. Nobody is, because the hard truth is that nobody really gives a fuck about anyone else in prison.

McAlister’s legs feel like wood.

The last time I killed someone, he thinks . . . Jesus, did I really think those words, “the last time I killed someone”? . . . It was an accident, an impulse. This time it’s intentional—flat-out murder.

That’s your civilian mind, he thinks.

Switch to your prison mind.

It’s self-defense, a preemptive strike.

Him or me.

So I pick me.

I want to get back to my wife and son.

So he keeps walking.

Two in the morning, most of the patients are asleep or whacked on dope.

Mulligan's out of it.

Eyes closed.

Oxygen tube in his nostrils, IV in his arm.

McAlister doesn't hesitate. He's afraid if he pauses, he won't go through with it. So he does just what Blanton told him. He looks around quickly to make sure no one sees him, then takes the IV needle out of the port in Mulligan's arm, detaches the tube from the needle, blows into it, refixes it to the needle and puts the needle back into Mulligan's vein.

Then he walks away.

He's in another part of the ward when he hears the alarm go off and sees nurses rushing to Mulligan's bed.

They give him CPR and then hit his chest with the defibrillator.

Too late.

Mulligan is dead from an embolism.

An air bubble blew out his candle.

Happy birthday to you.

END OF SHIFT. McAlister goes back to his house to get some sleep.

But he just lies there.

Thinking:

You're a murderer.

That's who you are now.

Yeah, maybe, he thinks.

But you're a murderer who's going home to his wife and kid.

NEXT MORNING, GENTRY says, "I heard Mulligan went home to his Viking gods."

"Is that right?" McAlister asks.

Gentry's looking at him with a smirk on his face.

McAlister asks, "What's it to me?"

Gentry smiles. "Now you got that prison mind."

He goes back to his book.

THERE'S AN INVESTIGATION into Mulligan's death.

Call it "cursory."

An inmate tapping out in the infirmary? Happens all the time. The thinking goes that these dirtbags have so many street drugs running through their veins it's more surprising when they *don't* die.

So this is strictly NHI.

No Humans Involved.

McAlister's name never even comes up.

IT DOES ON the yard, though.

The word goes out.

You do not fuck with McAlister.

It doesn't make him invincible, invulnerable or anything like that, but it does put an aura around him that he's not that much of a civilian, he's a killer.

You don't believe it, just ask Mulligan.

Oh, that's right—you can't.

McALISTER WATCHES PETTIFORD twist some toilet paper into a tight roll, then rub it with grease.

Then Pettiford lights it on fire and holds it under the metal frame of the bunk bed. Pretty soon, some soot appears. Pettiford scrapes the soot off with a spoon onto the cover of a glossy magazine. He dribbles a few drops of water and a little shampoo on the soot, gently mixes it, looks at McAlister and says, "Ink. Lampblack."

Because BGF has decided that if McAlister is going to hang with the family, even though he's white, he has to have some ink, has to represent.

McAlister doesn't want the tattoos but knows that they're necessary. He takes another swig of pruno, the booze inmates make by stuffing oranges, fruit cocktail and sugar into a plastic bag, heating it, and then letting it ferment for days.

A far cry from six-hundred-dollar Grand Siècle No. 23, McAlister thinks, laughing at himself. But the hooch will help fortify him against what's coming.

Pettiford picks up the tattoo gun.

The needle is made from the G string of a guitar, taken from the prison's music program. It was sharpened by dipping it in salt water that had been electrically charged with a B battery—submerging it over and over again until the electrolysis stripped away thin layers of the metal, making it, well, needle sharp.

The gun carriage itself is made from the tube of a ballpoint pen fastened to a toothbrush handle with tight rubber bands. A small motor, taken from a cassette tape player, is attached to the top of the handle. The needle is slipped through the pen tube, and the motor drives it up and down like a sewing machine.

Pettiford has already drawn the designs.

The first one features the letters "B," "G," and "F" around a machete crossed with a rifle. The second is a beautiful rendering of a dragon attacking a prison tower. The third is more basic: the number 276—the 2 representing "B," the 7 for the "G," the 6 for the "F."

"We'll start easy, with the 276," Pettiford says to McAlister. He dips the needle into the ink and raises the gun toward McAlister's left cheek.

"Not the face," Blanton says.

"Why not?" Pettiford asks.

That's where it goes, where everyone can see it and know the man's affiliation.

"You questioning me?" Blanton asks Pettiford.

"No."

"Because it sure sounded like a question," Blanton says. "Who, what, when, where, *why*."

McAlister stays quiet during this exchange. He knows better than to get involved in this.

"Where should it go, then?" Pettiford asks.

"Better question," Blanton says. "Only the chest and the stomach. I have my reasons. Take your shirt off, white boy."

McAlister takes his shirt off.

Pettiford dips the needle in the ink again and then puts the gun to McAlister's skin.

The motor hums.

McAlister's skin is the fabric under the sewing machine.

It hurts.

McAlister doesn't flinch.

Because that's part of it.

Gotta show you're tough.

It goes for days and he never flinches.

"Respect," Blanton says at one point.

McAlister shrugs like it's nothin'.

End of the process, the front of his body is covered with ink—the letters, the numbers, the machete, the rifle, the dragon.

Black Guerrilla Family.

"You ain't really a member," Blanton tells him. "You just sort of adopted. This is just skin-deep."

Blanton laughs at his own joke.

• • •

BUT IT'S SERIOUS.

McAlister is a unicorn—a white guy protected by the Blacks and Mexicans and still respected by the whites. He's an anomaly, a white convict who cells with a white guy but spends more and more of his time with Blacks. Plays basketball with them on the yard, listens to jazz with them, learns about Bird, about 'Trane, about Dizzy, about Miles.

"YOU PLAY CHESS?" Blanton asks McAlister one day.

"No. Why?"

"Passes the time. Keeps your mind sharp."

"Never played."

"I'll teach you."

He does.

Patiently teaches him the game, explains what he meant by Thirteen not castling their king.

"See, you want to keep your castle—your rook—close to your king, where it can protect him against an attack from a bishop, a knight, even a lowly pawn. Thirteen didn't protect they king."

Blanton usually wins, but he tries to teach McAlister the game. McAlister is smart, he learns, but Blanton learns more about *him.* He learns that McAlister is cautious, more concerned about protecting his king than about attacking his opponent's. Too worried about holding on to what he has to get any more.

Good to know.

McAlister learns about Blanton, too. Learns that he's aggressive, likes to take pieces off the board. That he's greedy.

BLANTON BECOMES LIKE a friend.

"There are no friends in prison," Gentry tells him. "Only allies. And the alliances are temporary."

"I thought *you* were my friend," McAlister says.

"You thought wrong," Gentry says. "That's your civilian mind. I don't have friends, I don't want friends."

He wants to be on his island.

Anyway, life goes on like this.

Chess, music, the yard, the meals, the showers, the long days, the endless nights.

McAlister does his time.

SO DOES RACHEL.

In the realm of This Isn't the Way It Was Supposed to Be, Rachel McAlister is the queen.

Because *this isn't the way it was supposed to be.*

What was supposed to be was that she would be a happy wife and mother in a stable marriage with a nice, predictable life.

This is not meant to convey that she is shallow or materialistic.

She isn't.

She is, in fact, quite deep, and her material wants extend only to the point where her family has what it needs.

This was *the way it was supposed to be.*

Then—

Everything changed.

In a single moment.

Her world crashed.

She literally thought she was dreaming, that she would wake up in the morning and tell Brad about the weird nightmare she had.

But the nightmare was real.

Her husband had killed somebody.

Then that gavel came down.

On her as well as him.

Eleven years.

She heard herself gasp.

But again, she sucked it up, she adjusted.

It was all so surreal, so unexpected, but she made love to her husband and saw him off to prison and knew that this was now her world, she was a convict's wife.

All right, she told herself, this is the "worse" of the "for better or worse" thing, and she renewed her vows, resolved to make every visit, to be upbeat and optimistic. And it wasn't just the marital vows—she *loved* this man.

So Rachel does her time.

She had to sell the house she loved, then get a job. There were no positions teaching French, so she found one selling medical supplies. With her salary and the profit she made from the house sale, it was enough for a smaller place in a lesser suburb, just enough to cover the cost of the day care she now needs for Wyatt, groceries and other expenses.

Rachel is strong, Rachel is tough. She handles it—the condescending sympathy of her friends, asking in faux-therapist tones, "Rachel, how are *you* coping?" as they drop off one by one; some of those same friends' husbands actually hitting on her: "It must get lonely, Rachel, huh?"

Yes, it gets lonely, thanks.

It gets damn lonely.

Lonely at night after Wyatt goes to bed, lonely in her own bed, lonely waking up by herself, lonely raising a child on her own, a little boy who can't understand—Christ, how could he, she thinks, *I* can't—why his father isn't there.

Once or twice she's tempted.

There's a guy in the office, good-looking, kind of sweet, who's let it be known in subtle ways that he's available for a matinee fling, and she has to admit to herself that, yes, she's tempted. It would be so nice to be touched, to feel another person's skin against her own, to feel . . .

She doesn't do it. Instead she fantasizes about Brad being with her, Brad being in her. A pale substitute that often leaves her feeling more sad than satisfied.

Mostly she just gets on with it, puts one foot in front of the other, the daily left-right-left-right of doing her time.

Rachel is strong, Rachel is tough.

But sometimes she wakes up crying, can't help but yield to the sorrow and, let's face it, *rage*.

This isn't the way it was supposed to be.

IT ISN'T SUPPOSED to be *this* way, either, on her second visit, eight months into his incarceration.

Brad has changed, she accepts that, but she never thought he'd change *this* much. She sat across the table from him and looked at his face as he tried so hard to make conversation with Wyatt.

It's not the crooked nose—which is sort of . . . handsome—it's not the faded scars, it's . . . this *hardness* about him.

What's shocking is what he says.

She had brought up the possibility of her relocating to Sacramento to be closer to the prison.

"It's a seven-hour drive now," she said, "without traffic. Sacramento is half an hour. Not to mention the cost of gas, a motel room. We could come a lot more often."

But Brad nixed the idea—he didn't want to rip Wyatt out of his surroundings, his school, his friends, whatever stability he still has with a working mom and an absentee dad.

Okay, she got that.

It's when time is up, he hugs Wyatt and then whispers in her ear. "I don't want you to come anymore."

"What?"

"I don't like the way these guys look at you," he says, "and at Wyatt. And you're right, the trip is too hard and too expensive."

"I want to do it."

"And these other wives—" he says.

"Time, McAlister!" the CO yells.

"—most of them are ganged up," McAlister says. "If they get to know you, they'll try to take advantage."

There's something else that he doesn't say.

It's too hard on him.

Seeing her.

Seeing Wyatt.

It's too painful a reminder of what he doesn't have.

And it takes him out of his prison mind—the mentality he needs to survive.

"We'll talk on the phone," he says. "I'll call every day. But the visits stop."

"Brad—"

"It's what I need to do," he says. "To come home to you. And I will. I promise. I'll come home to you."

Rachel accepts it.

What choice does she have?

But—

This isn't the way it was supposed to be.

FIVE YEARS.

His appeal was denied, one judge finding that another judge had done nothing at all wrong.

So McAlister has to wait for his first chance at parole.

Five years.

Sixty months.

Two hundred sixty weeks.

One thousand, eight hundred and twenty-five days.

Forty-three thousand, eight hundred hours.

Two million, six hundred twenty-eight thousand minutes.

You think it goes by fast?

It doesn't.

McAlister feels every one of them.

Does *every one* of them.

That old cliché "the minutes go by like hours"?

Fuck that, the minutes go by like days, like weeks, like months, like years.

Five years of the noise. The smells—the mixed stench of urine, shit, vomit, sweat, body odor, fear and desperation. The shitty food. The mind-numbing, soul-killing tedium. The casual violence. The loneliness that stabs like a knife. The missing his wife, the missing his son, talking to them only on the phone in the hall standing next to other inmates fighting with spouses, pleading, begging, having phone sex, and hearing his son's voice getting older, hearing about the moments he should have been present at, trying to explain why he wasn't, trying to explain why he can't answer "When will you be home, Daddy? I miss you."

Five years of that.

Changes you.

How can it not?

Then he comes up for parole.

HE WRITES HIS application.

Emphasizes his remorse for what he did, his spotless pre-offense record, that he has a family and a home to go back to, with the possibility of a well-paying job. He has a good prison record—in five years, the only 115 on him was from the mess hall fight five years ago—but McAlister is terrified that will be enough to get him denied.

His hearing comes up and he appears before the board: two old men and a woman sitting behind a table looking at paperwork.

McAlister sits and listens as the chairman reads the record of his offense and his prison record, noting the report for fighting but also noting the positive commendation from the prison infirmary.

Then he looks up from his documents at McAlister. "Inmate McAlister, it doesn't appear on the record that you have taken advantage of any of the institution's educational opportunities."

"No, sir," McAlister says. "I mean, I have a master's degree."

"I see," the chairman says. "You have one blemish on your record. It appears you assaulted another inmate? With a tray?"

"Yes, sir."

"Wasn't that the exact cause of your incarceration?" the chairman asks. "It doesn't appear that you've learned your lesson."

McAlister feels sick to his stomach. "It was my first week here, sir. My record has been clean since then."

"Does anyone else have any questions?"

They don't.

"Do you have anything you'd like to tell us, Inmate McAlister?" the chairman asks.

McAlister goes into the speech that he's rehearsed a few hundred times. "Only that I'm sincerely sorry for what I did. If I could take it back, I would. I've been pretty much a model prisoner since I've been here. I have a stable home and family to go back to, and I don't believe that I represent a threat to society."

"Thank you," the chairman says. "You can wait in the hall."

McAlister sits on a metal folding chair in the corridor and waits. It's only minutes but feels like hours before they call him back in.

"I'm going to be honest with you," the chairman says. "We have a split decision here. But two of us feel that you're ready to reenter society. Don't let us down, Inmate McAlister."

McAlister can barely choke out the words. "I won't. Thank you."

He walks back down the corridor like he's on air.

I'm going home, he thinks.

Well, the man I am now is going home.

The man I was is never coming back.

THE MORNING OF his release he says goodbye to Gentry.

"Thanks for everything," McAlister said. "I wouldn't have made it without your advice."

"Go fuck yourself," Gentry says.

Doesn't even look up from his book.

BLANTON IS A little different.

"My man," he says. "You take care of yourself in the world."

"I will," McAlister says. "You take care of yourself in here. And thanks, man, thanks for putting your arm around me."

Blanton nods. He turns away, chanting, "Free at last! Free at last! Thank God Almighty, I am free at last!"

McAlister hears him laughing as he walks back down the block.

"FREEDOM" IS AN ambiguous word.

It means so many different things to different people.

We tend to think of it in noble terms—political freedom, freedom of religion, freedom from want, for instance—but for an ex-con freedom means basic things.

The freedom to wake up when you want, the freedom to shower

and shave when you want, the freedom to eat when and what you want, the freedom to shut off the lights or keep them on.

The freedom to take a walk.

If you've been locked down for five years, like Brad McAlister has, this is heady stuff.

When he walks out the gates, gripping his old civilian clothes in the same plastic bag he went in with, Rachel is there to meet him.

They haven't seen each other in over four years.

By McAlister's choice, but still . . .

Of course time has changed her. But the tiny crow's-feet now around her eyes, the little frown lines around her mouth only make her more attractive to him.

He holds her so tight he's afraid he'll break her. Once again he feels her tears on his neck and maybe a few of his own on his cheek.

"It's okay," he says. "It's over now. It's over."

They get into her car. He wants to drive but no longer has a license, and the last thing they want is a parole violation two minutes after getting out.

"Wyatt's waiting at home," Rachel says. "He wanted to come, but I didn't think you'd want him to."

"You were right," McAlister says.

"I brought some new clothes," Rachel says. "We can stop at a gas station or something, you can change. I hope they fit, you're . . . uhhh . . . 'bulked up.'"

Five years of pumping iron on the yard.

Five years of building armor around himself.

The new shirt is a little tight in the shoulders and the collar when he changes in a gas station men's room. It's good, though, he doesn't want Wyatt to see him again in his prison blues.

But it's still awkward when they get home.

Well, the *new* home, a much smaller place in a modest neighborhood in Tustin, because Rachel couldn't keep up with the mortgage on the Laguna Niguel place with just one income as a medical salesperson.

But it's on a nice cul-de-sac, and Wyatt is waiting at the edge of the driveway, looking down the street, waiting for his dad.

He's been waiting for five years.

Half his life.

He's almost forgotten what it's like to have a father, and his dad has become almost a mythical figure to him, a hero he only knows from photos on the mantel and phone calls. A disembodied voice from far away.

Wyatt had been puzzled and hurt when they stopped visiting, at first angry at his mother, blaming her because she must have done something, then angry at his dad. So he had these conflicting feelings of anger, then guilt at being angry, and it was all pretty hard for a kid his age to sort out.

He's old enough now to realize that his mom has done her best—gone to every soccer game she could, signed him up for Little League, was almost always home to make supper, and there in the morning to make breakfast, pack his lunch and get him off to school.

Still, a boy misses his dad.

So he has mixed feelings—longing and resentment—when the car pulls up, and he doesn't know what he'll do when his dad gets out of the car. A part of him wants to hug his dad, another part wants to punch him, still another part wants to just turn and walk away. Like, you can't just *show up* after five years and expect me to run into your arms. I got along without you before, I'll get along without you now.

The car pulls into the driveway.

McAlister gets out.

He and Wyatt just look at each other for a couple of seconds.

Wyatt runs into his arms.

Presses his face into his father's chest and cries.

God, he's so much taller, McAlister thinks.

Ten years old now.

"Welcome home, Dad."

"Dad," McAlister thinks. Not "Daddy." Well, okay. "I'm so happy to be home. Back with you."

They hold each other for a few moments, then McAlister says, "Wyatt, look at me?"

Wyatt leans back and looks up at his dad's face.

"I owe you an apology," McAlister says.

"You don't—"

"Yes, I do," McAlister says. "My actions cost you a lot, and I'm sorry. I'm so sorry, son."

"It's okay."

"I know I can't make those years up to you," McAlister says. "But I'm home now. I'm with you now, and I'm going to be your dad again."

Wyatt smiles and nods.

"I thought maybe we'd go out for pizza," Rachel says, choking back tears. "How does that sound?"

It sounds great. It *is* great, although it feels weird to McAlister to walk into a restaurant and sit down where you want, order the food you want; to sit and enjoy a meal and not have your head on a swivel.

When it's bedtime for Wyatt that night, McAlister asks, "I guess you're too old for a story, huh?"

"I have a tablet."

McAlister doesn't know what that is.

Wyatt shows it to him. "I can teach you how to use it, if you want."

"Yeah, that sounds great," McAlister says. "Tomorrow. Bedtime now."

"Are you staying here?" Wyatt asks.

"I'm staying here," McAlister says. "I'm never leaving again."

McALISTER TAKES A shower.

Stands under the hot spray for minutes because it feels so good but also because he's nervous about going into the bedroom where Rachel is.

It has been five years since they've made love.

McAlister imagined it a thousand times, jerked off to memories, and now she's just a few feet away. But now he wonders if she wants it, is ready for it, because in a way they feel like strangers to each other. And he wonders if *she* wonders if he did anything else while he was inside, went "gay for the stay" like some guys did. He didn't, but he doesn't know if he should bring the subject up himself, like, *By the way, just so you know . . .*

He decides against it.

As he decides against asking her if *she* did anything while he was in. He really couldn't have blamed her, a young, attractive woman left alone for five years. He thinks that she probably remained faithful—she made a couple of jokes on the phone over the years about her attachment to D batteries—but he decides that he doesn't really want to know.

RACHEL WAITS IN bed.

Brad is taking a *long* time in the shower. She supposes that he's luxuriating, indulging in the new fact that he *can*, but she also wonders if he's stalling, if he's as nervous as she is.

She has her white robe on, the one that she's nicknamed "Viagra" because it's an automatic, and she realizes that she's probably more nervous now than the first time they made love back in college.

Now she listens to the water and thinks, Come on, it's been five years. Get the fuck out of the shower and . . .

He comes into the bedroom with a towel—white, fluffy, clean—wrapped around his waist.

She's in bed in that damn white silk robe.

And she sees his bare chest.

With all the tats.

"My god, Brad . . ."

"You don't like them?"

She gets up and walks over to him. Gently touches the tattoos with her forefinger. "They're . . . different."

So is his body.

Tight. Muscled.

"I mean," she says, "I don't *dis*like them, I guess. What's 'BGF'?"

"Black Guerrilla Family."

She traces the outline of the rifle. "You're Black now?"

"Sort of adopted."

She unwraps the towel and lets it fall to the floor. Then she runs her finger down his chest to his stomach, over the guard tower, then the dragon, down to the dragon's tail. "And abs now."

She runs her hand lower.

The white robe always works.

Rachel gently pulls him backward, falls onto the bed and pulls him down on top of her.

"Rache," he says, "I don't think I'm going to last very long."

"That's okay," she says. "I'll hold you more accountable the second round."

"There's going to be a second round?"

"Oh, yeah."

There is.

Afterward, he lies awake.

Can't sleep because it's too quiet.

No yelling, howling, sobbing, feet on the walkway.

Just the sound of her breathing.

After an hour or so, he takes the pillow and a blanket and stretches out on the floor.

Then he falls asleep.

IN THE MORNING they get Wyatt off to school and drive to the parole officer's where McAlister reports, fills out paperwork, confirms his address and discusses his employment possibilities.

"I have experience in the hospitality industry," McAlister says.

"What does that mean, you were a waiter?"

"I managed a five-star resort hotel."

"Well, I doubt you're going to get *that* job back," the PO says, sounding a little aggravated.

McAlister doubts it, too.

The corporation had dropped his big job offer the morning after his arrest—God, it feels like another lifetime—and in the five years since it has never contacted him. Not a call, not a letter, not a card.

He figures that door is closed.

But he decides to knock on it anyway because he doesn't know what else to do.

Rachel waits in the parking lot of his old hotel while McAlister goes inside on what they both think is probably a futile effort.

The new manager agrees to see him, though.

More out of curiosity than anything, because McAlister is a legend. First for what he did in restoring the hotel back in the day, but more from the delicious scandal of him having killed a guy and gone to prison.

"I'll take anything," McAlister tells him. "Desk clerk, night shift manager, I'll hand out towels at the pool."

"Brad . . ." the manager says.

Using his first name pisses McAlister off a little. He can remember when this jerk worked for *him*.

". . . I'm sure you of all people understand that in a facility of this standing . . . guests having a lot of valuables and all . . . it's hard to justify hiring a . . . convict."

"*Ex*-convict."

"Ex-convict, sure."

But it doesn't change his mind.

"Brad, I hate to rush this meeting, but corporate is here on a visit, and . . . well, you know how that is."

McAlister stands up. "Thanks for your time."

And thanks for nothing.

"We'll keep your application on file," the manager says, "and if anything changes, your current phone is on this, right?"

"Right."

McAlister walks out of the office.

Through the lobby.

It's surreal, the luxury of it. Compared with Folsom. And it strikes him that this used to be his life, his norm, and that he took it for granted, and now—

He sees Stacy.

Five years haven't done her any harm at all. Quite the opposite, in fact. She wears an expensive business suit, he notices the Louboutin shoes, and the short, stylish haircut must have cost a few hundred.

Stacy has done well for herself.

She looks shocked to see him. "Brad *McAlister*?"

"Guilty," he says, irony intended.

"It's so good to see you," she says. They stand there awkwardly for a few seconds, and then she adds, "I'm so sorry about . . . what happened."

"Thanks."

"But you're out now," she says. "Well, obviously. What brings you—"

"I was looking for a job."

"And they gave you one, of *course*."

"Not exactly." He tells her about his meeting with the manager.

"He's a dick," Stacy says. "And a limp one at that. I've been thinking about firing him. Maybe today's the day."

"You . . ."

"Oh, I'm the regional manager now," she says.

She ticks off the other six hotels—Las Vegas, Santa Fe, Cabo, Scottsdale, Jackson Hole, Beverly Hills—and McAlister realizes that she got *his* job. Well, the job that was his before . . .

Then he hears her saying, ". . . so you want the position, McAlister? Your old job?"

"Won't you take heat from corporate?"

"I can take the heat," she said. "Besides, between you and me? Gerard's on his way out. Dead man walking. He just doesn't know it yet."

"I mean, if you're sure."

"I'm sure," Stacy says. "I need a stud muffin to take over here, and you've always had that stud energy, McAlister." Her voice softens even more, to almost a whisper. "And, Brad, that night? I would have . . . you know."

"I don't think *I* would have, Stacy."

"Again, lucky Mrs. McAlister," Stacy says. "And lucky me, I don't have to worry about this property anymore. I'm going in to hand what's-his-name his walking papers. Welcome back, Brad."

McAlister hurries outside to tell lucky Mrs. McAlister the good news.

So now McAlister is back where he started.

He's okay with that.

Hell, he's thrilled with that.

Back in his job, back with his wife, back with his kid.

Freedom.

FOR SIX BLISSFUL months he's so goddamn happy with his freedom.

He takes over at the hotel, and although at first there are whispers among the staff, they soon fade as people realize how good he is, how efficient, how affable, how, while he demands the best from them, he actually makes their jobs easier, more fun and more fulfilling.

And he goes back to the role of being a suburban dad, Southern California version. True to his word, he goes to all of Wyatt's soccer games, hits the postgame pizza parties, makes small talk with the other parents, who soon forget his notoriety.

He and Rachel make a point of a weekly date night—usually Wednesdays—when they go out to a nice dinner, maybe a movie or moonlight stroll on the beach. Sometimes they'll hire an overnight sitter and take an unsold suite at the hotel, order room service, make love and fall asleep watching some dumb reality show on television.

McAlister learns to sleep again.

Even in a bed.

It takes time, but his mind stops waking at every little sound that might have been a threat, he gets used to the quiet, to the lack of noise, to the absence of smells other than the scent of Rachel's skin.

It's not like he forgets the past five years—that's not possible, and sometimes he wakes with a start, thinking he's back in his cell, and it takes a few moments to realize that he's not—but he starts to truly put it behind him.

It's in the past.

He starts to enjoy his freedom.

But freedom means different things to different people.

McAlister fully grasps this when he walks out to his designated parking spot at the hotel one night, gets into his car and sees a white paper bird on the dashboard.

THE NEXT NIGHT he walks out of the resort to find Blanton leaning against his car.

McAlister can't quite believe it.

Blanton is like some kind of human mirage.

An image totally out of context, as if he couldn't actually exist outside the environment of the prison. McAlister has only seen Blanton on the block, in the mess hall, on the yard. But here in the parking lot of an Orange County resort, with an ocean breeze blowing, among the Mercedes and the Land Rovers?

No.

But Blanton is real.

All too real.

"You surprised to see me," Blanton says, smiling.

"Uhhh, yeah."

"What, you thought I'd never get out?" Blanton asks. "Tell the truth, so did I. Something about 'prison overcrowding.' But you don't seem too happy to see me."

The truth is that McAlister has mixed feelings. On the one hand, it's the old nightmare coming back, the five horrible years he hoped to put completely behind him. And he's worried about associating with a known felon and breaking his parole conditions. On the other, Blanton was his protector for those five years, his friend. They'd spent a lot of time together.

And he's happy that the man—*any* man—has his freedom.

"No," McAlister says. "Of course I'm glad. Glad you got out."

"Life be full of surprises, huh?" Blanton says. He looks around at the hotel and the pristine landscaping. "Looks like you landed on your feet."

"I've been lucky," McAlister says, forcing himself not to ask the questions: What are you doing here? What do you *want*? After all, maybe Blanton has just looked him up for old times' sake.

"I hear you're in charge here," Blanton says. "You sort of the warden."

"Well, it's not a prison."

"No, it is not," Blanton says, looking around at the beautifully tended grounds. "No, it is most certainly not."

He's waiting McAlister out.

McAlister gives in first. "Did you just come by to say hello? Do you want to have dinner or something?"

"You gonna take me to dinner in *there*?" Blanton asks, pointing at the hotel. He sees the look on McAlister's face. "No, you not. Of course you not. You don't want your new associates to see you with your *old* associates. Don't look so guilty—I get it, I get it. It's cool."

"There's lots of good places around—"

"Fuck dinner." The smile is off Blanton's face. "I don't need *dinner*."

So let's get to it, McAlister thinks. "What *do* you need? You need money?"

"We had this conversation five years ago," Blanton says. "I don't need money, I don't need commissary."

"Then what?"

Blanton tells him.

LIFE CAN BE viewed as a series of collisions.

We think we live in one world, but we live in many.

McAlister, for instance, has his family world and his work world, but he also has this other world—his prison world, his killer world.

Those worlds can collide.

Blanton tells McAlister what he wants.

Bam.

Collision.

THERE'S THIS MAN. Blanton tells him.

Karl Metzger.

White man.

"Like you," Blanton says.

Metzger is not only white, it turns out. He's Swiss, which is about as white as it gets.

"*Yo-de-lay-hee-hoo,*" Blanton yodels. "He any whiter, he an albino."

They're sitting in McAlister's car now, because it wouldn't really do to have him out in the open seen talking with this guy for too long.

So they drive aimlessly down the PCH.

"What do you want?" McAlister asks.

"You in a hurry?" Blanton asks. "You got some side chick stashed away you got to get to? Patience, my man, a little patience."

This Metzger, Blanton says, has come over from Heidi-land to meet with Mexican drug sources to establish connections for the importation of cocaine and heroin into the European market.

What Metzger is trying to do is eliminate the middlemen.

"This is a problem," Blanton says, "because *we* the middlemen."

The established arrangement has been that the Mexicans sell to Blanton's outfit and Blanton's outfit sells to Europe.

"This sort of thing," Blanton says, "needs to be, shall we say, *discouraged.* Metzger gotta go."

"Why are you telling *me* this?" McAlister asks.

But he already senses the answer.

Blanton says, "Because you gonna kill him for us."

McAlister feels his world coming apart.

Two planets crashing into each other.

Worlds colliding.

"Why me?" McAlister asks, knowing it sounds weak. "You must have dozens of killers."

"Because you white, Bradley," Blanton says. "White can go places Black can't go."

Metzger always stays in the finest hotels. He never leaves his suite.

"No Black street motherfucker can ever get in one of those suites," Blanton says. "But *you* can."

Like he said, Blanton plays the long game. Spotted McAlister in the joint all those years ago and pulled him out of the shit because you never knew when you might need you a white boy.

"Sometimes," Blanton says, "I just don't give myself enough credit."

McAlister says, "I'm not doing it."

"Yes, you are."

"Why should I?"

"Because you owe us," Blanton says. "What, you think we kept you alive for five years because we liked you so much? Child, please."

"I have a life now," McAlister says. "I'm done with all that."

"Oh, you think so," Blanton says. "You have a life because we *gave* you a life."

"I already killed for you once," McAlister says. "That was our deal."

"Motherfucker, you killed for *you*," Blanton says. "Mulligan would have done you for sure. And *I'll* tell *you* what our deal is."

McAlister feels like a fish on the hook, twisting, trying to shake it out. "You said 'one small favor' and that would be it."

"I lied," Blanton says. "Deal with it."

"No," McAlister says. "I'm not doing it."

"Pull over."

"What?"

"I said pull over. You dumb *and* deaf?"

McAlister pulls into the little parking lot at Aliso Beach and stops. Blanton takes an envelope out of his jacket and hands it to him.

McAlister says, "There's not enough money in the world for me to—"

"Open it."

McAlister opens the envelope and looks.

A photo of Rachel leaving work.

A photo of her going into the gym.

A photo of her picking Wyatt up at school.

A photo of Wyatt at his soccer game.

"You son of a bitch," McAlister says. "You filthy piece of shit. Even you wouldn't—"

"We talking millions of dollars here," Blanton says. "I wouldn't *hesitate.* I kill your wife, I kill your kid. In front of you. You watch them die. Maybe then if I feel merciful, I'm in a good mood, I kill you. Maybe not."

McAlister looks again at the pictures of Rachel and Wyatt.

They're his world.

"Don't think about sending the family away to Cabo or one of your other resorts," Blanton tells him. "We see one thing out of the routine, we put a bullet in each of their faces. And there ain't anywhere they can go we can't reach them.

"And I don't need to add, do I, don't think about going to the cops. We'll find out. Same bullets, same faces, and besides, now I got you on tape confessing to Mulligan's exit from this earthly realm, and there's no statute of limitations on murder.

"Chillax, white, it's going to be easy.

"You have a VIP floor," Blanton says.

"We have a concierge floor," McAlister says. It offers the personal service of a concierge and a private lounge open twenty-four seven with drinks and food.

"Don't play me," Blanton says. "I know about your concierge floor. You also have a penthouse section that no one knows to ask for unless they know to ask for it or you offer it."

It's true, McAlister thinks.

One of those things that if you're supposed to know, you know. But how does Blanton know? The VIP section is on the south end of the top floor, and it has exclusive access through a private elevator.

The elevator has a special key card that it won't operate without.

There are three suites for the use of, obviously, very important people—oil sheiks, Russian oligarchs, movie stars down from L.A. who want their privacy. Each suite has a large living room, two bedrooms and bathrooms, an elaborate bar and a large balcony overlooking the ocean.

Blanton says, "You go to his suite to personally welcome him to your fine facility and ask if there's anything you can do to make his stay more comfortable. That way you absolutely sure what he look like. Wouldn't do to kill the wrong motherfucker.

"Next night, say two, three in the A.M., you use your elevator card and his room card to get in. Metzger probably be sleeping."

"You'll have the piece we give you, silenced, clean, untraceable. Like that *Godfather* movie you white guys love so much. Pull the piece, point, two in the head, drop the gun, walk out."

"What if he's not asleep?"

"Then you *put* him to sleep."

"The pass cards are coded," McAlister said. "They record every time they're used."

"Then I guess yours got stolen, huh?"

"There are security cameras in the hallway," McAlister says.

"They better not be working that night, huh?" Blanton says. "Technology be so *fragile* sometime. Frustrating."

"It will look suspicious."

"Probably." Actually, he doesn't give a fuck if McAlister takes the fall for this. If the cops press him, what's he going to say, his old Black prison buddy put him up to it? All Blanton's gotta say is *Bull*shit—*McAlister saw a man with money and decided to rob him. I ain't got nothin' to do with it, why you comin' at* me*?*

With that in mind, Blanton says, "The Mexicans come in on Friday. That means you do this by Thursday night, latest."

"Why?"

"Because Metzger ain't coming to the party with empty hands," Blanton tells him. "He brings earnest money"—millions of dollars in cash to spread around like candy in the piñata.

Blanton says, "*We* going to cancel Metzger's reservation. Why let the Mexicans have the money? You take it with you, you get a taste. Not a dinner taste, mind you, but at least a lunch taste. You can buy, like, a Subaru, decked out. Get you some cupholders and shit. I know you all like your cupholders."

"There's a safe in the suite," McAlister says. "He'll put the money in the safe and I won't have the combination."

"Safe is for jewelry and shit," Blanton says. "Too small for that amount of cash. Why you fucking with me, Brad? Quit trying to pussy out. You going to do this guy, you gonna take his money, you gonna bring it to me, or you gonna watch your wife and son die."

McAlister runs it through his head.

This Metzger's life versus Rachel's and Wyatt's?

No choice there.

If I get arrested and convicted, sent away for life?

I can do that.

Because my wife and kid live.

If I get killed?

My wife and kid live.

McAlister drives home.

No longer enjoying his freedom.

It's an illusion, he thinks.

My life is a prison and has been since that one drunken punch. One single moment in a lifetime of moments.

Even if I do this thing, there'll be a next thing and a next.

I'm not free and I'll never be free again.

HE DOESN'T SHOW it that week, though.

Something he learned in prison and hasn't been able to let go of yet: never show what you're thinking, what you're feeling, to anyone.

Rachel feels it.

His mask.

She's a realist, she knows that doing five years in that hell had to change him. Knows that he *had* to change to survive and come back to her. He's still Brad—he's sweet, he's loving, caring and considerate, and he's a great dad. But there's something new inside him now, a man whom she doesn't know and *can't* know, a persona hidden under a mask that sometimes comes over his face.

The week goes by normally.

The routine.

Get Wyatt off to school, then each of them to work, then home for dinner. Help Wyatt with homework, a little TV, then get him to bed.

Not that much later, to bed themselves.

There's the Saturday soccer game followed by Chuck E. Cheese.

Just the normal south Orange County suburban life.

Sunday they go house hunting. With his salary it's time to upgrade. Their old house isn't on the market, but they look in San Clemente, Lake Forest, Dana Point. A three-bedroom, two-bath "open floor plan" with at least a little yard, and McAlister can't help but wonder, can't stop himself from thinking, *Is this just another prison?* but then he feels like an ungrateful shit.

That night they're home discussing if they really need three bedrooms, and she brings up the possibility of having another child.

"You think so?" McAlister asks.

"I don't know, maybe," she says. "I kind of miss those baby days."

"Really?" he asks. "The diapers, the colic, the sleepless nights?"

"Yeah, sort of."

"Well, I wouldn't rule it out."

They decide to think about it.

He lies there thinking, though, about whether it's better or worse to kill a man when he's sleeping than when he's awake. On the one hand, the man won't know it's coming, he won't be scared, he won't feel anything. He'll just be dreaming and then . . . he just won't be. Or is it better that he sees it coming, that he does have that last conscious moment? But to do what with?

The horror comes up his spine like an electric jolt.

The realization that he's going to kill again.

The first time was an accident.

The second time was intentional, but he can rationalize that it was self-defense. A preemptive strike.

This time, though?

Straight-up murder.

He tries to think like an inmate again, get back into his prison mind. Like, the guy is a major drug dealer, he plays the game, he takes his chances, so fuck him.

It doesn't work. His prison mind and his civilian mind, well, collide.

Which one is going to come out of *that* crash?

On Monday afternoon, Metzger checks into the resort.

METZGER DOESN'T LOOK like an international criminal.

Then again, McAlister doesn't really know what an international criminal should look like. In any case, the man is fiftyish, short, plump, with curly gray hair that is just beginning to thin. He wears a bespoke gray suit with a blue shirt unbuttoned at the neck. Brown Hermès loafers.

McAlister introduces himself and gives Blanton's line about welcoming him to the hotel, if there's anything I can do . . .

He hands Metzger his card. "That's my private number. If there's anything at all you need—"

"Thank you," Metzger says with a wave of his hand.

Impatient to get the servant out of there.

McAlister is just as happy to make a quick exit. It's hard to look at a man you're planning on killing.

He gets home that night, and over dinner Rachel says, "I had something interesting happen today."

"What was that?"

"You know that intersection on MacArthur where the homeless guys hang out?" she says. "I was at the red light waiting to make the left turn, and I gave this guy a dollar—"

"Rachel, I've told you about this." She takes chances she shouldn't take and just won't believe that most of these guys use the money for drugs or alcohol.

"I know, but we're so blessed," she says. "Anyway, I gave him the dollar and he handed me this little paper bird. Wasn't that nice?"

McAlister feels rage but he keeps it off his face. "Was he a Black guy?"

Rachel looks at him curiously. "How'd you know?"

"I think I may have seen him out there."

"What would you be doing on MacArthur?" Rachel asks.

McAlister lies. "The freeway was a mess so I took surface."

That night when she's asleep he walks outside and calls the number Blanton gave him. "You keep my family out of this."

"Motherfucker, *you* keep your family out of this," Blanton says. "I'm just giving you a little reminder. Tomorrow be Tuesday. Tick-tock. Time go by when you having fun."

"Stay away from my wife."

"Wasn't me," Blanton says.

"Then it was one of your people," McAlister says. "Keep them the fuck away from my wife."

Blanton does.

But on Tuesday evening, Rachel is hanging up Wyatt's jacket that he'd tossed on a chair and finds a little paper bird in its pocket. "Wyatt!"

The boy comes in.

"Where did you get this?" Rachel asks.

"I dunno," Wyatt says. "I didn't even know it was there. What is it?"

"It's really weird," Rachel says.

She tells McAlister about it after dinner. "I don't like it. Someone must have been at the house, at his school . . ."

McAlister feels fury down to his bone marrow.

"Is this some prison thing?" Rachel asks.

"What do you mean?"

"You heard me," Rachel says. "Is this some sort of, I don't know, *message* or something? Some kind of inmate code?"

"Not that I know of."

"Don't lie to me."

"I'm not lying," McAlister says.

Except he is.

"Are you in some kind of trouble?" Rachel asks.

"No."

That night, Blanton calls *him.* McAlister had the phone on silent, so thankfully it didn't wake Rachel up, and he took it into the bathroom.

"You get my message?" Blanton asks.

"Threaten my son again, I'll kill you."

"First things first," Blanton says. "Tomorrow Wednesday. Procrastination is the thief of time, didn't nobody never tell you that?"

"You come near my kid again and I swear—"

"It's on you," Blanton says. "It all be on you. Get it done."

He clicks off.

McAlister gets back into bed, but he doesn't sleep.

He gets up in the morning and tells Rachel, "I'm going to stay at work tonight, check out the night shift. So I won't be home until four or five o'clock in the morning."

"Okay." But she's looking at him funny.

"What?" McAlister asks.

"What we talked about last night."

"Don't worry about it."

"I'm worried."

"You don't need to be," McAlister says.

"Brad," she says, "I lost you for five years. I can't lose you again."

"You won't," McAlister says. "I promise."

"If there's something you need to tell me," Rachel says, "please just *tell* me."

He tells her.

Everything.

About killing Mulligan, about hooking up with BGF, and now about what Blanton wants him to do—and what Blanton will do if he doesn't.

Rachel is strong.

Rachel is tough.

But now she breaks down and cries.

"We thought this was over," she says. "We thought we were free. And then it just reaches up and grabs us again.

"We'll never be free of it," she says.

McAlister knows it, too.

Blanton was using him the entire time—the protection, the chess, the music, hiding the tattoos, everything.

Biding his time.

I was just on layaway, McAlister thinks.

When that guy I punched died, I died right alongside him.

"What are we going to do?" Rachel asks.

She's terrified.

"What we have to," McAlister says. "Whatever we do, I'll protect you and Wyatt."

He tells her how.

THE DAY DRAGS like prison time.

Thinking about killing a man.

Waiting to kill a man.

McAlister has decided to do it tonight so that if something goes wrong he'll still have Thursday.

He's a careful person, a belt-and-suspenders kind of guy.

Thinks things through.

Now he walks out onto the beach and phones Blanton. "Tonight."

"You know Gelson's?"

McAlister knows it. It's on a small knoll off the PCH on the inland side. Only about five minutes from the hotel. "I know it."

"Meet me in the parking lot in forty-five."

McAlister drives there and sees Blanton sitting in a black Expedition. He gets in on the passenger side.

Blanton slides a pistol—a Beretta 92 FS with a sound suppressor—across the seat. "This is a nine. Two in the head will do the job. Anything more is excessive, just you being a dick."

McAlister takes the gun. It feels strange in his hand, cold and heavy. He's never used a gun before, not even on a shooting range. Never wanted a gun around the house, not with Wyatt there.

Blanton senses his nerves. "It's easy. Get up close, point and pull the trigger."

Easy, huh? McAlister thinks.

Easy to end a life. Just point and pull.

Then Blanton gives him a pair of nitrile surgical gloves. "Wear these. No prints on the door, no prints on anything. After you do the thing, drop the gun. As the man said, 'Leave the gun, take the cannoli.' By the cannoli I mean—"

"The money."

Blanton hands him a black ski mask. "I don't need to explain this, do I?"

"No."

"Meet me here by two forty-five, *with* the money, or—"

"I know the 'or.'"

"Do you?" Blanton asks. "My people will be outside your house. If you don't show up with the money, they go in and grab your little family."

McAlister just looks back at him.

"One more piece of advice," Blanton says. "Don't fuck it up."

McAlister gets out of the car.

WHOEVER SAID THAT time is relative didn't get it wrong, McAlister thinks. All night, every time he looks at his watch because an hour has gone by, five minutes have gone by.

He tries to stay busy. Makes rounds of the hotel, talks with staff, goes into the restaurant and samples the dinner items even though he has no appetite. Calls home to check in on Rachel and say good night to Wyatt.

"I'll be home to take you to school in the morning," McAlister tells him.

"Cool."

"Cool," McAlister thinks. Everything is "cool" with this kid these days. "Love you."

"Love *you*."

Wyatt hands the phone back to Rachel.

"Everything good?" McAlister asks.

"All good."

"See you when I see you." He clicks off.

THE DAY HAS dragged by for her, too.

The anxiety . . .

Anxiety? she thinks.

Pure terror.

A street gang, killers, outside her house watching her and her child?!

Get it under control, she thinks. You can't be scared now, you don't have that luxury. Do what Brad said.

She goes upstairs and packs.

FINALLY, *FINALLY*, AT 1:30 in the morning McAlister goes to the little security office. Hector Beltran is on duty, looking at the monitors for the security cameras.

Good man, Beltran.

One of those solid Mexican family men who make the whole economy around here run.

Father of two high school–age boys.

Good kids.

"Everything copacetic?" McAlister asks.

"Quiet night."

"I was walking the north end of the parking lot," McAlister says, "and there was a car nosing around, turquoise Jeep Wrangler.

Probably nothing, but you want to just take a stroll, check it out, please?"

"You got it."

Beltran grabs a flashlight and leaves.

McAlister leans over the computer keyboard that controls the security cameras, brings up the VIP section and disables the camera on that floor. Then he flips the monitor back to the second floor where it was. He leaves the office, walks through the lobby to the private elevator, touches his key card to the monitor and rides up.

He feels a little dizzy, light-headed, and wonders if he should have made himself eat more. The pistol is tucked in the back waistband of his slacks, under his suit jacket. Somehow it feels like an entity, a living thing with a will of its own.

The elevator door opens on the VIP floor.

McAlister forces himself to step out.

He looks at his watch.

1:47.

Metzger's suite is at the end of the corridor on the right-hand side.

McAlister puts the gloves on. Then the ski mask. Then he forces himself to walk. One foot after the other, he thinks—left, right, left, right—just keep moving.

He gets to the door.

Uses the same key card to tap the lock.

The lock clicks open.

McAlister nudges the door.

Metzger hadn't used the Modisch flip-lock bar. It had been one of McAlister's concerns and he had asked Blanton, "What if the flip-lock bar is engaged?"

"Then you ring the bell, and when he comes to the door, you shove him inside and you shoot him in the face. I gotta tell you everything?"

McAlister opens the door and goes in.

Metzger's not asleep.

He's sitting at his laptop on the sofa behind a glass table. Naked except for his underwear and a pair of reading glasses.

He looks up.

Understandably puzzled.

But seemingly more annoyed than scared.

McAlister pulls the gun from his waist and points it at him.

"Oh," Metzger.

That's it, just "oh."

Looks at McAlister like he's trying to figure it out. Is this a hit or a robbery? He tries to make it the second. "If it's the money you want, you can have it. It's in two briefcases in the closet. Take them and go."

Do it, McAlister thinks.

Don't hesitate. If you hesitate you won't do it, and then . . .

Think of Rachel and Wyatt.

There are people outside your house right now who will go in if you don't do it, and . . .

This is no different from Mulligan.

Just do it.

"You haven't done this before, have you?" Metzger asks. "It's all right, I'll talk you through it. The closet is behind you to your left. You take the briefcases and you leave. You don't need to hurt me, I'm not going to try to stop you. Let me give you a bit of wisdom, son. You can always make more money, but you can never make more life."

McAlister feels a sort of paralysis moving up from his feet.

Like he's frozen.

"Would you like *me* to go get the cases?" Metzger asks. "I will. I'm going to stand up, all right?"

Metzger raises his hands above his head, slowly stands up and comes out from behind the table. Hands still in the air, he walks to the closet.

Do it now, McAlister thinks.

While his back is to you and you don't have to see his eyes.

Two in the back of the head, do it now.

He aims the gun at the curly gray hair.

But he doesn't shoot.

Metzger opens the closet door and bends down to grab a briefcase. Instead, he turns with a gun in his hand and raises it at McAlister. "You stupid piece of shit, did you really think I would—"

McAlister shoots.

The first shot hits Metzger in the chest.

The second smacks him square in the forehead.

Metzger falls back into the closet.

McAlister grabs the cases and walks out.

TAKES OFF THE gloves and the mask, shoves them into his pocket.

Walks to the far end of the corridor out of the VIP section and onto the concierge floor. Goes to the service elevator and rides it to the basement laundry room. Then through the room to the other side to another elevator and rides it up into a small foyer, then walks out that door to the back side of the resort.

His heart races, and he forces himself to breathe to slow it down. Can't have a heart attack now, he tells himself. The job isn't done, your family isn't safe.

He looks at his watch.

2:07.

You have plenty of time, he tells himself.

Walk, don't run. Don't call any attention to yourself. He makes it around the building to the parking lot and heads for his car.

Then he sees Beltran.

McAlister drops the cases behind some shrubs and walks up to the guard.

"No sign of that Wrangler," Beltran says.

"Like I said, it was probably nothing," McAlister says. "Sorry to waste your time."

"I like getting outside," Beltran says. "You out of breath, Mr. McAlister?"

"Yeah, maybe."

"You should get that checked."

Is it my imagination or is he looking at me suspiciously? McAlister thinks. "How are the boys? Manuel and Fermin, right?"

"They're good, thanks for asking," Beltran says. "Both playing football. But they're teenagers, you know. Idiots. *Your* boy?"

"He's good, thanks," McAlister says. "Growing."

"It goes fast," Beltran says.

"Well . . ."

"Yeah, I should get back in."

"See you tomorrow."

Beltran heads back in. McAlister watches him as he walks past the shrubs. Please, please, God, don't let him see the cases. Please.

Beltran walks past the cases.

McAlister waits until Beltran goes into the building, then goes back, grabs the cases and gets into his car.

2:10.

You'll make it easily, he thinks.

"Easily."

Shit.

McALISTER PULLS INTO the Gelson's parking lot.

It's 2:25.

Sees a pair of headlights blink twice, drives next to Blanton's Expedition, gets out of his car.

Blanton rolls down his window.

"It's done," McAlister says.

"Our man be gone?"

"He's gone."

"You best be telling the truth."

"I'm telling the truth."

Blanton isn't that worried—he knows that he owns McAlister. "You dropped the gun?"

"Did you tell me to drop the gun?" McAlister asks. "There's your answer."

"I knew you had it in you," Blanton says. He juts his chin toward McAlister's car. "The money in the car?"

"No."

"Say what?" Blanton asks.

"The money isn't in the car," McAlister says.

"Give me my fucking money," Blanton says. "Let me rephrase that—give me my fucking money, motherfucker."

McAlister fills his chest up with all the courage he has. "Here's what's going to happen. I'm going to call my wife and tell her to take my son and go to the airport. She'll call me from there. When she does, when I know they're safe, I'll take you to the money."

Blanton's face curls into a snarl. "I'll have them killed right now."

"No, you won't," McAlister says. "Because you won't leave millions on the table just to make a point."

I know you from your chess game—you're greedy.

A stare-down.

McAlister sees that Blanton is thinking it over. He decides to nudge him.

"All I want is my family safe," McAlister says. "You can have all the money, I don't want a cut."

Blanton keeps glaring for a second, then he smiles. "Did I underestimate you, McAlister?"

McAlister shrugs.

"I should never have taught you to play chess," Blanton says. "Okay, call the little missus."

Then I'll get my money, Blanton thinks.

Then I'll kill you.

RACHEL ANSWERS THE phone.

McAlister just says, "Go."

"Brad—"

"*Go*," McAlister says. "I'll meet you there. Don't worry."

Rachel goes into Wyatt's bedroom. "Wake up, sweetheart."

Groggy, Wyatt sits up. "What's—"

"Get dressed."

Wyatt looks out the window at the darkness. "It isn't time for school."

"You're not going to school," Rachel says. "We're going on a little vacation. We're meeting Daddy there. You're all packed."

"Cool," Wyatt says.

THEY SIT IN Blanton's car and wait.

"What you want to talk about?" Blanton asks. "To pass the time."

"I don't need to talk."

"I do," Blanton says. "Nervous energy. Always been my problem. That ADHD shit. You see the Lakers game?"

"I don't watch basketball."

"Course you don't," Blanton says.

He sits silently, almost sulking.

RACHEL DRIVES TO the airport.

In her soccer mom van.

Classic.

It's a short drive, only about twenty minutes, but Wyatt's already back asleep in the passenger seat.

She looks into the rearview mirror.

The headlights are still behind her. The same car that started following her as soon as she backed out of the driveway.

She tells herself again not to be afraid.

Brad told her that it was going to be all right. He purchased their tickets online, the boarding passes are already on her phone. "If I don't meet you at the airport, I'll meet you at the destination. Just get on the plane."

She can only hope he was telling the truth.

McALISTER LOOKS AT his watch.

Rachel should be calling any minute.

Once she's at the airport she'll be totally safe, because no gang, no matter how brazen, is going to attack anyone at an airport, with cops and marshals everywhere. The penalties for even an assault would be a double-digit bit in a federal lockup.

But he does remember Blanton's threat that he could get to them anywhere.

His phone rings.

Rachel says, "We're at the airport."

McAlister feels like he can almost breathe again.

"Good," McAlister says. "Go through security."

It's even safer on the other side of that gate.

"When will you get here?" she asks.

"When I can."

"I don't want to leave without you."

"Rache, listen to me," McAlister says. "Whatever happens, you and Wyatt get on that plane. Tell me that you understand."

"Yes."

"I love you." He clicks off.

"How *is* the little woman?" Blanton asks.

"Keep my wife's name out of your mouth."

"Didn't say her name," Blanton mutters. Then he says, "Now take me where my money is."

RACHEL GOES THROUGH security.

When they're through, Wyatt says, "You said Dad was meeting us at the airport."

She can tell that he's getting anxious. He remembers losing his dad before, he doesn't want to lose him again.

Neither do I, she thinks.

"He will," she says.

"Where are we going?" Wyatt asks.

"It's a surprise," Rachel says.

McALISTER TAKES THE gun from his back and points it at Blanton.

The shot caller's surprised expression would be comical if McAlister had any humor left.

"Motherfucker," McAlister says, "you wanted the money so bad, you forgot to castle your king. Even against a lowly pawn."

He shoots him in the face.

Twice.

So now Blanton *can't* reach his family anywhere.

McAlister takes the little paper bird out of his pocket and lays it on Blanton's chest. A calling card of sorts. Blanton's people will comprehend it—you do not fuck with Brad McAlister.

He gets out of Blanton's car and into his own.

Drives to the parking lot at Aliso Beach and throws the gun

into the ocean. Then he walks over to the shrubs where he left the cases.

Puts them in his car and drives away.

He lied to Rachel. He can't go to the airport, not with that kind of cash. He'll need to go to Mexico, spend some of it on bribes, some of it on a new passport—it doesn't matter, he has more than enough money to last a lifetime. So sooner or later, probably sooner, he'll get on a plane or a boat and meet Rachel and Wyatt.

McAlister drives back up the PCH and onto the 5 South toward the border. It's going to take two or three hours, so he settles back. He rolls the window down and lets the crisp air flow in. It's noisy, but he likes the noise. It's cold and it's fresh and with the speed of the car it feels like freedom.

SOMETIMES IF YOU'RE hanging out in a bar in south Orange County, California, and it's late at night and everyone has had a few drinks, some of the locals might start telling a story that you're going to think is suburban legend, so to speak.

The tale will concern an executive who managed a five-star resort hotel—you might even be at the bar right there—who disappeared on the same morning a Swiss businessman was found shot to death in the hotel and a Black ex-con was also found shot to death in a parking lot just a few miles away.

Some people will say it was the same gun, that the crimes were connected; others will say that's bullshit. Some will claim to have known Brad McAllen—or was it Keith?—and tell you that there is no way he ever killed anyone—hell, they used to see him at his kid's soccer games. Others will swear that, no, McKee was an ex-con himself who had done ten years in prison for beating a man to death.

Some will say it was all about drugs; others that it was some kind of weird love triangle; others will insist that the whole story is apocryphal.

Whatever.

The truth of it is that no one in Orange County ever saw Brad McAlister or his family again.

STACY TOLLIVER WANTED to get away from it all.

Away from her position running the chain of luxury hotels, away from the board meetings, the endless texts and emails, the never-ending demands of her high-powered, high-pressure job at the Sterling Group.

It's the job that she always wanted, mind you, but six years of nonstop work will wear even the most ambitious woman out, and she just wanted a break. So she found a small, remote island off the coast of Java in Indonesia with a little hotel on the beach. No television, no telephones, no internet.

Just peace and quiet.

You can only get there by boat from a larger island, and when she arrives she finds that the hotel is actually a series of bungalows set in a line of palm trees, with a central house that serves as an office and a restaurant.

Stacy is enchanted.

The place is perfect.

An Indonesian man takes her bags to the office, and Stacy is a little surprised when an American woman checks her in.

The woman looks familiar, but Stacy can't quite place her.

"This place is paradise," Stacy says.

"It is," the woman says. She has short black hair with just a few streaks of silver. It's attractive.

"How long have you lived here?" Stacy asks.

"Long enough to know it's paradise," the woman says. She hands

Stacy a key. "Bungalow Three. I think you'll love it. Breakfast is from six A.M. to any time you want it here in the house. Dinner starts at eight. If there's anything we can do to make your stay more comfortable, please don't hesitate to ask. My son will take your bags."

A tall, gangly teenager comes out from behind the desk, gives her a winning smile, hefts her bags and walks her to the bungalow.

"How lucky are you to grow up here," Stacy says.

"It's way cool," the boy says.

Later, sitting on the lanai of her bungalow sipping a mai tai and watching the sunset, Stacy sees a man come out of the office, walk down to the beach and start setting up a dining table and chairs.

He wears a loose-fitting, sweat-stained flowered shirt, khaki shorts and sandals. The teenage boy comes out to help, and then the two of them talk for a minute and it's clear to her that they're father and son.

Something else becomes . . . well, not *clear*, but . . . close to that, because she could swear that the man is Brad McAlister.

And the woman at the desk . . . the lucky wife.

It's been years . . . six . . . seven? . . . but he has the same build, the same hair, the same smile. It occurs to her that she read somewhere that Indonesia doesn't extradite to the United States.

Stacy knows all the stories, knows what there is to be known. She was the one who had to deal with the fallout of the Metzger murder, the scandal, the harm in reputation to the property. She had to take the heat for having hired an ex-con, and if she hadn't known where all the metaphorical bodies were buried in the corporation, she probably would have been canned. But she did know, she kept her job, and, in fact, she took Gerard's corner office.

Now the man leaves the beach and walks up the pathway toward her, seemingly intent on some errand.

As he passes her veranda he smiles and nods.

Then he stops.

Looks at her.

She looks back.

There's a question in his eyes.

And an answer in hers as she says nothing, looks down, sips her drink.

McAlister keeps walking.

LATER, McALISTER SITS on the veranda of their house with Rachel to watch the sunset.

It's been their ritual for years now.

"She recognized you?" Rachel asks.

"I think so."

"And?"

"Nothing," McAlister says. "It's over, Rache. It's truly over now."

You see, life can be viewed as a series of collisions.

Collisions between who we want to be and who we are. Between what we want and what we don't. Between dreams and reality. Between wants and needs, good and bad, right and wrong.

Between the present and the past.

And sometimes these collisions are so violent, so strong, so powerful, that they destroy everything that was.

They break the bonds that chained us to what we were.

And in doing so, create something new.

Freedom.

ACKNOWLEDGMENTS

TO BRIAN MURRAY AND LIATE Stehlik at William Morrow, thanks so much for letting me get out stories that have been running around in my head for years.

Thanks, of course, to my brilliant editor and friend, Jennifer Brehl, for all her thoughtful and caring work and for her incredible talent and skill.

Likewise to my patient and thorough copy editor, Nancy Tan, and proofreader, Laura Cherkas.

To the good folks at William Morrow: Andy LeCount, Ed Spade, Julianna Wojcik, Kaitlin Harri, Danielle Bartlett, Jennifer Hart, Chantal Restivo-Alessi, Marleen Reimer, Nate Lanman—please accept my thanks.

To the unsung heroes and heroines of the sales, marketing, publicity, production, and design staffs at HarperCollins/William Morrow, my great gratitude.

To my lawyer, Richard Heller, my heartfelt great appreciation.

Likewise to Matt Snyder at CAA for the years of great counsel.

To Steve Hamilton, for his support and sage counsel.

To all the booksellers and readers—your support means everything.

To the many friends and places that gave me more support than they can ever know: David Nedwidek and Katy Allen, Pete and Linda Maslowski, Jim Basker and Angela Vallot, Teressa Palozzi, Tony and Kathy Sousa and their whole clan, John and Theresa Culver, Scott and Jan Svoboda, Jim and Melinda Fuller, Ron and Kim Lubesnick, Ted Tarbet, Thom Walla, Mark Clodfelter, Roger Barbee, Bill and Ruth McEneaney, Andrew Walsh, Jeff and Rita Parker, Bruce Riordan, Jeff Weber, Don Young, Mark Rubinsky, Cameron Pierce Hughes, Mark Rubenstein, Adam Rosen, Jon Land, Rob Jones, Ed Romano, Wayne Worcester, David and Tammy Tanner, Ty and Dani Jones, Deron and Becky Bisset, Ted Leittner, Bridget/Gidget and the whole Flipper Eddie Crew at East Matunuck, the Ocean State Waves, Drift Surf, Quecho, Las Olas, Java Madness, Jim's Dock, Cap'n Jack's, Phil's Diner and the Coast Guard House.

To the Story Factory—Deborah Randall and Ryan C. Coleman—my deep gratitude for all you do and everything you are.

To my brother in arms, partner in crime, world's best agent and dearest friend, Shane Salerno. Thank you for fighting so hard for a better tomorrow for me and my family.

To my son, Thomas, his wife, Brenna, and their son, Perry, you give me more pride and joy than you can ever know.

To my wife, Jean—ILYM.